Dorothy Uhnak and The Murder Room

>>> This title is part of The Murder Room, our series dedicated to making available out-of-print or hard-to-find titles by classic crime writers.

Crime fiction has always held up a mirror to society. The Victorians were fascinated by sensational murder and the emerging science of detection; now we are obsessed with the forensic detail of violent death. And no other genre has so captivated and enthralled readers.

Vast troves of classic crime writing have for a long time been unavailable to all but the most dedicated frequenters of second-hand bookshops. The advent of digital publishing means that we are now able to bring you the backlists of a huge range of titles by classic and contemporary crime writers, some of which have been out of print for decades.

From the genteel amateur private eyes of the Golden Age and the femmes fatales of pulp fiction, to the morally ambiguous hard-boiled detectives of mid twentieth-century America and their descendants who walk our twenty-first century streets, The Murder Room has it all. >>>

The Murder Room
Where Criminal Minds Meet

themurderroom.com

Dorothy Uhnak (1930–2006)

A native New Yorker, born and raised in the Bronx, Dorothy Uhnak attended the City College of New York and the John Jay College of Criminal Justice before becoming one of the New York Police Departments first female recruits in 1953. She wrote a memoir detailing her experiences, *Police Woman*, before creating the semi-autobiographical character of Christie Opara, who features in *The Bait*, *The Witness* and *The Ledger*. Opara is the only woman on the District Attoney's Special Investigations Squad, and applies the same cool, methodical approach to hunting down criminals as she does to raising a child on her own and navigating complex relationships with her colleagues. During her 14 years in the NYPD Uhnak was promoted three times and twice awarded medals for services 'above and beyond'; she also earned the department's highest commendation, the Outstanding Police Duty Bar. Her writing was equally highly regarded: *The Bait* was widely praised by critics, and won the Edgar Award for Best First Mystery of 1968. Dorothy Uhnak died in Greenport, New York, and is survived by her daughter Tracy.

By Dorothy Uhnak

Policewoman (1964)
The Bait (1968)
The Witness (1969)
The Ledger (1970)
Law and Order (1973)
The Investigation (1977)
False Witness (1981)
Victims (1986)
The Ryer Avenue Story (1993)
Codes of Betrayal (1997)

The Bait

Dorothy Uhnak

An Orion book

Copyright © Tracy E. Uhnak 1968

The right of Dorothy Uhnak to be identified as the author of this work
has been asserted in accordance with the Copyright, Designs and Patents
Act 1988.

This edition published by
The Orion Publishing Group Ltd
Orion House
5 Upper St Martin's Lane
London WC2H 9EA

An Hachette UK company
A CIP catalogue record for this book is available from the British Library

ISBN 978 1 4719 0648 0

www.orionbooks.co.uk

This book is for my daughter, Tracy – just as I promised.

CHRISTIE OPARA sat in the small seat outside the empty motorman's cab of the nearly deserted, post-rush hour, downtown IRT local. Her shoulder was pressed against the warm steel wall and her long slim legs, bound by faded green dungarees, tensed against the pitch and sway of the train. Her bare feet felt moist and itchy in the ragged black sneakers as they pressed against the floor. Her hands rested lightly on her schoolbooks and she felt herself becoming part of the motion and monotony of the all-encasing speed which, unmeasured by landscape or anything else framed by the small dirty window facing her, gave no feeling of speed.

The train jerked to an unanticipated stop and Christie's right hand shot out to catch the shoulder bag which slid off her left arm. She caught it before it hit the floor, then biting her lower lip in annoyance, she leaned forward and collected the books and papers which had fallen between her feet. Although the shoulder bag hadn't opened and there was not the slightest possibility that anything had fallen from it, Christie's fingers automatically slid into the bag and identified each item: the small makeup case, the wad of tissues, sunglasses, ball-point pen, the rough textured butt of her .32 service revolver, the collection of keys on her rabbit's foot chain, the small spiral notebook, then, finally, beneath everything else, the small leather case that held her detective shield.

She snapped the case open within the depths of the bag and through habit, her fingers traced the embossed lettering: New York City Police Department, then sliding over the word "Detective," she lightly touched the four numbers "4754" which were cut into the small rectangle at the lower edge of the shield.

Christie dropped the leather case and pulled her hand free. Absently, she pushed the long, dark blond bangs from her forehead and her fingers wandered through the thick, short hair. It was a fruitless attempt to look a little less disheveled and actually, she looked exactly the way she was supposed to look for this assignment.

At twenty-six, Christie Opara, with her slight, flat-chested, long-legged and almost hipless body and still freckled face, devoid of any makeup except for an excessive amount of white eyeshadow and black eyeliner, appeared to be the bored, desultory twenty-year-old college student she was impersonating. It hadn't been too difficult for her to edge her way into the group at City College. Christie had a talent for picking up not only patterns of speech and gesture, but the more subtle attitudes and postures which could make her an almost faceless, yet vaguely accepted and unsuspected member of any particular gathering. Her presence at City College was for the purpose of identifying and arresting the source of LSD-saturated sugar cubes. This morning, in a particular corner of the school cafeteria, Christie and certain other students with whom she had established a casual and easy rapport, were prepared to purchase these cubes at five dollars each.

It had been a long investigation, requiring over four weeks of careful, tedious work and she was glad it was coming to a climax. It had been even more tiresome and routine for the four other members of the squad working with her, for as Christie supplied them with names of the students involved, they had to check each suspect's background from the exact moment of birth up to and including the present day.

Ordinarily, this would have been a routine case for Narcotics, so the mere fact that it was being handled by the D.A.'s Special Investigations Squad meant that one of the students was "somebody's" son or daughter and *that* meant things were to be handled tactfully. The arrest this morning was to be effected so discreetly that the prospective purchasers would not even be aware of what had happened to their supplier.

Christie adjusted her body against the hard wicker seat and tried to figure out which student was "somebody's" offspring. She gave up the attempt in irritation. Although she was instrumental in this investigation and was to be credited with the arrest, Supervising Assistant District Attorney Casey Reardon did not see fit to tell her exactly which student's presence in the group had caused the case to be bucked to the D.A.'s Squad. After nearly a year of working for Reardon, Christie knew she should be able to accept the way he ran things: he asked the questions, his people supplied the answers. Period. She knew Reardon considered his selection of her as the only female detective in his squad of sixteen men a very great compliment. It was the only compliment he had extended to date. No matter how competently she accomplished any of her assignments his reaction was always the same: she did only what was expected of her.

Christie hadn't noticed the sound of the door between the connecting cars slide open or even felt the rush of air, but the door was slammed shut with a loud metallic clanging at the same instant that a shrill, piercing voice streaked through the car.

"In-the-midst-of-Life-we-are-in-Death! I-am-the-Resurrection-and-the-Light! I-am-God-and-you-shall-know-me-or-you-shall-perish!"

Startled by the sound and then by the presence before her, Christie looked up directly into the angry, somewhat glazed eyes of the small man. He was dark and the bones shone through the tightly stretched skin of his face. His body was covered by a huge, dirty white sandwich board which was emblazoned in jagged red and blue lettering: "Repent! His Day is at Hand! I am Life! I am Death!" He whirled around sharply and before her eyes was a terrible Christ-head, badly drawn and colored in furious streaks of poster paint and yet, incredibly, the face was his: the thin bony cheeks and dark glaring eyes.

The man spun about again, his words now a spate of hissing Spanish. A thin brown hand, roped with blue veins, was thrust from beneath the sandwich board as though to conduct the cadence of his words. Christie sought his eyes but they were focused on some far-off vision of his own. The train lurched to a stop. The doors slid open. A few passengers boarded the car, warily eyeing the now silent and

3

motionless little man and his sandwich board. They carefully found seats at the far end of the car and bent over their morning newspapers.

When the doors closed, the man, as though a switch had clicked inside of him, issued forth with a terrible wailing sound. His hand rose up again and his eyes, burning with frenzy, saw no one. As though he did not exist, no one seemed to see him. He stopped speaking as abruptly as he had begun. A smile pulled his tan lips and his eyes narrowed over some secret which seemed to give him great pleasure. His right hand disappeared beneath his board, then emerged waving a small American flag with a golden tassel. He clicked his heels together smartly, nodded his head twice and marched down the length of the car.

After a moment of silence, his voice ripped through the car again in his steady, high chant, "In-the-midst-of-Life-we-are-in-Death! I-am-the-Resurrection-and-the-Light! I-am-God-and-you-shall-know-me-or-you-shall-perish!"

Christie Opara's fingers tightened along the edge of her textbooks and she tried to force the insistent words from her brain. She didn't need anyone to tell her about death. Not today. Not on Friday, May 6: Mike's birthday. Thirty years old. He would have been thirty years old if he hadn't been killed when he was twenty-five years old.

She forced her teeth together and raised her chin so that her face was tilted toward the dim light overhead. She breathed the words into her lungs: in the midst of life. Mike was not in the midst of life: he had *been* life and now he did not exist. Christie closed her eyes tightly but that did not ease the reopened wound anymore than her resolution not to notice his birth date each May. She strained against the darkness of her eyelids forcing all images away, trying not to try, just to let it come to her: the fullness of him. But only a flat photographic likeness, unreal and untrue, engraved into her memory by hours of staring at black and white snapshots, appeared. Not the essence of him, not the feel, touch, sense, life of him. She felt a wave of panic. She could not remember what her dead husband looked like.

At twenty-six, Christie was older than Mike had ever been or ever would be. She had become a member of the

Police Department because of him. Together, Mike had said, they might become the Department's first husband and wife team. They could make a real contribution in the area of preventive work among juvenile delinquents. Now, nearly five years after his death at the hands of a juvenile narcotics addict, she was a second-grade detective on her way to an assignment involving addicts. Christie shook her head; no. They're not addicts. Reardon had explained that LSD users were not addicts in the true sense of the word.

Christie inhaled sharply and opened her eyes. She was being studied by a middle-aged woman seated diagonally across from her. She was a heavy woman, obviously encased in bulky corsets beneath her two-piece navy-blue crepe dress. The woman regarded the torn black sneakers, the long slender legs covered by taut faded green denims, the black cotton turtleneck and finally the face of the young woman, with that particular expression middle-aged people reserve for the new and terrible generation. The woman's eyes, when they met Christie's, encountered an expression of such cold and unanticipated hostility that her lips twitched compulsively and her head ducked back into her *Reader's Digest*.

Christie stood up abruptly and walked into the vestibule of the train, leaning her narrow body hard against the steel panel. She stared, unseeing, through the smudged window as the tunnel wall raced past and by a conscious, deliberate and fierce act of will, forced herself into the reality of the moment. She glanced at her wristwatch and tried to remember whether it was running four minutes slow or four minutes fast. Not that it really mattered; she had plenty of time. Nine-fifteen, more or less.

Nine-fifteen. That meant Nora and Mickey would be on their way to Mr. Stone's house for their guitar lesson. Christie's eyes traced the image of her small, round mother-in-law against the flat green panel in front of her. Nora Opara, white-haired and pink-faced and filled with as much vitality as her tireless little grandson. Christie smiled at the thought of her son, Mickey, biting his lip in concentration as Nora guided his small, inexperienced hands over the chords.

Again, she looked at her watch. She was getting a little

DOROTHY UHNAK

tense, which was good, because that meant she was getting involved and that was essential. She pushed her feet out along the scarred floor, the base of her spine supporting most of her weight. She lowered her head and stared, expressionless, into the car. She began to feel the character, build the mood, go along with it, so that by the time the subway train would arrive at 23rd Street, she would emerge completely transformed into the particular identity required of her. She would be ready to play it.

MURRAY ROGOFF stood on the subway platform and pressed his shoulder hard against the lumpy steel rivets which protruded every six inches down the length of the black-green pillar, trying to concentrate with every fiber of his body and mind on just that one sensation: that one uncomfortable physical contact, because concentrating on just one particular sensation, he could slow down the steadily building panic which must not be allowed to control him. He visualized the impressions that were being dug into his shoulder and down the hard muscles of his long arm: they would be concave and white at first, the blood forced from the area and then, later, if he pressed hard enough, there would be small reddish-blue bruises at the center of each point of contact. He forced his shoulder cruelly against the pillar but the pain did not stop the questions: how had he come to be here on this station? How long had he been standing here? *Why was he here?*

Why was he here? That, of course, was the question he must destroy with the strength of his body. His strength was so great, his body so powerful and so responsive to the demands he made on it, that Murray considered for a moment what would happen if the steel pillar could no longer resist his efforts. Shifting his body, Rogoff pressed his hip and thigh and calf and foot against the pillar and a small grunt escaped his lips. He could feel within himself a low growling sound, a steady rumbling sound which started at the soles of his feet and vibrated upwards through his body. He slowly realized that the sound was not coming from himself. A subway train was echoing far down the black tunnel and the sound changed: it grew and swelled and the long shining tracks reflected the light which preceded the entrance of the train into the station.

Rogoff backed around the pillar and stood behind it, easily flattening his body so that he was part of the steel

7

which held the station together. He pulled the plaid peaked cap down firmly over his forehead, feeling the leather band constrict the steady beating pulse at his temples. Hearing the subway car so close to him, emitting strange noises like some huge animal, breathing and gasping, Rogoff impulsively came from his hiding place and bent forward and through his thick glasses he saw a face staring blankly out of a window. It was a sleepy, vacant, dazed subway-face, but the eyes, confronting him, suddenly blinked rapidly and were alerted by a strange and urgent alarm. The doors of the train slid closed and the face inside the train gaping at him—it was an old man's face—triggered within Rogoff an anger and he lurched toward the window and pressed his face against the sticky warm glass and the old man recoiled in terror, as though some missile had been hurled at him. The train, moving from the station, flung Rogoff back against the pillar and he stood, hunched now, breathing shallowly, trying to fill his lungs, to hold down the pounding anger within his chest.

He yanked the cap off his head, jamming it under his armpit, and rubbed a calloused palm over his thick-skinned naked skull. His eyes ached and burned beneath the safety of his glasses. He took them off and, knowing he would only make the pain worse, he dug his fingers into his unprotected eyes anyway. With the edge of his dirty tan cotton-knit shirt, he scrubbed at the lenses, then at the special plastic sides which fitted firmly to the contours of his temples, like a welder's eyeshields, helping to build essential moisture inside his lashless and tearless eyes.

There was a clattering of running feet and the excited laughing voices of a young couple. Murray watched them, concealed behind the pillar. They were holding hands and gasping and pressing and bumping their bodies against each other. He wondered what the boy was whispering into the girl's ear. Or was he merely nuzzling her, tasting her, getting the smell and feel and breath of her? She was fat and cinched in at the waist by a narrow belt and her hips were lumpy, but the boy, skinny and sharp-boned, dug his hands into her flesh eagerly.

Murray locked his eyes within the enclosure of his glasses

8

but he could not close out their sounds; heavy, thick obvious sounds. He jammed his cap over his ears, then pressed his hands against the fabric, listening only to the hollow roar within his head.

All he had to do now was to let himself fill completely with the craving he had tried to hold down. Let it rise upwards through him from his loins with the sharp tentacles of need wrapping around his stomach and clenching like tight fists over his heart and lungs so that his breath came painfully hard and his heart throbbed in sharp stabbing bursts. His mind dissolved fully into his body as it had so many times before, bringing him into the night-quiet streets where the shadows would conceal him; into parks, where he could hunch his body behind shrubs in some lonely spot and watch and wait.

And sometimes, like now, when the bright sun cleared the streets of hiding places, the terrible need would send him into the still-cool damp closeness of a deserted subway station where he would watch the stairways and the passageways and the passing trains. For something.

The lust sharpened his brain with its demands, destroying all other thought. It raced through his blood, touching all parts of his body, but crystallizing into a shrewd awareness which he recognized and was willing to accept. It would not be *satisfied* now. That would come later, the complete and wonderful and joyous emptying of himself. But it *could* be sated and relieved.

Murray Rogoff watched the flashing lights of the train approaching the station and he moved to the edge of the platform because he knew that he had to get on the train. And, without thought, he knew *why*.

9

[3]

CHRISTIE STARED vacantly into the darkness that slid past the window of the vestibule, leaning her body into the steel corner. She didn't realize that she had been aware of the large figure approaching her until the man entered the vestibule, hesitated at the door leading to the next car, then, looking at her, dropped his hand from the brass handle and moved into the corner of the vestibule diagonally across from her. She had seen him in an automatic, encompassing glance down the length of the car, her mind not particularly registering the tall, lumbering figure: neither wary nor curious. But now, the man, hovering in the semi-darkness, pressing himself into a corner, came sharply into focus.

Christie felt herself tensing, the old familiar readiness, that peculiar sense of warning which started at the back of her throat and ran downwards into her stomach. She breathed easily and steadily trying to slow down the quickening senses of her body. She shifted her books to her left hand: her right hand was free now and rested lightly on the flap of her shoulder bag. Not looking at the man, her face averted from him, she could see his body reflected in the window of the car door directly to her right. The small vestibule was filled with his presence: by the heavy, deep-breathing, living sound of him and the pervasive, acid odor of him. Christie's eyes scanned the length of the car, darting along both sides of the nearly empty, past-rush hour, downtown local. There were five, maybe six, passengers, each carefully avoiding contact with anyone else: faces vacantly regarding the colorful advertisements or heads bent over morning newspapers.

Even without directly observing him, Christie knew the man was a degenerate. It was the kind of knowledge that she had absorbed day after day in the movie houses, the parks, along the side streets near schools, an awareness as intangible but as definite as a radar flash. There was a small.

sharp, breathy sound from the corner where he stood: the man was exposing himself. With certain, harsh clarity, Christie acknowledged two facts: the man was a degenerate performing a degenerate act; she was on her way to an assignment where four Squad members awaited her arrival and she could take no official action.

Without a sound, without another glance toward him, without any indication that she had been even slightly aware of him, Christie moved casually from the vestibule and entered the car, sitting halfway down the length of wicker seats, on the left side of the train so that she faced the empty portion of the vestibule. She felt a helpless anger. None of the passengers in the car was aware of the man in the vestibule; nor, for that matter, would they have acted any differently had they been aware of him. Christie sat stiffly, eyes averted from the end of the car, regretting her inability to act. The train pulled into the station and she glanced toward the vestibule. He had not exited.

Two small girls entered the car by the center door. Dressed in crisply identical uniforms of navy-blue school jumpers, white blouses, little blue bow ties and berets, emblazoned in gold with school emblems, the children were chattering excitedly and clutching their schoolbooks to them.

Sit down, sit down; oh, come on, little girls, sit down. Christie pleaded with them silently but their skinny legs couldn't stand still. Radiantly alive in the deadness of the yellow-lit subway car, their bright faces overly animated compared to the sleepy dullness of the older passengers, the children seemed unable to settle down. Looking up and down the subway car, trying to decide in which direction they should go, they turned and headed toward the vestibule.

Christie moved rapidly toward the subway map at the end of the car. The man had switched sides: he was leaning into the corner, facing into the car now, waiting. The two young schoolgirls, trying to get their footing as the car lurched into a turn, moved toward him.

Acting swiftly now, as the small girls approached the vestibule, Christie turned from the map, confronting them,

11

blocking their way and their view into the vestibule. Confused, the two children tried to walk past her, but Christie, with the graceful force of her body, spun them about so casually that no one but the children was aware of her actions. "Stay out of there," she commanded in so low and harsh a whisper that the children, startled, didn't look back at her, but took seats midway down the car.

In a determined motion, Christie, her hand extracting her detective shield from the small pocket inside the shoulder bag, pushed the schoolbooks under her arm, transferred the shield to her left hand, right hand free. She moved swiftly into the vestibule, confronting the man directly.

"Police officer," she said quietly, the flash of shield confirming her words. "You're under arrest." Her right hand grasped the man's belt, her fingers twisted into the leather. Her eyes searched for his face, hidden somewhere beneath the plaid cap and strange goggles. "Close your trousers. We're getting off at the next station." Standing close to the man, she was sickeningly aware of his size. Her voice wavered and she spoke lower. "I have a gun in my pocketbook. I don't want to use it, but that will be up to you."

The man's hands moved and he zipped his trousers. Wordlessly, he seemed to be regarding her but Christie could not see his features. She was only conscious of the massiveness of his body and she swallowed dryly as the station slid into place outside the door. Still grasping his belt, she tugged at him and he exited with her through the opened door.

"Nice and easy," she intoned. It was more of a prayer than a command, but the man, stooping forward slightly, obeyed her. No one else got off the train and the station seemed deserted. Christie, with a sinking sensation, heard the doors close behind her, felt the rumble as the train pulled away from the station. She looked about with an empty feeling and stepped away from the edge of the platform and the very real possibility of being tossed against the rapidly moving train. With her still holding his belt and him still obeying every tug and direction, they moved against the wall. Down the far end of the station was a tall, easy-moving figure in a blue uniform. A Transit Patrolman. The

12

patrolman stiffened curiously, approaching them now, his chin raised in question. Christie directed her prisoner to place his hands against the tile wall, high over his head, feet apart and well back, his weight balanced on his fingertips. She slid her left foot sideways against his left toe, feeling her schoolbooks edging from beneath her arm.

The policeman, as tall, but lighter than the prisoner, was beside them.

"What's this all about?" he asked warily. Christie could sense the sharpening of the policeman. She unclenched her left hand, the shield pressed against the flesh of her palm, aware that the officer was making a curious appraisal of her levis and sweater and sneakers.

"I'm Detective Opara, District Attorney's Squad. I just took this man off the train—indecent exposure."

The policeman was very young; his face was as pink and smooth as those of the two small schoolgirls. He whistled softly in admiration and surprise. "He's a big one." He measured himself against the height and bulk of the prisoner, then quickly, expertly, the Transit Patrolman ran his hands down the length of Murray Rogoff, shaking his head. "He's clean. Turn around, fella, let's see what you look like."

Rogoff obediently turned and faced the two police officers, his hands dangling at his sides. His face was still obscured by the cap which rested on the edge of his glasses. The young policeman squinted, peering for a better look, then asked Christie, "He give you any trouble?"

Christie glanced at her watch and moved back a few steps. She signaled the cop nearer to her and spoke quickly and quietly. The policeman's eyes remained riveted on the prisoner. "He hasn't caused me any trouble yet, but he's going to. Look, officer, I'm on an assignment. I'm supposed to be down at City College in about fifteen minutes. I'm on a set-up." Watching the clean, intense young profile, Christie clenched her teeth, then said, "Officer, this fellow is an 1140; have you ever had an 1140?"

"No, ma'am," he answered, his eyes not leaving Rogoff. "In fact, this is my first collar. I mean, I'll get an assist, won't I?"

Christie took a deep breath and the words came out

13

without pause. "Look, how'd you like the collar? Your first pinch, as a gift. He's yours."

The policeman's eyes left the prisoner for just an instant; his face stiffened. "How's that?"

Trying to read his profile again, Christie said, "I'm on an assignment. Something very important, for the D.A. We have four men staked out, waiting for me to make a connection, in just about fifteen minutes. We've been on this case for nearly a month and today's *the* day." She realized her voice was getting a little shaky. There was an intelligent awareness about the young patrolman that unnerved her. Not stopping to measure his reaction, she continued, "When he got off the train he was exposed—you saw that when you approached us, right?"

The cop's bright face was a frozen mask; the eyes, like two points of ice, stayed on hers now. "I didn't see him exposed. I can't make the collar. *You're* the arresting officer. *I* have no complainant and *I* can't take him on observation because I *didn't* see him exposed: you did. *He's your prisoner. I'm assisting.*"

Christie's breath exploded into an irritated whistle between her teeth. She could hear a train approaching from the tunnel. All she wanted was to get on that train and ride one more stop to where she was supposed to be: to where the Squad men were waiting for her.

"All right, officer, my mistake. I thought you had observed him. So you didn't. Look, I'll tell you what. He's been a nice, quiet fellow. He isn't going to give me any trouble. You go on with your patrol. There might be a mugger or something down the south end of the station. Why don't you just go about your job and I'll take care of this, okay?"

"No good," he said in a voice so familiar to her: the voice of every cop who knew he was being conned. "He's a prisoner. You placed him under arrest. His next stop is the precinct, which you know better than I do, officer. If he was to dump you or something, that would be my responsibility."

With a feeling close to despair, Christie watched a train pull into the station, saw the doors slide open and then shut;

14

watched it leave the station heading toward 23rd Street . . . without her.

The Transit Patrolman had a firm grasp on Rogoff's arm now, then his face broke into a grin. "Hey, Sarge," he called, waving to a stocky blue-clad figure who had just gotten off the train. His voice lower, he said to Christie, "This guy's a corker; he gives us a look every hour on the hour." Then, to the sergeant, who came toward them, "Look what we got here!"

The Transit Sergeant, a compact man of about fifty, with the springy bounce of a light heavyweight, professionally narrowed his eyes which raced from Rogoff to Christie, trying to size up the situation. "What's this?" he asked sharply, his chin pushing in her direction. "Couple of beatniks acting up?"

The patrolman grinned. "She's a detective, Sarge. D.A.'s Squad. Took this guy off the train all by herself. An 1140," he added.

"Yeah?" the sergeant growled, unconvinced.

Christie held up her shield; then, regarding the shrewd, weary, wise face hopefully, she moved away, motioning him toward her. "Sergeant, can I talk to you for a minute?" She looked at her watch, groaning. "Oh God, I'm going to get murdered." The sergeant regarded her without expression. "Sergeant, I'm supposed to be down at City College right now. We're on a big case. Confidential, involving some students and LSD; some big people are pushing this investigation and today is wrap-it-up day. My squad is down there, waiting for me. Casey Reardon is my boss and . . ."

The sergeant's face collapsed now into a different face altogether: the human, warm, pleasant face of someone who has just recognized a friend. "Casey Reardon?" The smile recalled some private memories. "Hey, he still a regular hell-shooter? Geez, I could tell you stories about him."

Clutching at a sudden, unexpected, possible hope, Christie's voice became conspiratorial: the sergeant knew Reardon. "Well I'm the one who is going to get shot right straight to the devil if I don't get myself to where I'm supposed to be. It's not just a case, Sarge, you understand that." He nodded sympathetically and she began to feel a little better. "Someone 'very high up' is waiting on this, Sarge, and putting real pressure on all of us."

The sergeant's face had its professional look again. "Why this then?" His thumb jerked over his shoulder, toward Rogoff and the young officer.

Christie explained about the schoolgirls, watching the sergeant's face relax again. "I wouldn't have touched him with a ten-foot pole otherwise. Believe me, Sarge, I don't want him. I would have called your headquarters and I'm sure your teams would have picked him up in the act another day. I was just afraid he'd expose himself to the kids —or maybe worse—after I detrained at 23rd Street." Then, not hiding her bitterness, "I didn't expect to run into your bright, efficient and very helpful young patrolman. Sergeant, I'm in a jam."

The sergeant thoughtfully rubbed the back of his neck. His face was sympathetic. "I understand the situation. Casey Reardon!" His soft whistle did not help Christie. "You see"—his eyes flashed over to the young cop—"we just turned these kids out. Two weeks on the line; bright-eyed, bushy-tailed young turks, most of them. This one is a good kid; going to make a real good cop out of him. Book smart and head smart."

Christie felt the subway platform being pulled from under her and it was a long, long way down.

"If it was *me* had been on the station, well, I *might* have seen him exposed, you know? But these new kids—it's a big deal. First collar. And these are *good* kids, know what I mean?"

Christie nodded with heavy resignation. "I know what you mean, Sarge. And thanks for the ear, anyway." More to herself, she said, "Reardon might bounce me all the way back to the Woman's Bureau."

Without conviction, the sergeant tried to comfort her. "Aw, maybe it won't be that bad, kid. Under the circumstances, what the hell could you do?"

The agent in the change booth, a wiry man with a thin leather face, pushed the telephone on the little steel revolving platform from his booth so that the Transit Patrolman could call his Headquarters. The agent continued counting his tokens, his fingers automatically pushing them two at a time from one part of the smooth wooden board to the other, not missing count but also not missing a word being said into the telephone.

"That's right, Lieutenant, 1140, Indecent Exposure. On southbound IRT local en route between 33rd and 28th Street. Arresting Officer, Detective Christie Opara (he spelled it phonetically into the phone "O-per-uh" and Christie didn't correct him, because then he would call her, as everyone did, O'Para); shield number 4754, D.A.'s Squad —Investigations." The patrolman listened for a moment, then, "Oh, all right, I didn't know you wanted the prisoner's pedigree now, just a minute." Carefully cradling the telephone against his shoulder, he turned the pages of his notebook. "Here we go: Murray Rogoff—two f's—male—white —36 years—born U.S.; height, 6'1", weight, approximately 185." Then turning to Rogoff, "Hey, fella, what color are your eyes?"

The sergeant peered at Rogoff. "Take off your cap, mister."

Rogoff reached up and removed his cap. The sergeant whistled in blunt surprise at the stony skull. "You wouldn't miss this guy a mile away. Those special glasses, buddy? What have you got, trouble with your eyes?"

Rogoff removed his glasses without being told and his lashless eyes blinked rapidly, unprotected now. His face was browless and as smooth as his head with no stubble or indication of any beard growth. The sergeant called out, "Eyes, light brown. Go ahead, buddy, put the glasses back on if it hurts your eyes." Then, to Christie, who at the moment couldn't care less, "Those are special moisture glasses; I've seen them before. Guy I know got burned in a forest fire once—pal of mine, used to be a ranger. Holds the moisture in, right, Rogoff?" The sergeant wasn't annoyed by the unanswered question. He whispered to Christie, "This guy's in a fog; acts like a robot; gotta watch them when they're like that."

Christie looked around the station again: no telephone. The sergeant, catching her distress, hurried the patrolman off the phone. "Come on, come on, you can give them more

17

details from the precinct; hell, you can tell them what color shorts he's wearing if you want to."

Christie took a deep breath, inserted her index finger in the dial, spinning it completely for an outside line. She heard the steady buzzing of the dial tone, then dialed her office number.

The first ring was interrupted by the slurred words: "District-Attorney's-Squad-Detective-Martin."

"Stoney? This is Christie."

There was a silence lasting approximately two seconds. "Is it now?"

"Yes. Stoney, listen . . ."

"Christie, where the hell are you? It's after ten. Marty called twice; Ferranti called once; O'Hanlon's been ringing steady and Mr. Reardon is getting what you might call a little tense, only that's not what you really might call it."

"Well, Stoney, a funny thing happened to me on my way to City College." Her voice fell as she realized he wasn't responding. "I'm at the 28th Street station of the IRT subway."

Another voice blared into her ear, harsh, cold and deliberate. "And exactly what the hell are you doing at the 28th Street station of the IRT subway?" Casey Reardon demanded.

Christie caught her breath. The sergeant, standing next to her, was pointing at himself. Would it help if he spoke? She shook her head. "Well, sir, it's a long story."

Irritably, she was ordered to tell it fast. "Well, I got this 1140." She hoped the sergeant hadn't heard the words that were blasted into her ear. He probably had, for he was strolling discreetly toward the prisoner. Christie's mind went blank and she felt the words struggling inside her mouth, not forming first carefully inside her brain. She wondered if Mr. Reardon even heard her: it seemed as though his steady, furious cursing continued as she spoke, trying to tell him the facts. "And this Transit cop gave me an assist, and . . ." This triggered another barrage of words and then the voice receded and Stoney's voice spoke to her again.

"Christie," he said carefully, "Mr. Reardon says as soon as you get your prisoner arraigned you get yourself into the

18

office. Hold it a minute." She heard an angry consultation, then Stoney again. "When you get to court, see Tommy Kalman, you know him, the blond court attendant. Have him get you in and out fast—tell him Mr. Reardon's orders, then you come in, right?"

"Right. What about the other fellas?"

"Yeah, how 'bout them?" Stoney asked her. "I'll probably be hearing from them in the immediate future and I'll call them in." She heard Reardon's voice moving further away, then cut off completely by the explosive sound of a slamming door. Stoney sighed and his voice was softer now. "Christie, you better wear a suit of armor; Mr. Reardon is what you might say 'unhappy.'"

"Thanks a lot." Christie hung up the phone and pushed it back into the booth. Mr. Reardon's unhappy.

Regretfully, Christie waved to the sergeant as he stood looking out the window of the subway train which was picking up speed, hurtling toward 23rd Street.

"Good God," the desk lieutenant at the precinct said, "look what Transit is sending us now: a twelve-year-old cop and a beatnik female detective. What's your prisoner, a circus strong man? Look at the build on this guy!"

The uniformed clerical man lifted his head from the large sheet of paper he was charting, nodded without comment, and continued his work.

Christie held up her shield. "I'm P.D., Lieutenant. D.A.'s Squad. Prisoner is an 1140. I took him off a train and this officer from Transit is assisting me."

"An 1140? Off a subway train? And you're D.A.'s Squad?" The lieutenant's voice was loud in contrast to her own.

"Yes sir," Christie said shortly. "I was heading for an assignment and came across this man. Can we bring him up to Detectives now?"

The lieutenant waved in the direction of the iron staircase and Christie signaled for the young officer to follow her with the prisoner.

Transit Patrolman Alexander looked a little upset. He was seeing for the first time the translation of the crisp, cold official words of police procedure into reality and he was

19

groping. "He gets printed, doesn't he?" he asked Christie.

She nodded, then stopped in the dampish, musty hallway. Ptl. Alexander was trying very hard. "Look," she explained, "remember Section 552 of the Code of Criminal Procedure?"

Ptl. Alexander tried to remember. "Code of Criminal Procedure . . . 552 covers certain misdemeanors and offenses."

"Section 552 of the Code of Criminal Procedure is probably one of the most important sections you're going to deal with." She tried to keep the impatience from her voice. "It covers various misdemeanors and offenses that require the fingerprinting and photographing of a prisoner, remember?"

Ptl. Alexander brightened. "Yes. Included are jostling, certain forms of disorderly conduct, possession of certain drugs not covered by narcotics laws, indecent exposure and . . ."

"I *know* what's included," Christie said. "The main point for you to remember is that although 1140 of the Penal Law is an offense, the prisoner is processed exactly as though it were a felony. He is printed, photoed and arraigned in Felony Court."

The young officer nodded. He remembered now.

The detective from the squad neatly and expertly rolled Rogoff's fingers on the ink pad, then carefully transferred them to the official Criminal Identification form. "You know how to back them up, don't you, Transit?"

The patrolman nodded uncertainly and Christie took the sheets of fingerprints to the typewriter, while the detective led Rogoff to the men's room, to wash his hands. Filling in the required information; name, description, address, scars, characteristics, Christie was unaware of the sensation Rogoff was creating among a newly arrived group of detectives from the precinct. Unrolling the pedigree sheet from the machine, she looked up curiously, getting a good look at her prisoner for the first time. He was rubbing his wet fingers along the seams of his trousers.

His face was large and expressionless, the broad bony structure clearly outlined beneath the taut stretch of yellow skin. His eyes blinked incessantly beneath the unusual glasses, appearing to see no further than the smudged limits of the lenses themselves. Though he responded to the orders and requests of the detectives who were studying him, he did not speak or seem to be aware of his surroundings. As he turned toward her, she noticed a bulge of heavy bone at the top of his forehead, then as his head moved toward the sound of his name, Christie observed that the mass of bone flattened out at the base of his skull. His head was like a piece of sculpture roughly shaped by an artist who had abandoned his work without polishing it into a finished symmetry.

"Jesus, not a hair on him," one detective said. "Any hair on your body, mister?"

The naked head swung back and forth. Rogoff removed his glasses, letting them examine his lashless eyes, then, wiping the lenses against his dirty shirt, he wedged them on again and jammed his cap over his skull. His ears were bent by the pressure.

"You're entitled to a phone call, buddy. Who do you want to call? You just tell me, and I'll make the call for you."

Rogoff shrugged, his long, powerful arms falling on either side of the wooden chair where he sat, slumped to one side. The detective pulled up a chair beside him, his voice patient, and he began moving his hands, as though speaking to one who didn't understand English. "Here's a piece of paper and a pencil. You write down who you want to be notified and the phone number. That's right." Then, examining the words on the paper, the detective asked, "David Rogoff, huh? That your father? No? Your brother, huh? Okay, Murray, I'll give him a call and tell him you'll be arraigned in Felony Court."

The detective stopped beside Christie. "He's a real beaut. He give you any trouble?"

"Not a sound out of him. As you see him, that's how he's been."

The detective turned and regarded Rogoff across the room. "You're pretty lucky, kid. That's some powerful guy." Then, pulling at his mouth, "You were crazy to take him alone."

"Crazier than you know," Christie said. Rogoff's arms, hanging limply, were long and hard and tautly muscled, the

21

fingers long and thick, the wrists powerful. It was the complete hairlessness that made his body look so dangerous:
like some indestructible living stone. If there was anything
to be grateful for in all of this, it was that Rogoff had been
so submissive. For an instant, it flashed through Christie that
it might have been better if he *had* resisted. At least, if she
had a bloody nose or a black eye, she might get some sympathy from Reardon and the men in the Squad. But looking
again at those powerful hands and arms and wide shoulders
and strange, hoodlike head, Christie dismissed the thought.

They waited at the precinct for over an hour before a
patrol wagon picked them up. "You ride in the back with
him, Patrolman Alexander. I'll be up front with the driver.
First stop is the Photo Gallery. One of the squad detectives
dropped the prints at the B.C.I., so if Rogoff has a yellow
sheet, it will be in the complaint room at Felony Court by
the time we get there—I hope."

Transit Patrolman George Alexander nodded solemnly.
There was a marked change in him now: *he* was responsible
for Rogoff.

Gripping his prisoner firmly, Ptl. Alexander emerged from
the rear of the patrol wagon, his eyes searching for the entrance to the Photo Gallery, located in the basement of
Police Headquarters. Following Christie, he escorted Rogoff
into the confusion of the room where prisoners from all over
the city were milling about, each one individually guarded
and watched in varying degrees of intensity by the particular arresting officer. The photographer waved Alexander
away from Rogoff, who had been placed, face-front, small
name-board and identification number strung around his
neck.

"C'mon, Transit, move it," the detective-photographer
yelled. "You want to be mugged too?"

"Gee-zus, look at the light bounce off that guy's skull. He's
a weird one, ain't he, with those glasses?" A runty little
prisoner with tiny rat's eyes nudged the lanky detective who
had arrested him for attempted robbery. "How'd you like to
meet *him* in the dark?"

Christie checked her watch against the wall clock. It was

nearly 11:30. Someone grabbed her wrist, holding her hand over her head.

"Hey, who belongs to this? Who you with, sister?"

Wrenching her hand free, Christie glared at the detective. "I'm with *my prisoner*, brother, do you mind?"

The detective grinned good-naturedly. "Can't tell the good guys from the bad guys anymore."

They waited another twenty minutes for the patrol wagon to fill with prisoners heading for Criminal Courts Building. Seeing the fleeting panic on his face as Alexander emerged once again from the patrol wagon, Christie impatiently explained, "Follow the parade to the Detention section. You sign him in and then Correction has him. Then ask somebody, or just follow the cops up to the Complaint Room. I'll be up there getting the complaint drawn up."

The young officer moved resolutely into the crowd. There was a long line in the Complaint Room and Christie looked around rapidly, spotting a familiar form on line amidst the many uniformed and plainclothes police officers, and the bewilderment of frightened complainant victims. Crashing through the milling confusion, Christie came alongside her target.

"Excuse me, mister, could you help out a poor girl who's lost?"

The large head turned, a suspicious scowl pulling all the blunt features. "What?" The eyes, narrowed, recognized her and all the features of his face, everything—mouth, brows, cheeks—turned upward. "Well, I'll be damned! Christie Opara. My God," he said, looking her up and down, "things that tough in the D.A.'s Squad?"

"Guess I wouldn't pass muster back home at BOSSI, huh?"

"Well, we never had you down that low, kid. The Squad Commander wouldn't let you past the door in that get-up." The warm brown eyes rested on hers, and the heavy neck leaned to Christie's face. "What you got, Chris—something special?"

Making a face, Christie muttered, "1140."

Jack Maxwell raised all his features in surprise. "You're

23

kidding—1140? D.A.'s Squad? They send you out on that stuff?"

"No, just something I ran into. Look, Jack, I'm in a jam; very long story, very short on time. Can I crowd you out, Jack, old friend, old former teammate. Please?"

Detective Maxwell stepped back, forcing the line in back of him to stagger a little more. He ignored the hard glares he was getting from two officers directly behind him and he called out to no one in particular, "You guys don't mind, do you? We'll help the little lady out." Then leaning forward again, "How's things over there, Christie? I hear Reardon's still going full-steam ahead. What kind of boss is he?"

Christie forced a smile. "Okay. He's okay. But I do get a little homesick. Say, Jack, keep an eye out for a young Transit cop, will you? He gave me an assist and I'm trying to show him the ropes. First time out for him."

"Transit? You training Transit cops now? That what they got you doing?" Jack spotted the tall, clean-cut young officer. "Holy mackerel, he looks twelve years old."

"He's thirteen," Christie said. "Hey, George, over here."

Relieved of his prisoner, Patrolman Alexander looked around the room with interest, "Wow, lot of action, huh? This go on every day?"

"Every day and every night, Saturdays, Sundays and holidays included. Patrolman Alexander, meet Detective Maxwell, Bureau of Special Services."

The policeman, boyishly unguarded, shook hands with Jack. "Special Services? BOSSI? Wow!"

Jack shook his head wearily. " 'Wow,' " he repeated softly, then to Christie, "It's a sign of advancing age when you look at a kid like this and he's in a policeman's uniform. How old are you, son?"

Patrolman Alexander's chin raised slightly and his lips tightened. He pulled his hand from Maxwell's grasp. "Old enough."

Maxwell studied the smooth young face with something close to sympathy. His expression was thoughtful, remembering some other time, some other young cop. "Relax, officer, you're among friends," he said, not unkindly.

"Come on, George, watch how it's done." She leaned over

the high counter, recited her information to the bored clerk who punched the keys of the typewriter, handed Christie the affidavit and the yellow sheet which one of the detectives had dropped off for her. "No previous," she said. "Just our arrest. Jack, see you around, and thanks again."

"Take care, Christie; you too, Junior."

"Now," Christie told Patrolman Alexander, "go back to Detention, show the affidavit to the Corrections man, get Rogoff and meet me up in Felony Court. Follow the signs or ask someone; I'll meet you right by the detention pen in the front of the court."

Christie went into the ladies' room, ran cold water over her wrists, splashed her face and swallowed a mouthful of water from her cupped hands. Patting her face with tissues, she wrinkled her nose at her reflection in the mirror. She pulled a comb through her thick hair, trying to soften the straight disheveled bangs. With a tissue, she wiped the pale eye-shadow from her lids, then dug again into the shoulder bag, finding a turquoise shadow stick. Christie rubbed her finger on the makeup, then slid some color onto each lid. That looked a little better. The only lipstick she could find was a medium pink: at least, it was a little deeper than her colorless lips. Tugging at the jersey turtleneck, she craned her neck, then decided she had to make the best of things. Christie looped the shoulder bag over her arm and absently reached for her textbooks, which weren't there. She stood motionless for a moment: damn. She had lost two textbooks and one spiral notebook somewhere along the way.

She walked down the wide, high-ceilinged marble-walled corridor, pulled the heavy oak door and entered the cathedral-like courtroom where felony cases and certain misdemeanor cases were arraigned. Walking silently on the sneakers, Christie felt the familiar sensation that always overtook her when she entered this place. It was like being in a church or in a museum or in some sacred, ancient tomb. The ceiling was two stories high; the windows began midway up the side of one wall and extended almost to the ceiling, letting in long narrow slashes of dust-filled light. The chandeliers, massive and systematically ranged across the ceiling, glowed with a dim tanness which did not penetrate

25

the semi-darkness. The benches filling the room were of a smooth, polished wood. Over all the whispered, worried, earnest conversations taking place throughout the room, a heavy layer of silence seemed to press downward like a lid over the bowed heads and cupped mouths.

Avoiding the center aisle, Christie walked close to the right wall, feeling invisible. No one noticed her or was interested in her; everyone here had his own concerns. Court Attendant Tommy Kalman spotted Christie at the same moment she saw him, raising her hand to attract his attention. He motioned her forward inside the gate which separated the long rows of benches from the area reserved for officers of the court, police officers, attorneys and prisoners. Immediately behind this section was the high, long desk where the Magistrate, robed in black, was presiding.

"Hey, Christie, come on. I got your docket number moved up." Noting her surprise, he added, "Stoner Martin called me. Seems like Reardon wants you out fast."

"Thanks, Tommy. My prisoner is with a young Transit cop. Has he come up yet?" Then, seeing Alexander resolutely hanging onto Rogoff's arm, she nodded toward the detention cage. "There he is."

Kalman ushered the Transit officer and Rogoff into the courtroom, clanging the cage door behind him. Alexander glanced back at the meshed-steel cage which protruded into the courtroom, set over a stairway leading to the detention cells. The prisoners, lining the stairway, awaiting their appearance in court, were craning their necks in hope of spotting someone—wife, friend, attorney—anyone, within the courtroom.

"Take your cap off, mister. Judge sees that and he'll flip." Kalman regarded Rogoff's odd skull without expression of any kind. There was nothing that Tommy Kalman hadn't seen before. There was nothing, no person, no deed, no crime, no event, no deformity, no beauty, nothing that would ever register on Kalman's placid features.

Christie kept her eyes on Kalman, watching him move easily among the people milling before the Magistrate's bench: speaking quickly with the court clerk, indicating her, handing him the affidavits, crossing to the Assistant District

Attorney, standing on his toes, speaking up to the Magistrate, then signaling for Christie to approach.

"Let's go," she said softly to the Transit Patrolman who moved forward with Rogoff. "Stand to his left and slightly behind him," she instructed.

The young A.D.A. raised his face from the affidavit. "You the arresting officer?" She nodded and he lifted his face questioningly toward Alexander. "He assisted," she explained.

The court clerk rapidly read the complaint in a monotone of mumbling and Christie, holding up her right hand, answered, "I do" when asked to swear to the truth of the words. So indistinguishable had his reading been—it always was—she could be swearing to the fact that she was a spy from another planet.

Rogoff, head down, seemed unaware that any words had been directed to him. The D.A. repeated, "Mister, the judge wants to know if you want Legal Aide assigned." Rogoff regarded him blankly. "Can you afford an attorney? If you can't, the court will appoint Legal Aide." Rogoff blinked rapidly but remained silent. The D.A. turned impatiently to Christie. "What's the story here—he psycho or what?"

"He hasn't opened his mouth since we arrested him."

The magistrate leaned forward, his horn-rimmed glasses resting on his forehead. "Did he have any identification on him, officer? And has anyone been notified of his arrest?"

"Yes, sir, he had identification. A call was made to his brother, your Honor."

The magistrate slid his glasses over his eyes, addressing the D.A. "What is your pleasure, Mr. Martinelli?"

The D.A. consulted his calendar pad. "One thousand dollars bail, your Honor—adjourn to May tenth—that okay with you, officer?"

Christie nodded. "Wait a minute," she whispered to Patrolman Alexander. "Stand over there, I'll get the commitment papers." She took the papers, which the magistrate had signed, from Tommy Kalman and thanked him for saving her a few hours' waiting time. "Here, George, bring him back down to Detention, give these to the Correction officer, sign him in and you're on your way."

Alexander seemed a little nervous again. "Look," she said, glancing at the large round clock embedded high in the wall at the back of the courtroom, "that's all there is to it. You won't be called on the case. It's adjourned back to this court for the twelfth. Then he'll probably waive to Special Sessions for a plea. He'll probably get bailed out later in the day when his brother, or whoever, shows. When the case is disposed of, I'll call your command with the details, okay?"

"Okay." Then, his youthful excitement overcame his strenuous attempts at professionalism. He leaned forward, whispering to Christie, "Hey, Detective Opara, you know who they have down there? You know that guy all over the *Daily News* this morning—murdered his wife and drowned his four kids? *He's* down there," Patrolman Alexander said, as though the detention pen in the Criminal Courts Building was the last place in the world he'd expect to find a murderer. "I guess that's why all the photographers were hanging around out back." He shook his head in wonder. "Boy, you know something—he's just a medium-sized guy. I mean, he looks just like *anybody* else, you know? Stabbed his wife twenty-two times, then drowned his four kids, then made himself some scrambled eggs! The detectives were telling me, down there. He looks just like anybody else," he repeated.

"Yes, I'm sure he does," Christie said. "*Everyone* looks just like *anybody* else. Well, I better get to my office. Thanks for all your help, officer." He looked so earnest; it didn't seem possible that he was only five years younger than she. But then, she had five years more on the job than he had. "Good luck in your career," she said, "I'm sure you're going to be just fine."

He grinned, holding his prisoner with his left hand, so that his right hand was free to grasp hers. "Thanks a lot, Detective Opara, this has all been very interesting. Oh, and good luck with your boss."

Transit Patrolman George Alexander, age twenty-one, disappeared with his prisoner into the detention cage. Detective Christie Opara looked at the clock on the wall, and wished she could disappear too.

[4]

IT WAS 1:00 P.M. when Detective Christie Opara turned the cold brass doorknob to the drab, green-walled office identified by the neatly stenciled legend in the smoked-glass upper half of the door: "District Attorney's Squad—Investigations." She was prepared for the reaction of the members of her Squad. She had worked too long with men not to anticipate exactly what her reception would be.

Detective Marty Ginsburg was leaning over the battered old wooden desk in the far corner of the Squad room. It was a relic handed down from generations of municipal offices and, out of respect for the uniform gray metal and black-rubber-topped newer standard desks, it had been placed in the least conspicuous area of the room. Invariably, Marty, when in the office, claimed it for his own. Each of the four scarred drawers contained a nondescript collection of things held in value by Marty Ginsburg. At the moment, half of the desk top was covered with coins: nickels, dimes, quarters. The other half was covered with large grains of salt and pretzel crumbs. A large cardboard carton bulged with thick, doughy pretzels. Peering from beneath a heavy, lank strand of dark hair, Marty rasped, "Yeah, kid, what do you want? You the delivery boy for the 'Quik-Lunch'? Where's the coffee and how come it took you so long?"

Christie held up her large leather shoulder bag. "Mailman, mister. Say, are you selling those pretzels?"

Marty dug his arm into the box. "These are *bagels*—not pretzels. Italians sell pretzels. Jews sell *bagels*. Two-fer-a-quarter, three-fer-fifty cents." Marty winked. "That's how we make all our money. You want the bargain deal or what?"

"I don't think I could swallow anything right now, but thanks anyway."

Pat O'Hanlon, a tall man with a light voice and a bland

29

pale face, pointed a long index finger at Christie and asked no one in particular, *"What-is-that?"*

Stoner Martin, first-grade and senior detective in the Squad, finished the sentence he had been pounding out on the five-year-old Royal, the best typewriter in the Squad and his by claim of seniority. He stood up and walked over beside O'Hanlon. *"That,* Patrick, is a second-grade detective. A *female* second-grade detective. Opara, I believe. Am I correct, officer?"

Stoner's black eyes glinted in his dark face. He was a handsome, dark-skinned Negro, a powerful man, his lean hard torso outlined by a narrow custom-made white shirt. He was the only man in the Squad who could successfully wear close-fitting, beltless slacks: he was absolutely hipless and stomachless.

The three men regarded Christie as though she were an inanimate curiosity. She hoisted herself easily onto the long table against one wall, her sneakers dangling a good six inches from the floor. She leaned the palms of her hands on either side of her body, hunching her shoulders against their words, which were good-natured, but sharp.

"We had a second-grade female detective in this Squad once, remember, Stoney?"

Stoner scratched his chin thoughtfully, then snapped his fingers. "Oh, yes, that's right. She was a real ace, wasn't she?" Stoner's musical voice played over his mockingly admiring words. "I remember now. A regular one-girl crime-buster. 'Lock-'em-up-Susie'—that's what we used to call her."

O'Hanlon nodded earnestly. "She sure made the Squad look good. Lifted the Squad's activity record way up, carried the rest of us non-productive foot soldiers."

"Yeah, and us bagel vendors," Marty chimed in.

Stoner fixed his eye on Ginsburg, who was eating another pretzel. "Marty, if you think you are going to fill your already adequate stomach with enough of that poisoned dough to get you on sick leave, forget it. Mr. Reardon is not in a particularly sympathetic mood as of this moment and if you begin to feel a little queasy, you better not get a little queasy on these immediate premises."

Marty gasped, "I don't feel so good. When I don't feel so good, I eat. I can't help it. I'm a compulsive eater."

"I've heard of compulsive eaters," O'Hanlon said. "Stoney, have you ever heard of compulsive lock-'em-up second-grade female detectives?"

Christie sighed. "Okay, fellas. Anyone want to hear what happened?"

O'Hanlon looked at Ginsburg. "Marty, do you want to hear what happened?"

Marty shook his head. "Not me. I don't want to hear what happened. Do you want to hear what happened, Paddy?"

"Hell, no, I don't want to hear what happened. Stoney, do you want to hear what happened?"

Motioning Christie toward his typewriter, Stoner Martin said, "No, I don't want to hear what happened. But Mr. Reardon in there, *he* wants to hear what happened. But first he wants to *read* what happened, Detective Opara, so will you just put your typing fingers on this keyboard and type up a 'complete-the-Man-said' report of what happened, so that the Man will know completely what happened?"

Christie set up the papers: one original and two onionskin copies, and found some small consolation in the fact that Stoney had relinquished the Royal and now muttered over the inadequacies of the ancient Underwood. She typed: "From: Detective Christie Opara, Shield #4754; To: Mr. Casey Reardon, Supervising Assistant District Attorney, Investigations." Turning the paper down four spaces for the body of the report, Christie looked up and flexed her fingers. "Fellas—Stoney, Pat, Marty—I'm sorry that you got hung up because of my arrest. Really."

Stoney stared up for a moment, then unlocked two keys which had stuck together. O'Hanlon, without stopping his search for some address in the Manhattan directory, began singing in his soft tenor, "Who's sorry now? Who's sorry now?"

Marty, a piece of pretzel in one hand, a clutch of coins in the other, came over to her desk. "For myself, Christie, I don't really mind." He opened his large hand, revealing a palm filled with money. "See, I figure I'm about a buck-twenty ahead. And I got breakfast and lunch out of my

31

box." He leaned toward her and whispered loudly. "But Bill Ferranti is the guy you're going to have trouble with."

"Ferranti? Why?" She pictured the mild, clean-cut partner of Marty Ginsburg.

"Well, Bill *looks* like a very nice guy. I mean, gee, no matter where you go with Bill everybody figures—salesman, librarian, IBM technician. He's got that nice manner that makes everybody else look like a bum. But boy, is that a cover-up." Marty looked around, whispering even louder. "You see, I've worked with him for five years now, so I know better. What happened was, see, Ferranti with that white hair of his, well, he couldn't be taken for one of the college kids, and it seems somebody got a little nervous, with this dapper white-haired guy hanging around the school cafeteria. Like, if he was a professor or something, he'd be in the teachers' lounge, not in the students' cafeteria."

Christie frowned. "What happened?"

"Well, I guess I better tell you. Someone got nervous, like I said, and called the security guard and they gave Ferranti a fast toss and Ferranti blew a fuse. I mean, how would a guy feel, them acting like he was some kind of a nut— hanging around the young college girls, you know?"

"You're kidding?" Christie asked hopefully. Then, seeing Marty's mournful face, "You're not kidding?"

"I'm telling you what happened is all. So listen, kid, you just stay away from Bill, see, that's the best way. Don't say nothing to him, not even a word. He cools off in complete silence. Mr. Reardon sent him uptown for some information on something, but he'll be back soon, so you just ignore him, okay?" Marty patted her reassuringly on her shoulder and returned to tally up his profits.

Christie called to O'Hanlon. "Pat? Is that true? What Marty said about Bill?"

O'Hanlon's eyes scanned the ceiling, his mouth stretched. "Just give him a wide berth, Christie. He always simmers down." Then, softly to himself, "After a while, that is."

The sharp voice cut through the room over the clattering of typewriters. "Hey, Stoney, is what's-her-name here yet?"

Christie's fingers leaped from the keys. Stoner quickly

crossed the room and depressed the key of the call box on his desk. "Yes, sir, she's just typing up the report you wanted."

"Well, tell her to make it snappy!"

"Yes, sir." Releasing the key, he turned to Christie. "The Man said to make it snappy."

"Yes, I heard him. They probably heard him in Canarsie. What's-her-name is typing as fast as she can."

Christie typed steadily, then rolled up the paper to read her report. Her fingers found an eraser in the top drawer, her eyes fixed on an error. Carefully, she placed scraps of paper against the carbon and scrubbed away a letter, then, lining the paper up, hit the proper key sharply. "Damn." She had placed the letter in the wrong spot, causing a strike-over. Slowing herself down, she neatly erased the strike-over, then repaired the damage as best she could. She pulled the report from the machine, signed her name. "Okay, Stoney, here it is."

Stoner took the report and held the first copy up toward the light. His voice was sad. "Nearly made a hole in the paper. Mr. Reardon doesn't like near-holes in his reports. Oh, well, I better get it in to him anyway."

She watched Stoner walk down the connecting corridor, rap once on the smoked-glass door and enter Casey Reardon's private office.

Christie walked to Marty's desk, absently pressing a few salt crumbs on her finger tips and licking them with her tongue. "Marty, what do you think?" she asked, trying to sound casual.

"Well, I think I must have eaten about twenty-two bagels so far and I think I don't feel so good."

"Come on, Marty, no more jokes." She hadn't intended to sound quite so urgent.

Marty pressed his hands against his large stomach, then, peering at her through his thick hair, his voice changed, becoming serious. "Okay, kid. Let's say that you're not officially a member of the Squad until you've been through the fire initiation. We have—one and all, at one time or another—been through it. Now, it's your turn." He stood up, his heavy hand on her shoulder. "He's rough, but he's a

33

good boss. Fair. Just don't try to fool him. Tell him what happened straight out, no excuses."

"Thanks, Marty. I will."

Stoner rolled into the office with the easy, rhythmic step of an athlete. "Okay, little one," he said softly to Christie, "the Man says *now.*"

Christie swallowed, looking around the room. The men were all very busy; too busy to glance at her.

Christie knocked twice on the door. She didn't realize how loud the second tap was until the voice bellowed out, "For God's sake, don't break the door down—just come in!"

She entered the large square room, which was a strong contrast to the dinginess of the Squad office. It was flooded by light from windows on two sides. The walls, a light beige, were filled with framed photographs, shiny metal plaques presented to Casey Reardon from an assortment of fraternal, civic and ethnic organizations; certificates, documents, law degrees, diplomas, citations. His desk, a large, modern oiled walnut, was cluttered with an assortment of papers, folders, case files, a haphazard stack of books, two pen sets, and a small, double-framed picture, probably of his family. There was a dark green leather couch against one wall and two straight-backed, wooden-armed chairs, upholstered in the same green leather, directly before the desk.

Reardon was leaning back in his tilt chair, his feet crossed on the top of a desk drawer that had been opened just for that purpose. He was scanning Christie's report through horn-rimmed glasses. He looked up, motioned her toward a chair, then, pushing his glasses up into his dark red hair, he said, "Wait a minute. Hold it right there." He stood up, hands on his hips. "My God. Walk across the room."

Christie uneasily followed his hand, which waved her from one side of the room to the other.

"Turn around. Go ahead, just turn around. Now, back here."

Christie's fingers nervously settled on the heavy side seam of her levis. Self-consciously, she hooked her thumbs into her side pockets. Reardon ran his hand roughly over his face, then dug at his eyes for a moment. "Turn off the radio, will you?"

Christie walked to the cabinet and turned the knob the wrong way. The music blasted into the room. She snapped it off immediately, and muttered, "Sorry."

"Sit down. Go ahead, relax." Reardon leaned back again, silently rereading her report.

Christie lifted her eyes from the edge of his desk and studied his face. It was the kind of face which had probably improved with age. The paleness of the typical redhead had deepened. There were still clusters of reddish freckles across the bridge of his short, pugnacious nose, but they too were dark. His eyes, an almost transparent amber, could range from honey to fire-red and they dominated his face. Light darted from them in sharp flickers through the thick, short red lashes. His hair was as dark as bottled iodine and thick and unruly. His face was strong, revealing much of the character of the man: there were some small lines along the edges of his eyes and the start of some heavy expression lines across the forehead. The chin was square and firm with just an indication of light red stubble. It was still a boyish face, yet at forty years of age, there was also a touch of maturity beginning to dominate.

If time had mellowed the visage of the man, it did nothing to blunt the imprint of the West Side longshoreman's son. He still spoke in the flat, tough slangy voice of the street, flavored by four years in the Marine Corps. During Reardon's courtroom years, many a magistrate and judge had demanded in anger or requested in despair that he modify—if not his manner—at least his vocabulary.

Reardon pushed the glasses back into his hair again, and tapped her report on the edge of his desk. "Very explicit, concise. You write a good report, Opara."

Christie breathed evenly. "Thank you, Mr. Reardon."

He regarded her for a moment, then glanced back at the report. "He was a big guy, this Rogoff. Let's see: six foot one; 185 pounds. Big solid guy, huh?"

His voice betrayed none of the anger she anticipated from their telephone conversation. Possibly he had reconsidered

35

the situation, a condition for which Christie felt grateful. "Yes sir, he was a big man."

"Mm-h'mm. Well, I'd like you to give me a different kind of rundown now. In your report—and very efficient too— you describe what happened and what action you took. Now, I'd like you to tell me a couple of things not included in your report. *Rightfully* not included," he amended quickly. "Just a few things to satisfy my curiosity, right?"

That seemed reasonable; he just wanted some more details.

"Now, you started from your home with enough time to get to your assigned location, right?" He accepted her nod. "Judging from your attire, you were fully prepared to report to your scheduled assignment. I assume you're dressed the way you are in anticipation of a 'trip party'? Your contacts advised that everyone wear casual clothing?"

"Yes, sir," Christie said agreeably. "I wouldn't be dressed like this otherwise."

"And of course, you hadn't anticipated going into court today under circumstances other than those connected with the pinch we expected at City College?"

"No, sir. The last thing in the world I expected to be doing today was arraigning an 1140."

His voice was edged with sympathy for her predicament. "I imagine you must have felt pretty embarrassed, dressed like that. Christ, you look like a little boy."

There was nothing in his voice to indicate his words had been meant unkindly. "Yes, sir. They sure gave me the business—in the precinct and at the Photo Gallery and all."

"I guess they did. And I guess they were especially surprised when you told them you were from the *D.A.'s Squad.* Dressed like that. Collaring an 1140. On the subway."

The pacing of his words had changed. Each phrase was a little more precise. The pause between each statement was just a little longer. Christie felt her fingers tightening around the arms of the chair. Reardon stood up, loosened his tie, opened the top button of his shirt. He walked to the window, gazed out for a moment, then, rubbing the frame of his glasses along his chin, he turned his attention back to her. "At what point—*exactly*—did you decide that collaring this 1140 was more important than continuing on to your assignment?"

The unfair question had to be weighed carefully. "Mr. Reardon, if those two little girls hadn't been on the train, I wouldn't have touched him."

"Yeah, but the two little girls *were* on the train, weren't they?" His eyes were motionless on her face. His voice switched to an interested, inquiring tone. "Tell me about those two little girls. Describe them."

Christie felt her voice going hollow, the way it did when she was testifying on the witness stand. She was being baited; she wasn't sure, yet, where his questions were leading. Carefully, she said, "They were about eight or nine years old. Two little girls." She lifted her hand, palm down: "About this tall. One blond girl; one little brunette. And—well—carrying their schoolbooks—and—" she faltered under his continuing stare.

"Describe what they were wearing. In detail."

If he were testing her accuracy of observation, she could meet him easily. "They had on school uniforms. Parochial school. Navy blue jumpers, white blouses with navy bowties and navy berets."

"Any school emblem or insignia?"

She nodded, recalling; her hand touched her head, then her chest. "Yes, on the jumpers and the berets; gold insignia."

"What school was it?"

Closing her eyes tightly, straining for the bit of information he was demanding, knowing it had registered somewhere in her brain, she blinked, then said, "Holy Sepulcher Academy."

"Uh-huh. Where is the Holy Sepulcher Academy located? On what street?"

Responding to her blank expression, Reardon tapped the walnut cabinet against which he was leaning. "Get out the Manhattan directory and look it up."

Christie knelt down, pulling the telephone book from under a pile of books and magazines; still kneeling, she could sense his eyes on the back of her head. She flipped the pages, then her finger ran down a row of tiny print, stopping at a pencil line, which underscored the words: Holy Sepulcher Academy, followed by a Lexington Avenue address and a telephone number. "Do you want me to write it down?" she asked stupidly; it was obvious he already had the information.

Reardon shook his head slowly, walked to his desk, held up a small scrap of paper. "No, thank you. I have it here. Come on, put the book away and sit down." She jammed the phone book into the cabinet, shutting the door firmly so that it wouldn't topple out after her. "Do you know what street that's on? Let me tell you. Holy Sepulcher Academy is located on Lexington Avenue between 22nd and 21st Street." She sat tensely in the chair. "What's the matter, Opara? You look a little confused, like you can't figure out what I'm talking about. Think about it for a minute. I have every confidence that you'll come up with something."

Christie covered her forehead with her hand for a moment, and he prodded, "Well, how about it? Come up with anything? Any conclusions?"

Resigned, she stated the obvious fact flatly. "That means the children would have gotten off the train at 23rd Street."

His voice was falsely pleased. "Hey, good. *Very good.*" Then he cut back into anger. "And if you had ridden one more stop, instead of taking this bum off at 28th Street, *if you had ridden just one more stop,* instead of rising to the challenge of protecting the public well-being—you would have seen that these vulnerable little children, whose welfare caused you so much concern, were getting off at 23rd Street—which is where *you* were supposed to get off. And this, this *Rogoff* could have gone on his way. *Right?*"

"I . . . guess so."

"*You guess so?*"

Quickly, she amended her reply, but it seemed to Reardon that there was something oddly harsh in her clipped words. "Right. Yes, sir, that's *right!*"

Leaning back, he rolled her report into a cylinder and rested it against his chin. "And you wouldn't have had to bother to write this up. And I wouldn't have had to bother reading it."

Christie breathed slowly; a small cough caught in her

throat and she swallowed hard. When she raised her face, Reardon caught the change. Her chin was tilted to one side, the head slightly back; there was a steady pulling at her jaw line and her eyes had darkened. "And those men out there wouldn't be left hanging," he continued, "and the whole investigation wouldn't be exactly *nowhere*, which is exactly where it is, as of right now."

He sensed the careful weighing of her words, the effort at control. "Mr. Reardon, the facts are that I *did* run into this degenerate and there *were* two young girls involved and I *did* act in what I felt to be a proper manner as a police officer."

Reardon smiled without amusement. "You acted in what you felt was a proper manner at the time. Reevaluate your action now, in the light of all the circumstances involved."

"I acted in a proper manner," she insisted.

"Technically?"

"Yes, sir."

"All right. Now considering the fact that four other Squad members besides yourself have conducted an investigation for nearly a month, building up to this particular day, and aware of the fact this was a 'pressure assignment' directly from 'upstairs,' what's your evaluation of your action?"

"I had no way of knowing those children were getting off at 23rd Street and in light of the situation in which I found myself, I acted properly. *Considering all the circumstances.*"

Reardon let the report uncurl on his desk. He stretched his arms, then locked his fingers behind his head. He began a different line of questioning. "When you placed Rogoff under arrest, he was standing against the door that was to open, right?" She nodded. "Okay. Now, when the train stopped at 28th Street and the door slid open, did it ever occur to you to wait until just before the door was about to close and shove him off the train? Dump him out and continue on your way?"

His words were so reasonably stated: the considered offering of one possible solution to a dilemma. Unguarded, Christie answered quickly, confidingly, "Mr. Reardon, I wasn't going to take this Rogoff. I just wanted to get him off the train. I nearly died when I saw the Transit cop."

He said softly, "I bet you did."

Encouraged by his renewed sympathy, relinquishing her own anger, she crossed her ankle to her knee, her hands moving over the denim unselfconsciously. "I was going to let him run. That's what I expected him to do anyway. He was tremendous; I couldn't have taken him alone. I was amazed that he even got off the train when I told him to."

"Yes," Casey said, "that is amazing."

"I think he would have run as soon as the train pulled out and he got his bearings. If it hadn't been for the Transit cop. Then, I would have gotten on the next train and would have made it in plenty of time to my assignment."

"If only the Transit cop hadn't been there," Casey said, almost to himself.

"Yes, sir," Christie agreed easily.

Casey placed his hands deliberately on the desk before him, his weight on his palms, and leaned toward her. "Then, in effect, the whole situation was the fault of the Transit cop?"

He recognized the sudden wariness, the realization that she had been led to say too much, to reveal what she should not have revealed. She bit her lip, not answering him.

"And further," he accused her, "you're telling me that your intention, after having placed a man *under arrest*, was to let him escape. Is *that* what you consider *proper police action?*"

Christie felt a cold disgust: she had given him his weapon. She had set herself up; but he had given her a weapon too, and without hesitation, meeting him head-on, she said, "A minute ago you asked me why I didn't just dump him off the train. Would *that* have been proper police action?" she demanded.

Reardon shook his head slowly. "That isn't what I asked you. I just asked you if it hadn't *occurred* to you to do that. I didn't even *suggest* that would have been a proper course to take."

He wondered if she were counting: five seconds, six seconds, or if it was an instinctively timed hesitation. He had seen her do it in court: the gathering of a protective cloak of calmness when she had spoken too hastily, rising to the

40

questions calculated to destroy the validity of her testimony. Her face was red but her eyes met his steadily and without excuse.

"Mr. Reardon, are we playing that old game: heads-you-win, tails-I-lose?"

"I don't consider this a game, Detective Opara. Do you?"

"Well, it seems that no matter what I would have done, I would have acted improperly."

"And it seems to me that there has been a drastic change in your attitude from the moment you entered this office up to this minute. It seems to me that you came in here seeming to feel that you owed me and the members of this Squad an explanation of why you failed to follow through on your assignment. And that now, you seem to feel that no explanation of any kind is in order."

Her voice no longer able to conceal the anger which had been glaring from her eyes, she said, "You're accurate on that score, Mr. Reardon. I walked in here this morning feeling like some kind of a culprit. Well, I'm *not* a culprit and I'm *not* a defendant in a courtroom!"

"Jesus, I'm glad of that. You've made several incriminating admissions relative to highly improper police action which you intended to take and I hope to God you never make those admissions on a witness stand in a courtroom."

Disregarding some small sense of discretion still warning her, she said, "In a courtroom, I would hope to have someone on my side. Like the *District Attorney*, so that when counsel for the plaintiff is trying to make *me* the culprit, I would have legal counsel to protect me!"

Reardon stood up. "It's a little difficult to protect a witness who doesn't know when to shut up!" He walked to the window, his eyes fixed on two yellow taxicabs fighting for position along Foley Square, inching so close they seemed to touch, then bounce apart. He turned, switched the radio on, tuned the music low, listened for a moment, then recognized the melody. He looked back at Christie Opara and noted with astonishment, anger and some amusement: *the little bastard is furious.* She had slid down in the chair, resting almost on the base of her spine, and one long slender leg, outlined by the pale green denim, was crossed on the other, which was stretched out, the foot hidden under the desk. Her hands were gripped around her raised knee and she was completely absorbed in her own thoughts.

Reardon walked behind his desk and she looked up at him, not raising her face, just her eyes. She released her knee, pushed some hair from her forehead, rested her chin against her thumb, the index finger pushing into her cheek. She nibbled absently on her pinky. Her eyes, which had seemed gray, now, in the clearer light of the sun which had shifted to touch her face, were a clear, cold green.

"For Christ's sakes, sit up and take your finger out of your mouth!"

It was like speaking to one of his sixteen-year-old twin daughters, and her reaction was what he had come to expect from them. Deliberately, she shifted her position in the chair, placed her feet flat on the floor, slid her hands along the armrests and lifted her body so that her spine hit the back of the chair and she was rigidly straight. Her face had a familiar expression, too: a kind of pleased awareness that she had been able to irritate him. He reached for a scrap of paper.

"When does this guy go to court again?"

"May 10," she answered, "Tuesday."

"You expect him to cop out?" he asked coldly.

"That's up to him, isn't it?"

Casey Reardon looked up. "Look, Opara, don't get *too* fresh with me, okay?" She focused her eyes on the edge of the desk. At least she knew enough not to engage him again. She'd better not. Not now. "Wednesday, okay." He consulted his calendar. "You can pick the investigation up on Monday and—" He was stopped by the complete change of her expression: the complete absence of any mask. "Well, what's the matter *now?*"

She shook her head. "Nothing. Nothing."

Her eyes were shining and her face, he noticed, had been steadily getting paler. He walked around the desk, standing in front of her. "Opara, did you think I was going to *dump* you? Jesus, look up at me." She was trying hard to keep her face expressionless and he was curiously touched by her rapid blinking and the quick licking of her lips. "Did you really think I was going to dump you for what happened today?"

She shook her head, shrugged, then whispered, "I don't know. I guess the thought did occur to me."

He smiled at her bowed head: that was why she had fought him, then. Because she felt it didn't matter. Realizing her struggle to keep the tears back, his voice changed sharply. "Oh, boy. Hey, Opara, I think I owe you an apology." Her chin lifted, her eyes narrowed warily. "You know what the trouble has been here?" He slapped the top of his desk, walking across the front of the room, berating himself. "Damn it, I'm so used to talking to the *guys*, you know, the other Squad members, as just guys—detectives. When I talk to you as a detective, as a detective second-grade, I talk to you as if you were—just another member of the Squad." He could see the green eyes hardening. "You see, I forgot, I think we *all* forget that you're a girl. A female. Hell, dressed like that, you can't blame us. You look like one of the guys!" Sitting down, leaning forward, his voice apologetic, "You'll just have to give us all a second chance to get used to you. You know, to give you the special considerations a girl is entitled to. We just tended to think a cop is a cop."

Her voice was low but furious. "I'm a second-grade detective, Mr. Reardon, and I got second grade on the basis of my *ability* as a *cop*."

Reardon's face relaxed and Christie was startled by the sudden sound of his deep, hard laugh. "Opara, don't ever play poker. You can't hide a thing. I can hear you loud and clear: 'You bastard, Reardon!'" He pointed a warning finger at her. "Don't say it, honey, but when you're thinking it, don't let it show so clearly." He looked at his watch. "Look at the time. I have to get going." He waved her toward him. "C'mere a minute. Put out your arms."

Watching him closely, Christie extended her arms as he roughly pushed up the sleeves of her black jersey, his fingers pressing her wrists. "You ever have a busted wrist? Wait a minute—the *left* wrist?"

She nodded, trying to withdraw her arms, but he held her, his fingers pressing hard on the left wrist. "Okay. You're

43

going to break it again. Hey, put the chin down. *I'm* not going to break it. Hell, I wouldn't tangle with you, you're probably a karate expert." Releasing her wrists, looking her up and down, he told her, "You ought to take vitamins or something, Opara." Then, to himself, "Or something."

"How am I going to break my wrist, Mr. Reardon? And why?"

"I was afraid you'd never ask," he said, buttoning his shirt, tightening his tie. "You're going back to City College Monday morning with your arm in a cast. That's why you couldn't show today: it would have to be something drastic to keep you from It Day. Ginsburg has a cousin who's a veterinarian or something. Marty will take you over there Sunday night and get you into a cast." He grinned. "It'll be a nice heavy cast—we want it to look authentic, right?" He slipped on his jacket. "Then, you get back into your little group of pals and we'll play it by ear from then on."

"Yes, sir. May I leave now?"

Reardon adjusted the jacket, smoothing it across his shoulders, then he nodded, waiting until her hand was on the doorknob. "Oh, Detective Opara, just a moment." He held the report which she had typed, carefully removed the first page, held it up toward the light and squinted at it. "Here"—he extended the papers to her—"the original copy almost has a hole in it. I don't like reports that almost have holes in them; retype it." Still holding the report as she tried to take it, he said, "Relax, tiger, you're getting off easy. And watch the expression, kid, I can read you like radar."

"Yes, sir. Is that all?"

"For now. Tell Stoney to get his . . . tell Stoney to come in. In a hurry."

Stoney tapped and entered Reardon's office, offering him some papers. "Here's the info re the gambling matter on the East Side."

Reardon stuffed Stoner's information into his battered attaché case, along with a collection of papers from his desk top, then pushed his hat low on his forehead. "What a fresh little bastard. I mean, *really* fresh." Then, looking up, "What's your opinion?"

Stoney grinned. "I would say—she took you on."

44

"Like a tiger cub." He pressed his lips together thoughtfully. "No, more like a flyweight who sneaked into the heavyweight class." He laughed, remembering the angry face. "Wow, what guts! She's pretty cute. How'd she take the guys? They give her the business?"

Stoney considered for a moment. "Well, I would say we were up to our usual form. She's played boys' rules before, Casey. She can handle herself."

"No feminine wiles?"

"Well, she's got a way with her, boss, but I wouldn't say feminine wiles, exactly. Pretty good-natured. You know— one of the guys."

Reardon nodded, concentrating now on jamming his overstuffed case shut. "I think she'll be okay. Make sure Ginsburg gets her to his doctor cousin or whatever the hell he is. This damn thing doesn't hold enough."

"You put too much in it is the problem."

"Nope. I am never at fault," Reardon said, accepting Stoney's casual salute. "Let's move."

Stoner Martin followed Reardon into the main office where the Squad was expecting him: there was no sudden ducking of heads over suddenly important work, no changing of attitude, yet everyone was aware that Casey was striding through the room, his eyes taking in everyone present, fully cognizant of what was happening in every corner. He nodded at O'Hanlon, who glanced up from the pad on which he was sketching circles and squares while listening to the voice on the telephone. He knew that Christie, staring blankly at the paper in her machine, had hit a wrong key and would correct it as soon as he left. He took the scrap of paper Ferranti, who had just arrived, handed him, scowled, then nodded at the information he wanted. Shoving the paper into his pocket, he waved at Ginsburg, who waved a pretzel back at his boss.

"Hey, Mr. Reardon, you want to buy some bagels?"

"What do you get for them, Marty?"

"Two-fer-a-quarter, three-fer-a-half, but seeing as how you're the boss, a special price: fifteen cents each, flat rate."

"You crook," Casey called out, "you'd swindle your own

mother." Then, "Stoney, you're top man here. This is a very motley looking group of people. See if you can't clean them up a little, huh?" His eyes swept the room. "Get Ginsburg out of that apron, he looks like a cook in a greasy-spoon joint." He looked at Ferranti, then back at Stoney. "No ties, no jackets, what is this? And try to get Opara into a dress: it might help a little." His eyes stayed on Christie, but she refused to look up from her steady typing. "And if Ginsburg makes any sales, you know, for cash, right here on the premises, have Opara write up a summons, or make an arrest, if she feels it's warranted." Christie stopped typing and glared up at him. "We want to build up the Squad arrest record. She might make us all look good one day." Reardon walked out without looking back.

Christie stared at her report, reached over and pulled the papers from her machine, squashing them into a ball which she tossed at the wastebasket. It bounced against the wall and onto the floor. Whispering to herself, she bent down and dropped the papers into the basket, pulled open the drawer and prepared another set of papers and carbons.

Stoney's voice, beside her, was musical and pleasant but something made her stop and listen closely to him. "You type up a nice report for that man, Christie. Oh, I know you're steaming a little from the pressure cooking he gave you, but I want to tell you something. Casey Reardon spent about forty-five pretty hot minutes himself, upstairs." Stoney's thumb jerked toward the ceiling, indicating the "top floor" where the District Attorney of New York County held domain. Stoney's black eyes caught her surprise at his next words. "*Defending you.* Yeah, that's right, defending Detective Christie Opara, who is a member of this here Squad. You see, the Great Master of Us All up there on that top floor, he wasn't too interested in anything except that the case didn't come off today. And he wanted to know *who?* and *why?* but mostly *who* and then why the *who* wasn't removed from the Squad—forthwith." Stoney flexed his shoulders, straightening his spine, and sighed. "Now, Mr. Reardon *never* tells *who* to the fella up there, and as to the *why*"—he smiled—"well, Mr. Reardon has a pretty good backlog of convenient *whys* that he can draw on, so we still have the investigation and the wind-up has just been put off, temporarily. So if he was a little rough on you, you might feel, under the circumstances, that the Man was entitled, no?"

Christie took a long, deep, grateful breath, nodded wordlessly at Stoney, who winked and moved back to his own desk. Taking her papers with her, she crossed the room, to stand alongside of him. "Stoney, can I use your typewriter? I'll make it fast. The Royal does a better job"—she grinned —"and I want to give Mr. Reardon a mistake-free, hole-free report, no?"

Stoner Martin groaned wearily. "Ah, my words always can be turned against my own best interests. Make it quick, Christie, I don't want to spend the rest of my days and nights here, lend-leasing my typewriter."

She was nearly finished with her report when Bill Ferranti approached her. She turned quickly, catching some wild hand signals from Marty Ginsburg.

Detective Ferranti was a slender, neatly dressed man who wore dark horn-rimmed glasses. His face had a mild, pink-skinned, owlish appearance, and he had thinning, pure white hair. He was always immaculately groomed. "Christie, did you have your first go-round with Mr. Reardon today?" His voice was friendly and concerned.

"Yes, but it wasn't too bad. Bill, I'm sorry about this morning. I hope . . ."

Ferranti waved his hand in the air. "So we waited a while; the cafeteria was nice and cool and the coffee is very good. No damage, as long as you got off the hook with Mr. Reardon. He can be very rough, but he's fair."

Christie grinned and in a loud voice said, "Well, your partner back there"—turning, she discovered Marty had disappeared from sight—"I think he's hiding under the desk. Bill, you better have a long talk with him. He's been spreading some pretty awful stories about you!"

Ginsburg made groaning sounds, and his hand emerged from under the desk, grasped at a pretzel, then disappeared. The wisecracks began to crisscross the room, from O'Hanlon, who held his hand over the mouthpiece of the telephone, from Christie, between Bill and Marty. Finally,

Stoney called for order. "Let's hold it down in here! Let's try to act like professional law enforcement officers, gentlemen. And you too, Christie. Let's have a little decorum *if* it isn't too much to ask. After all, we *are* a rather select little group, though we do, some of us anyway, appear a little motley today, like the Man said."

Christie finished her report without a mistake: the margins neatly lined up, the paragraphs properly indented. Handing the report to Stoner Martin she felt, for the first time since she had been assigned to the District Attorney's Squad, that she was, in fact, a member.

[5]

DAVID ROGOFF, a pale man of forty, pressed his forehead
into his hands, which clung to the steering wheel of his 1965
coffee-color Dodge Dart. He could feel the streams of sweat
running under his arms, along the sides of his body, down
his chest, making the Dacron shirt cling to his body like a
thin layer of clammy paste.

It was totally silent in the cavernous parking lot, two
levels below the street. The trip in from Manhasset had
been unreal: a mechanical maneuvering of the car along the
Expressway, the sudden realization that he was hitting
nearly seventy, the jamming on of the brakes, the anger of
some indignant housewife, her hair flapping wildly in her
convertible behind him as she simultaneously braked and
honked to keep herself from racking up on him and to
let him know what she thought of him. The sudden
maze of lower Manhattan traffic, which hadn't been sudden
at all; actually, a slow, steady, continuous building up of
traffic and side streets, but David had noticed all of it at
once, as though he had been miraculously transported from
the cool, dark, understated, elegant showroom of "Tastefully
Yours" in the shopping center to the inexplicable commotion
and heavy heat of Canal Street. Consciously fighting traffic,
consciously forcing his way through the narrow, congested
streets, he had found this municipal garage, had accepted
the small pink ticket from the uniformed man in the little
glass booth, had followed the endless series of arrows that
kept pointing: around, around, lower and lower, to this final
depth of white-marked rectangles. Somehow, not scraping
either the large gray cement pillar to his right nor the care-
lessly parked Cadillac to his left, he had brought the Dart to
a halt, turned off the motor and sat now in the silent deadness of his car, trying to pull himself together.

David Rogoff rubbed his forehead, trying to erase the
panic that had been building from the instant of that fan-

tastic phone call: that hard unfamiliar, unsurprised, unconcerned voice telling him that *Murray had been arrested.*

He took a long and steadying breath, recalling hard-won conclusions, certainties, drawing on them after so many years, trying to form them into a shield around himself:

Murray is not my fault. What happened to Murray is not my fault. Murray is what he is because of what he is: what he had been before the accident and because he could not cope with the thing that happened to him. And there wasn't even real medical proof that the accident initiated Murray's strange, progressively rapid, complete hairlessness. None of the experts could pinpoint it; none of them had pointed a definite finger at the cause. There was no proof. *Was there?* Murray is Murray's own fault. The irony was that he, David, had undertaken long years of therapy when it was Murray who should have learned to accept himself: not David. It wasn't David who needed the help: it was Murray.

David Rogoff bit down on his index finger, trying to let the pressure of his teeth biting into the bone keep him here, now, in the moment, but the scene was before him, before his eyes, which he kept locked tightly behind his horn-rimmed glasses. It *had* been an accident, for who in this world could possibly have imagined that David Rogoff could have caused irreparable physical damage to his young giant of a brother? It came back to him again, as it had come back to him time and again through the last seventeen years, as it would come back to him periodically through all the years of his life.

Murray, sixteen years old, tall, his great height absorbed by the power of his body. His shoulders like carved stone yet flexible as wire, his chest, broad and massive, outlined by the narrow shirt which fitted into his tight pants without a break in the smooth line of his body. Standing outside the Loew's Delancey movie house that hot July night, surrounded by his usual crowd of adolescent worshipers. Murray, running his large hand through his thick mop of yellow hair: the golden boy. That's what Mama always called him: my great golden boy, and Murray's golden glow protected him from all the responsibilities, all the requirements which he, David, small and narrow in the mold of his father, had to meet, but Murray's splendor, stared at and admired by family and neighbors and even by total strangers, passing him on the street, glancing at him, then turning to gaze at him openly, as though he were some natural wonder. Murray didn't have to worry about how he could finish N.Y.U. at night, working as an accountant during the day; about how to pass that lousy C.P.A. exam; about how to plan and scrounge and get the money together so that one day he could have a business of his own. Murray worried about nothing but Murray.

He didn't have to worry about Edna and her tricks. If only Edna hadn't led him on that night. David Rogoff let his body relax, loosened the grip on the steering wheel, let it run through him, let it play itself out.

That August night, Edna had been up to form with her usual teasing and light touching. It was her idea of innocence, to express shock and anger when one careless, unguarded slip of her hand, one playful quick darting of her tongue against his teeth, aroused him. They had quarreled and he had left her in tears and professed confusion and he had sat swaying in the dirty heat of the "D" train all the way from the Bronx with all those needs and hungers tensing up inside of him. He had gotten off two stations before Delancey Street, needing to run a little, to walk it off, because he knew, as she did, that if it killed him, she wouldn't let him have her until after the wedding in September.

But the jogging walk through the August streets of the lower East Side hadn't helped. The stoops were lined with Puerto Ricans, twining arms and legs around each other easily, rubbing, touching, nuzzling. The sidewalks were filled with Italians, the men patting their women, the women warning that the children would see but smiling when the men shrugged: so what? Then, coming upon Murray and his cronies; the kid all flushed and smug, running his fingers inside his opened shirt, playing lightly over the golden strong curls of his chest, sliding his fingers along the fly of his trousers and then, telling—*telling* and all his pals, their eyes narrowed and excited, picturing what Murray was

51

saying: that he had laid those little spic sisters, Maria and Delores Gonzalez, twice each in the period of two hours and mockingly had asked *them* to pay *him* and they, seriously, said they would be glad to because Murray was a great, golden god, a gift to them on a hot, languid, uneasy July night. David had tried to shake free of his brother's grasp. He didn't want to hear about Murray's filth. He had pulled away from Murray, warning him, but Murray was too caught up in his story and all his pimply, snotty friends, gleaming their lewd interest, prodded him on.

Then, Murray, the small golden hairs along his cheeks and chin glittering in the flashing lights of the movie marquee, had reached down, grabbing at David playfully, disregarding David's anger, David's warning, and Murray, in surprise, had let out an obscene howl of delight, had made some stupid, lewd, taunting, crude accusation about David's condition and then about Edna. And David had pushed him.

That was all he had done, his 140 pounds of anger (but had it been deeper than anger? had it been some cumulative force of unknown rage?) had shoved at the massive chest and Murray slid on the slippery smoothness of the pseudo-marble floor under the marquee of the Loew's Delancey and he went into a coma caused by an unanticipated, uncalculated, unimagined crashing of the back of his skull on the curbstone and Murray had remained in a coma, still and lifeless on the flat white bed at Bellevue Hospital for three days and three nights.

David Rogoff stared through the windshield of his car, not seeing the concrete wall directly before him: seeing the image of his brother, Murray, flatly huge beneath the white sheet, breathing fitfully, the bottles arranged about his bed, sending fluids into his body through transparent tubes.

David had talked and talked and talked with Dr. Arono-witz: for four and a half years, digging up all the hidden thoughts, all the unknown resentments of the eleven-year-old boy with white skin and sharp elbows and bony legs who was told over and over again, "Like a little god he is, David, your baby brother! Like Uncle Moishe in the old country, a wonderful great giant!" While he, David, having heard the wondrous stories of the great, unbelievable Uncle Moishe, whose legends ruled his mother's heart, stared at the rapidly growing, powerful child who at seven could easily knock him down.

He had denied the unsuspected words: he hadn't hated Murray. *He hadn't.* That was what Aronowitz had wanted him to say. God, hadn't he taken the kid everywhere with him? Hadn't he lied for him, time and again, when he got into wild scrapes with the neighborhood hooligans? Stealing, pinching things from the candy store, even lifting coins from the register in Papa's fish store, and David, covering it up, making good the coins so that Mama would never know the reincarnation of the legendary Uncle Moishe was just a common little crook. (But Mama would have said she told Murray he could have some loose change: that's what she would have said.) And he had said, "Stealing from your own parents, Murray—*from your own parents.*" But the light tan eyes regarded him in that special way, the golden lashes blinking up and down, the mouth, ready with a quick, pleading smile, the face so innocently sorry.

Of course I loved Murray. Everyone loved Murray.

But not now. No more. David eased his body from beneath the steering wheel, struggling into his lightweight suit jacket, the sleeves sticking against the dampness of his shirt. Murray was Murray's fault. He wasn't blind or crippled or disabled. He had refused to wear the dark blond hairpiece which David had bought for him years ago: for three hundred and twenty dollars. He ruined every decent suit David had bought him; walked off every job David had schemed and begged to get him; had antagonized every doctor David had taken him to with the same reaction: bullshit. Now, Murray was on his own. I will go bail for him and get him out of this and then I am finished with him. *This time: finished.*

David carefully checked the front door to make sure he had locked the car, then tested the rear doors. He glanced at his watch. It was three P.M. Murray had been arrested, the policeman's voice had said, at about nine fifteen. Well, he couldn't have gotten into the city any earlier. He had had to sit and think, after the call, what to do: whom to contact.

How he had remembered Frankie Santino was still a mystery to him. How he had even vaguely recalled that Frankie Santino, that skinny, sleazy little Italian kid who worked part-time in his parents pizza joint on Sheriff Street, was now a lawyer, was one of those peculiar little bits of information he had absorbed somehow. When the secretary had said, in a cool, unsurprised way, "I'll see if *Mr. Santino* is in, just a moment please," he had sat there in his office, watching through the lush artificial rubber plant so that his partner, Jerry, wouldn't see him. He could not picture Frankie Santino, a lawyer now.

He couldn't have called their attorney, Sam Gerstein. My God, what could he have said to Sam: what would he know about a brother who got arrested on a subway train for being a degenerate?

Frankie had said he would meet him outside of Felony Court, like that was under the Statue of Liberty: anyone would know where.

David stood immobilized in the center of the square lobby of the Criminal Courts Building, his eyes seeking some direction, some sign. People were moving, quickly, slowly, lingeringly, hurriedly, like ants from one side of the lobby to the other, arms around shoulders, voices urgent. Breathing with a slight wheezing sound (that's all I need, an asthma attack), feeling the beginning light-headedness of nausea, David emitted a startled gasp at the unexpected clutching of a hand at his shoulder. Turning around, he regarded the man before him without recognition.

He was a short, stocky man with a thick neck emerging from a tightly buttoned white-on-white shirt worn beneath a shiny black Italian silk suit. An inch of pure white emerged at each sleeve and the hand, which reached for David's, had a large, grayish-blue star sapphire ring turned outward on the pinky. David squinted, trying to see Frankie Santino somewhere in the face which was nearly strangled by the silvery white silk tie at the neck. It was a broad, blunt, dark face with black eyes which danced all over David, and the thick, curly black hair was now a heavy fringed semi-circle accenting the swarthy skull.

"Davey Rogoff! You haven't changed, you haven't

54

changed," the unfamiliar voice informed him loudly. The skinny, blotchy kid with the greasy curls had had a shrill, tough little voice. "A little filled out maybe, but then aren't we all?" The laugh was unpleasant.

"Mr. Santino?" he asked uncertainly.

"Hell, what is this 'Mr. Santino' crap?" the lawyer bellowed at him, seeming delighted to see David. "I'm still Frankie, *Frankie*," he said expansively. "My God, Davey, you look great." Stepping back, he surveyed David shrewdly, noting that David's dark gray suit fitted a small but compact body which had not succumbed to the years. The dark tie was neatly correct against the expensive shirt. The horn-rimmed glasses added a certain polish and refinement to David's face. The dark brown hair, Santino noted, had been razor cut: the sonuvabitch took good care of himself. Probably went to a health club and took sauna baths.

"Davey-boy, you look real Long Island suburbs. Manhasset? You said the furniture business? You got your own place?"

Carefully, David said, "Not really my own—I have a partner. We have a small showroom in Manhasset. My home is in Great Neck."

Santino shook one hand lightly—the hand with the ring —letting it dangle from his wrist. "Hey! The million-dollar mile—Manhasset!"

David spoke rapidly, putting things in their proper place. "Well, not exactly. We're sort of on the fringes of the million-dollar mile. Showroom is in Manhasset and we have a small plant in Jersey. It helps with the tax structure to have the factory in Jersey." He could see the small dark eyes calculating what his business was worth. "We do small stuff— an occasional office, but mostly dens and playrooms."

"Sure, sure." Santino nodded. Then he took David's shoulder, leading him to the large, flat, wide stairway, his voice dropping now, his face pulling into a look of urgent concern. "Hey, tough shit about Murray, huh? The kid never really pulled out of it, huh? Jee-zus I remember old Murray-the-Norseman: that's what we used to call him. I haven't seen old Murray for years. Never got over the accident, huh?"

David, walking close to the wall, tried to ease himself from Santino's grasp. Just let me get through all of this, he pleaded, just let me get through this minute, this hour, this day, and let me get back home, back into my own life.

He followed where Santino, obviously at home and comfortable and familiar with the workings of the vast building, led him by a series of pressures on his elbow and arm. He sat in a small room with benches where Santino had placed him, handed him the crisp, freshly withdrawn fifty-dollar bills, while Santino set about getting a bail bondsman.

Thirty-five minutes later Santino slid himself next to David, exhaled his minty breath into David's face and told him, in that same, loud, whispering, confidential way which David observed all around him, "The kid'll be out in about twenty minutes." Santino winked, holding his right eye closed for several seconds and jabbed David's ribs with a well-padded elbow. "Old Frankie's got the right connections, kid. We got the bond and the kid comes up for pleading next Tuesday, May 10th." David stared blankly at the lawyer. "Don't worry, don't worry. This is all a formality, all in a day's work, nothing unusual, nothing spectacular. Now, I saw Murray." His expression was somewhere between pity and disgust. "Wow, he is some helluva mess: dirty. He still living with mama and papa?"

David winced. "Yes."

"Helluva thing for them, but you don't have to tell them nothing—say he got a ticket for jay-walking or something and didn't have the price of the fine, you know? And Dave, clean him up for court on the 10th: get him showered and into a suit and shirt and tie. He sure is a mess, but man, he still got the built!"

"What happens then, Frank, on May 10th?"

"Formal arraignment—we waive to Sessions." His voice softened, apologetically acknowledging David's puzzled expression. "He was set bail this morning, but he wasn't represented by an attorney so what happens is, they put the formal arraignment over to the tenth. Then, we show up with him and what we do is we waive him to Special Sessions, Part One. Then, in about another week, he comes before the magistrate and makes his plea."

David felt his stomach beginning to rumble and his chest felt heavy. Next week. And then another week. And then another.

Hurriedly, confidentially, his hand covering the lower half of his face, Frankie told him, "I know the cop who locked him up. A sharp little cookie, this kid—a girl cop. She bagged him off the train; I've tangled with this kid a few times in court, on cases like this."

The phrase was repeated over and over inside David's head: cases like this; cases like this. Murray was a case, like other cases like this.

"Some of these cops are no good, hell in my book, they'd all frame their own fathers for a pinch. But this kid is straight—strictly on the level. There's no doubt that Murray waved his jewels at her so I think we better cop him out." He smiled and patiently explained, "Plead him guilty and take our chances. He doesn't have any previous, thank God, so he'll probably get an S.S.—suspended sentence. In fact"— he looked around, his eyes darting in circles, his voice falling a pitch or two—"I'm *sure* I can get him an S.S. I got a few contacts." The hooded slow wink of the right eye: *"You know."*

David could feel the heat pressing around him, inside his clothing. His mouth felt yellow and sticky. He nodded: anything, anything, okay, Frank, okay. He walked a few steps to the water fountain, leaning his face low into the small, hollow alcove. Depressing the shining steel handle, he sucked at the small, inch-high stream of warmish water, holding the water in his mouth, around his teeth, then swallowing. He watched Frank Santino: he was hanging on to the shoulder of some fat man with a spiral of wavy yellow hair, winking and nodding and smirking.

"Okay, Davey, let's go. Murray will be out soon. We go around to the side of the building; the bondsman will point him in the right direction. I told Murray we'd be waiting."

David shielded his eyes with his forearm against the glare of late afternoon sun, avoiding the glances of the other people who were standing uneasily at the gate where prisoners were being released on bail. A skinny Puerto Rican girl, her thin hand clutching the collar of a bright-eyed little boy, her other arm holding a sleeping infant against her body, let out a high sound: some word, some name, and a pale, emaciated, boy-sized man rushed through the gate, breaking into a toothless grin, jabbered at her in a rush of incomprehensible words and embraced her so tightly that the infant was crushed and shrieked itself awake with an angry scream. They both laughed, the man took the infant, ruffled the head of the little boy, and the girl placed her thin arm around his narrow waist. The family walked off, directly into the sunlight.

"Hey, here we go, Davey," Frankie said, his eyes darting from the prison gate to his watch. He had other things to do this afternoon. "Hey, Murray, over here, boy."

David Rogoff steeled himself against the sight of his younger brother, raised his eyes slowly, swallowed hard.

Murray, directed by Frank Santino, who half-embraced him, shuffled, blinking in the strong light, toward David. He looked down blankly at David, who had drawn back but then with effort stepped toward him and reached for Murray's hand, which was cold and limp.

David hadn't seen his brother for more than a year. The sun, shining directly onto his glasses, sparked out Murray's eyes; all David could see was the large head and the yellowness of Murray's face and the broad expanse of thickened bone extending backward like a hood into his filthy shirt. His eyes ran over the soiled and stale clothing and he looked away nervously, nodding and muttering at the final directions Santino was giving him. He shook hands with Santino, accepted his rough slap on the shoulder and tight squeeze on his upper arm, then didn't look after him as he hurried off.

David, his voice unfamiliar in his own ears, not looking at Murray, said, "I have my car around the corner in the Municipal Parking Garage. I'll drop you off at home."

Murray followed wordlessly. David, staring straight ahead, was aware of the stooped, forward shuffle, the sliding of the large heavy feet along the pavement, the lurching movement slightly to the right and slightly behind him. He could hear the deep intake of stifling air as they thudded

58

down the iron-caged stairway that led, prison-like, to the lowest level of the parking lot.

Opening the door on the driver's side, David stretched himself across the front seat, pulled up the door lock and motioned Murray around the car. Sitting now behind the wheel of his car, David forced his mind to hardness: to steel. He would drive Murray home; let him off on the street, not see his parents. He couldn't face that. He would do only what he was capable of doing: no more, no less. He could feel Murray settling his large body into the seat beside him; shuddered at the explosive sound of the door being slammed.

And then, for the first time, he heard his brother's voice. Unwillingly, he turned toward the words and looked directly at Murray.

"Gee, Davey, I got a terrible headache," Murray said, the large hand brutally rubbing the top of his skull, the fingers pulling the glasses from his face, digging at the closed eyes, trying to rub the pain away. The voice was from some long dead, long buried time and Murray's face, twisted now into a look of utter, complete bewilderment, asked him, "Davey, what was that place? I can't figure it out. I just got this terrible headache, like pounding the top of my head off."

David said nothing, fighting back the flood of words. He forced his lips tight against each other, kept his hands rigidly on the steering wheel. Murray's hands swept upwards over his face, then down his head and pressed hard on the back of his neck, then suddenly, he opened his eyes and his expression changed, his entire face changed. He smiled a delighted, purely happy smile. "Hey, Davey, you know what? I got this *feeling:* you know, like something *really good* is going to happen to me today."

It all collapsed. Somewhere inside of David, it all fell apart. All the years of all the Wednesday nights with Dr. Aronowitz; all of his resolve, firmness, decision. It all collapsed.

The face before him, large and yellowish, the nose too prominent now, the eyes frantically blinking, the mouth, smiling like a child's, guileless and mystified, the powerful hand extended by the long and still strong arm to the back of his bare neck, the strong legs, bent at the knees sideways so that his body could settle into the smallness of the car: it all rushed at him and David pulled his own glasses from his face, pressed his hand into his eyes, not trying to stop the tears, just spreading them over his face.

"Hey, Davey," the voice, concerned, frightened, called to him. "Don't do that, Davey, don't do that."

David's right hand reached out blindly, touching the cheek, the neck, the powerful shoulder of his kid brother, and over and over again, he sobbed, "Murray—Murray—Murray. Oh God! Murray—why? Murray—why?"

[6]

CHRISTIE OPARA stood facing her body in the full-length mirror set into the door of her bedroom closet, ignoring the small puddles of water forming around her feet. The towel wrapped around her was practically dry: she was usually in too much of a hurry to dry herself after a shower, though now she wasn't in a hurry. She had a date to meet Dan Biers at eight; Nora wouldn't be back with Mickey from their dental appointment until 5:30.

A date with Dan was always a relaxing experience; the conversation, over good food, interesting, informative. Being a corporation attorney, Dan never baited her, never provoked her into those touchy arguments about the role of the police officer in a changing society. Nor did Dan ever suggest they should end their evening, after the theater, in his apartment. (Just that first time, and he accepted her refusal good-naturedly, filing it away for future reference.) She considered Dan, who was legally separated from his wife and son, as an attractive, pleasant, intelligent, good friend. If he were to telephone ten minutes before she left the house, begging off on their date for some reason or other, she would experience no stabbing resentment, no bitter wound, just mild disappointment. In five years of widowhood, she had suffered a few such wounds and had learned how to avoid them.

When she was with Dan, thirty-two years old, darkly good looking rather than classically handsome, Christie was aware of her femininity in a way that did not relate to any of the more basic female needs: his consistent courtesy, his unassuming natural awareness of her intelligence, his planning for an evening that she would find entertaining, made her feel attractive. And yet, at the same time, did not make her feel particularly desirable. This was exactly the way she wanted it.

Standing alone in her room, the house silent except for

the soft music of the radio, Christie ignored the fact that she was soaking wet, that her short hair, clinging to her head, was dripping, and she critically studied herself, drawing the towel tightly around her waist so that there was a sharp, bony curving out at the hips. Finally, she let the towel fall to her feet.

Regarding her naked body, she stretched her arms over her head with an athlete's sense of well-being, aware of her own easy flexibility, pleased with the trim firmness of her stomach and thighs. Christie let her head fall back, enjoying the pull along her throat and the pressure at the back of her neck. Leaning forward, she placed the palms of her hands on the floor in front of her, then slowly uncoiled her spine: not just standing up, but unwinding herself in specific sequence. Turning sideways, stretching her arms over her head, she frowned. The slight contours of her body flattened: like a boy's. She leaned forward from the waist, placing her hands on her knees. There. Now she had breasts. But she couldn't very well walk around bent over like that. Straightening up, she rotated her shoulders backwards. That was supposed to help. But she had tried that before: all she had gotten out of that particular exercise was aching shoulders.

Christie picked up the towel with her toes, flipping it through the air, so that it landed on her head. She rubbed her short hair vigorously until it was damp, then brushed it. Well, it might be short, but it could still be sexy. She set a series of rollers across her forehead so that the bangs would be soft, then four rollers at the crown. She pulled a few hairs forward on her cheeks, setting them in place with Scotch tape.

She opened her lingerie drawer, sniffing at the clean, fresh fragrance of Tweed. She pulled out the flame-red Vanity Fair bra and matching pantie girdle, sprinkled herself freely with the toilet water, drying her fingers on her underwear. I *feel* sexy and I *smell* sexy. I can't help it if I don't *look* sexy.

Absently, she fingered her left wrist, feeling the slight indentation where the bone had been fractured when she was twelve. She had run the football right through the line, right through her older brothers, right through all of them, to score the point, even though she had felt her wrist snap. She had gotten up and wouldn't stop and wouldn't let go of the ball until she had passed the playground goalpost. To make the point.

Christie stepped into the half-slip, pulling it up over her hips. "Now that," she said into the mirror, "looks sexy."

By the time Nora and Mickey returned, Christie had her hair brushed and placed just the way she wanted: soft and casual. She slipped on a jersey shift: bright orange-red. It fitted her easily, outlining her small breasts, resting lightly on each sharp hipbone, her waist suggestively ignored by the fabric. Not bad.

"For heaven's sakes," Nora Opara said as she sank into the rocking chair by the window of Christie's room, "I thought you were going out with Dan Biers tonight."

"I am. Why?"

Nora surveyed her daughter-in-law carefully. "I don't know, it just looks like you had someone else in mind besides 'ole buddy Dan.' You're wasting that dress on a *pal*."

Ignoring Nora's familiar taunt, she asked, "Any cavities?"

"Me, no. As for our little hero: nobody knows. He began screaming the minute Dr. Endleman said, 'Well, now, young man, let's have a look at you.' That's all the poor man said. Mickey yelled like he'd been stuck full of darts. Frankly, I think we ought to just let his teeth rot or make him brush with all the magic anti-cavity toothpastes and chew Dentyne gum."

"Oh, Nora. I should have taken him."

Nora shrugged easily. "Don't worry about it. I just shoved him back into the waiting room and glared around at everyone there and asked if anybody knew this terrible child. Of course, everyone immediately denied responsibility for him, so I told him to sit and read a magazine until the child authorities showed up for him. Then I had my teeth cleaned and collected Mickey from a coloring book he was sharing with a little curly-headed girl. Very cute, too. He has good taste. We'll go back and try again next month. What a little character."

The clear, watercolor-blue eyes narrowed with amusement, recalling her grandson's rebellion. Nora Opara, at nearly fifty (her exact age was Nora's secret), had bright pink skin over a face unlined except for laugh crinkles at the sides of her mouth and eyes. Her face was constantly in motion, registering the expression of every fairytale character she created for her grandson or in perfect imitation of every sales clerk, deliveryman or neighbor with whom she had dealings. In every incident she related, she pointed up the comical aspect of the human condition, with kindness and understanding. There was no trace, no slight hint that the clear bright face had ever experienced tragedy or discomfort of any kind. There were no visible scars of the sudden, violent widowhood she had suffered nearly sixteen years ago; no mark of the grief and torment of having endured a second inspector's funeral some five years ago when she saw her only son, Mickey's father, buried "in the best traditions of the New York City Police Department—killed while performing his duty," with the added distinction of following the tradition of his father before him.

Yet, sometimes, in the late evening, when she seemed engrossed in the latest lending-library novel, her face, in repose and unaware, revealed a great and heavy sadness. This childishly slender woman, with her female awareness of the continuity of life, had been Christie's strength during those unbelievable days when Mike had been killed and had to be buried and the whole situation had to be borne.

Nora kicked off her shoes, stretched her toes, then regarded Christie thoughtfully. "Well, your mind isn't on your son's rotting teeth. What's the matter, Chris?"

"Nora, I want to ask you something. Oh, something silly, I guess."

"I'll probably have a silly answer for you, so go ahead."

Christie seemed fidgety, her fingers poking at her hair. "Nora, when—when Mike first told you about me, you know, that we were serious, what did he say?"

It was one of the strong bonds between them: their resolution, through the years since Mike's death at twenty-five, that they would speak of him easily, naturally. It had been Nora, cutting through the shock and pain, with the sharpened experience of her own widowhood, who had told

64

Christie that they *could* speak of him. Nora studied Christie's face intently; it wasn't the 'Mike blues'; not this time. There was something else bothering her daughter-in-law.

"Well, he came home one night, all flustered and talking his fool head off about 'this girl, Christie Choriopolous,' and of course, I said, 'Christie What-ee-opolous?' and then I shut up because I saw he was really saying something. *Something important.*"

Impatiently, Christie shook her head. "No, that's not what I meant. Nora, did Mike ever say—well—I guess a man doesn't say that to his mother." She made an annoyed clicking sound against her teeth, then blurted out, "Did he ever describe me as 'sexy'?"

Nora's spontaneous laugh was clear and honest. "My God, no! He said, 'Mom, this kid is so damn cute: a regular little tomboy!'" Nora bit down on her lower lip. "Oh-oh. I think I said exactly the wrong thing, didn't I?"

"No," Christie said shortly, "you just told the truth, dammit, like you usually do. Nora, do I still look like a 'regular little tomboy'?"

Christie jutted out one hip, shifting her weight, her hands resting on the back of her hips. She lowered her head, striking a pose, peering at Nora, who studied her.

"Not exactly. But honey, let's face it. There's not a damn thing you can do about your bustline or that flat fanny, so make the best of what you have." She stood up, turning Christie around. "At least, you won't get all saggy and sloppy. You're built to last. You're the slim type. You'll never have to worry about the calories, like some people do." She thumped her own round rear. "And I'll tell you a secret: I think I would have hated you if you had been a real sex-pot, one of those sweatery, curvy gals."

"Oh, swell. I was good for *your* morale."

"Honey, it wasn't easy facing mother-in-law-hood and possible grandmotherhood in my early forties. Christie, I know what your problem is. You don't get around enough." She held her hand playfully over Christie's mouth, stifling her protests. "Oh, I know, good old Dan takes you out regularly. But you know as well as I do that Dan is *safe:* all tied up and unavailable. And such a perfect gentleman that he would never say, the hell with what you *say*, kiddo, I'm male, you're female."

"Nora, you're beginning to sound like my-mother-the-matchmaker. I remember your friend Mrs. O'Donnell's son, Jeffrey with the curly blond hair. And the opinions." Her mouth pulled back. "Jeffrey O'Donnell had more opinions than there are subjects to have opinions on. Particularly about the New York City Police Department and all members of that 'authoritarian, perverted' city agency. He and I sure had something in common: a natural antagonism for each other." She put her arm affectionately around her mother-in-law, giving her a sharp pinch. "Stop playing the nervous mother with me, okay?"

"Okay, okay. But you tell me then: when are you going to meet some men? And don't tell me that you're around men all day. They're either married cops or loony criminals. And what about Mickey? You know as well as I do . . ."

"Nora, don't preach what you didn't practice. You were a widow when Mike was fourteen years old; you were still young, but you didn't remarry."

Nora brushed that away. "I was afraid Mike would have a resurgence of his Oedipus complex; after all, he was in the throes of adolescence." Then, flippantly, "You know, I think I read too much in those days. But anyway, even if I didn't remarry, I had *fun*. Remind me, sometime, to tell you a few things."

Christie grinned. "Nora O'Malley Opara, you are an Irish phony."

Nora winked. "That's what you think." Then, she stopped at the doorway and turned, her voice serious. "Listen, you just keep on being *Christie*, you hear? That was good enough for Mike, and he was a pretty discerning fellow. I know—I raised him. There'll be another man—a perfectly *available* man—who is looking for *exactly* the same Christie who knocked Mike Opara silly. Don't change yourself: you just be you. That's what makes you the very special girl you are."

Christie blotted her lips on a Kleenex, thinking of Nora. Whoever invented all the nasty mother-in-law stories hadn't met the likes of Nora. She started down the stairs, but was halted midway by Mickey, his face steamy with dirt, his baseball cap tilted over one eye.

"Ah, gee whiz, Ma. Gee whiz, why are you all dressed up like that? Gee whiz," he muttered disgustedly.

"Well, ah gee whiz, I thought maybe you'd say your mother looked just a little nice."

Wrapped up in his own problem, Mickey said, "Mr. Silverman was supposed to pitch for us in the driveway and he had to go somewhere for his wife and I told the kids my mother would pitch." Mickey banged his glove against the banister, his face pulled down. "Gee, Ma, it's the *big* guys —eight and nine years old—and the only reason they're going to let me play is if you pitch. Can't you change into pants or something?"

"Sorry, my boy. You scout up somebody else's father. I'm somebody's mother, remember?"

The small face crumpled. Mickey rubbed the large glove across his forehead, leaving long dark streak marks. He let Christie steer him to the door, then wriggled free of her hand, darting to the kitchen. "Hey, Nora? Gran? Can't you get Mom to come out and play ball with the guys?"

Nora, her hand on Mickey's neck, called, "Hey, Mom, can't you go out and play ball with the guys? They need a good pitcher."

Christie looked at the two of them, Nora's face warm with amusement, Mickey's heat-flushed and hopeful. She glanced at her watch. "For one half of one hour—not a minute more. Not one single minute more. I *do* have a date in Manhattan. Remember, now, Mickey, at *exactly* six-thirty, I have to drop out and shower *again* and get dressed *again*." As she spoke, Christie turned and ran up the stairs. "Go on, Mick. I'll be ready in a minute."

Changing rapidly, Christie tossed her jersey dress over the rocking chair, slid the dirty jeans and a fresh shirt over her flame-red, Tweed-impregnated lingerie. She said mockingly to the face in the mirror, "Well, can *I* help it if I happen to be the best pitcher in the neighborhood?"

67

[7]

MURRAY ROGOFF leaned his hip easily against the glass
wall of the phone booth. It was a nice feeling, enclosed in
the small cubicle, with people walking past, cars gliding
along right outside, yet he, Murray, all protected, all closed
in while they were all closed out. No one could see him but
he could see all of them: the punk kids whispering against
the wall, their eyes darting away from each other, their
faces mean and sharp; the thin, hollow-eyed junkies, yawn-
ing and scratching, waiting for their fix-it man. What a hang-
up that was. The bleached-out little queers, wagging their
tight little cans at each other. Murray let his breath out
slowly. He'd like to lift up three of them at a time, way over
his head, and smash them down into the gutter. Murray
flexed the muscles in his arm, ran his fingers over his biceps.
God, he felt strong. *God, he felt so good.*

He slipped the dime into the slot and dialed carefully,
closing his eyes. She always answered on the second ring,
like she wanted to be sure the first ring was her telephone,
not some neighbor's.

"Hello?" The small, soft voice, questioning. From just the
one word, she formed within his brain. A bright girl with
nice, natural color and flashing dark hair, all shining and
clean. That was what Murray liked most about her: that
glowing cleanness, the fresh sweetness. Everything about
her honed and nice, not an extra ounce of flesh. Her legs,
long and straight, the thighs tapering neatly to the slight
flare of her hips, and the small waist, not all pulled in with
wide belts the way the cheap girls were, just curving in the
way a girl's waist should and her breasts a nice size to cup
into a man's hand and a white neck and not too much
makeup on her face: just on her eyes, so that they flashed
with bright live color.

"Hello?" Again, the voice, only trembling a little.

68

"Hello, Carol Logan." Murray's voice was full and gentle, his hands cupping the mouthpiece, his eyes closed.

He didn't hear the sharp intake of breath or even catch the sense of her words. "Who is this? *Please*. Who is this?"

"I love you, Carol Logan."

Murray heard the click in his ear, the dead sound where her voice had been, but he understood. His tongue flicked out, touching, just touching the earpiece, where her lips had been, then he carefully replaced the receiver. He looked at his watch. He had a lot of time. She couldn't speak with him now because she had a dancing class at eight. He understood.

Murray walked along Broadway, stopping briefly at the corner of 51st Street, craning his neck, counting four stories up. That was where she would be for her hour's session. She never missed a lesson: three times a week—Monday, Wednesday, and tonight, Friday. It must cost most of her salary. How much could she earn working in an advertising agency? But he knew Carol was a smart girl. Those ad agency people had connections; they sponsored TV shows and things and maybe her boss could get her a spot somewhere.

But she stayed out too late after those dance lessons: particularly on Fridays. Murray rolled his fingers into fists. She shouldn't go out with all those boys from the dance school: they were all fags. Even the big guys: couldn't she see that? No. A kid as clean and pure and young as Carol, she probably didn't even know about those things. But didn't she even wonder why they never took her home? They probably felt that the Bronx was too far to travel: those moles, all digging into some little rats' nests in the Village—with each other.

She was lucky he had seen her home every Friday night for the last month.

Murray glanced at the clock set in a flickering advertisement high above the street. He had plenty of time to go over to the Automat for some coffee. It wasn't even starting to get dark. Murray hated daylight saving time. The streets were just as bright, though cooler than afternoon. Murray unbuttoned his collar. The shirt was starchy as were his

immaculate chinos, and beneath his clothing he still felt as
scrubbed and clean as when he had stepped from the tub an
hour ago. He stood for a moment, absently fingering the
crisp short sleeves of his shirt. Some little guy lunged into
him, letting out a curse word at the unexpected obstacle,
and Murray turned, bending forward to look directly at his
face. The man gasped, hanging onto the arm of a cheap
little broad with high, stiff, whitened hair. She yanked at the
man's arm, her eyes wide, her mouth redly opened. Murray
made a deep hard sound way down in his throat and he
heard the broad say, "My God!" Murray stood in the middle
of the street, watching them hurry into the crowd, and he
began to laugh. He raised his arms over his head, freely
reaching, feeling the stretch from the waist up, along his
torso, pulling his lean flesh along his ribs. He felt so good.
So great.

Murray Rogoff did not see the faces of any of the people.
He did not notice the usual loungers, hunched against open-
front hot dog stands and penny arcades, taking him in with
swift, evaluating eyes, then discounting him, or the bland-
faced tourists who moved in startled detour from his path,
staring at him with the same sense of wonder and incredul-
ity with which they had regarded the Empire State Building
or the Statue of Liberty or the hollow immensity of the
Radio City Music Hall. Murray saw only his destination, the
Automat, and he whirled through the revolving door, faintly
amused that he had sent two indignant, potty women spinning out onto the sidewalk, mouths sputtering and packages toppling.

He jammed his two nickels into the slot and watched the
coffee squirt into the heavy battered cup. Carol drank too
much coffee. She should drink more milk. For energy. A
dancer needs a lot of energy. She should eat only food containing a lot of vitamins, like an athlete; when you use your
body a lot, you have to give it the right fuel. Like he did.
No matter what Mama said, Murray would not eat the
heavy swill she tried to load him with; his hand would
sweep away all the starches and his fingers would pounce
on the meat and chicken and fruit and milk. Milk: boy, he
drank it down by the bottle, right from the bottle, a quart

straight down without stopping for breath, the way some guys drank beer. They were crazy to drink beer: fat bellies, that's what they were. Young guys, growing, should take care of their bodies. Like he did. Everyone should do routines: muscle-flexing and bends and stretches and resistance. It made a guy feel so great. Almost as great as when you took a girl.

Murray Rogoff sat down at a table near the large floor-to-ceiling window. He did not think it was strange that the man and woman and little girl who had been sitting there, eating from a collection of dishes on their trays, had gotten up, staggering off with their heavy trays. He liked having a table all to himself: it was like having a private box seat on Broadway. He drank his coffee in a few hot gulps. He didn't like coffee, but he was feeling a little tired and he needed something to keep him awake. It was Friday and it would be a long night for him. He sat watching for a long time, then looked at the clock in the Automat. It was time for him to go to 51st Street. He had to make sure Carol got to her dancing class.

For Murray Rogoff, time began and ended now at the particular moment. Living was walking along Broadway, right now, to 51st Street, to wait for Carol Logan. There had been no morning on some subway station with the terrible, confusing, unknown dread whirling through him, eating away at his body, devouring his brain; there had been no collection of people, moving him within the depths of his nightmare to strange rooms, telling him to move here, put your fingers on this pad, on this paper, sit there, look at this camera, turn sideways, look up. There had been no small, narrow room with a hard platform bed and dirty uncovered toilet and no clanging of steel or long barred corridors and no large and dusty courtroom filled with men who spoke around and at him.

There had been no hot and blinding afternoon and no Frankie Santino, fully grown into semblance of manhood, whispering some words at him, pinching his arm and shoulder. And there had been no David, clenching his shoulder, his knee, his neck. There had been no screaming in the hot small rooms on the top floor of the tenement on

71

Rivington Street where his mother, lighting the Sabbath candles, had dropped the taper at the sight of David, unexpected and unseen for more than a year. For Murray, time had canceled out and his day had been as all his days: an automatic enduring of the hours in his father's fish store, toward the time when the sun would finally let go, darken things down so that the lights would flash on all over the wide and busy streets and Murray Rogoff feeling young and strong and great like he could throw off whatever crazy shroud-like thing seemed to encase him and he would emerge as he truly was, at the center of himself as he always had been: Murray the Norseman, Murray the Great, filled by that special and good and joyous feeling which was fully his now, no longer hiding beneath a furious jumble of sounds and voices and hard-faced strangers, and he could identify joy and savor it and know it: *Carol Logan*.

He pressed against the fender of a light blue Buick convertible, watching the street, his eyes blinking away all the unimportant people who tried to fill his vision. *There*. Murray held his eyes steady, sharply set on her. With the first far-off glimpse, he knew it was Carol as surely as if a spotlight had picked her up and hovered over her in the beginning dimness. His eyes fastened to the top of her head, which was the first part of her he could see, bobbing in and out among the faceless bodies. She moved surely, easily, steadily, emerging whole and beautiful, half a block away: dressed in a blue shift which hit her slender thighs as she walked that nice, ladylike walk, her face held high, her eyes not caught by any of the punks and bums, her ears not aware of the dirty remarks and crude passes. She could walk through mud and come out clean.

Murray slid his body down so that his lower spine rested against the fender; his arms folded into each other. As she passed directly in front of him, he dropped his head so that he appeared to be dozing, but his eyes, beneath his glasses which were half-hidden by the peak of his tan cap, were steady on her and she kept going, her face straight ahead and held high. He watched, straightening up now, watching those legs in the nice little heels, not high and spiky, just medium heels and firmly hitting the pavement. The dress touched along her body and you could tell she wore a girdle, probably just a soft little girdle, but just right so that it gave her a smooth line across the backside and the little waist could be seen, not all pulled in, just nice and natural and wonderful.

Murray smiled, watching her safely into the building. He pulled himself from the car and took a large breath, filling his lungs with the sooty air. He rubbed his chest with both hands, laughing a little, looking at the creeps pushing along the sidewalks with their dirty little pickups. He walked about aimlessly: down a block, across Broadway, stopping to look into a window where they sold the type of underwear prostitutes wore: little black things on skinny little strings. Murray shook his head. It was disgusting. He turned, looked across Broadway, over the tops of the cars and taxis and buses. Carol was up there, dressed in her dancer's leotards, which she carried in that little leather satchel, and he could see her: firm and neat in command of every part of her body. He shook his head again at the terrible things in the window.

The hour went by quickly. An hour is a short time and Murray Rogoff had endless patience during that particular hour. But the rest of the evening was too long and he was beginning to get tense. Just because it was Friday, that didn't mean she should stay out so late. Not with those punks, anyway. And not in that dump: all those ham-and-egg joints were the same. He stood, leaning against the closed-down, deserted newsstand, shifting his weight from time to time. He didn't like that girl with the red hair. It was a cheap, obvious dye job and if Carol hung around with someone like that, some of these Broadway sharpies might get the wrong idea about her, might think she was like that. Murray wondered how she could eat that crappy food, all greasy and heavy with rancid oil. But Carol only played with the food on her plate, occasionally taking some into her mouth, chewing slowly, her lips slightly parted. She leaned across the table, her eyes on the boy with the white skin and the black hair. One of those: Murray knew the type. God, Carol was a baby. That guy was turned on himself. One of those pretty boys who looked around constantly to see who

73

was watching him, speaking with his hands, his eyebrows, his shoulders, then breaking into one of those wide smiles, but always making sure that everyone else was giving him the right reaction. Carol certainly was. He was one of those weirdos who could make it with a girl or a queer or maybe even all by himself.

Murray rubbed his hands along the seams of his chinos; his palms began to feel sticky. He closed his eyes, putting his hand over his glasses, smearing them. He rubbed his wrist over the lenses, batting his eyes rapidly. They were leaving. God. He almost missed that.

Murray Rogoff walked slowly through the wandering, aimless crowd, not feeling an occasional pocketbook bang against his thigh, not hearing any stray remarks directed at or about him. Not daring to take his eyes from her head, which was all he could see except for a quick glimpse of her upturned face now and then as she listened to the black-haired boy, Murray moved steadily into the mass of bodies. At 42nd Street, as he had expected, they turned left, toward the subway at the end of the block. Some seedy old panhandler approached them, his hand outstretched, his face polluted. The boy, smiling, said something to him, extending his own hand. Murray's fingers curled into the palms of his hand.

Murray walked slowly down the subway steps, hearing Carol's voice beyond the two middle-aged couples directly in front of him. The men, walking behind their women, gesturing and arguing about something, edged nearer to their wives, taking their elbows and steering them clear of him, and Murray cut through the sharp, sudden silence, ignoring their rounded eyes and opened mouths. He slammed his quarter at the agent in the change booth, slipped his token in the slot, pushed himself through the turnstile, right past Carol, who lingered inside the controls, still talking to the black-haired boy whose fingers were moving, through the iron bars, along her bare arm.

Murray walked right past them, slowly down the subway steps leading to the uptown platform, without looking back. He heard her quick step, running for the train which was pulling into the station. Murray boarded the "D" train at the center door, aiming for one of the few empty seats. The woman who had gotten directly in front of him raced him for it, but he got there first and he sat, pulling his cap over his forehead, sliding low in the seat so that the woman, glaring, had to move away because his feet took up all the space directly under the handstrap. Murray turned his face toward the front of the car. Carol was standing, holding one of the enamel loops, her face gazing at the subway map. His eyes moved along the line of her arm, bare at the shoulder in the sleeveless shift. Her raised arm hid the neat breast, but the shift, pulled up now, dove in at the waist and glided along the hip and just a tiny fraction of blue slip showed.

He felt a tightening in his thighs and in the pit of his stomach. He closed his eyes. It would be a long ride up to the Bronx.

By Kingsbridge Road, the train had nearly emptied but three other people got off besides Murray and Carol. She had a firm grip on her leather satchel and little pocketbook and she didn't look around, just straight ahead. Murray walked behind the other people, some tired-looking men, elderly, dazed strangers. He lost sight of her momentarily, but it didn't matter. He knew where she was headed.

The cool night air hit his chest and the back of his neck. The sky was deep black now with little holes of light, like sparks from the full moon whose glow did not extend much beyond a wide circle. The sound of Carol's shoes across the street was steady and a little rapid, but not scared and panicky like some girls', alone on the side street, three blocks from home. She walked in the center of the sidewalk, not against the parked cars pressed tightly into one another, and that was smart, because you never knew who might be sitting in one of those cars, waiting for some girl.

Murray walked faster now so that he was well ahead of her. He was on the side of the street where her building was, close against the wall of apartment houses. It was strange that she always got out at the exit across the street, but people do funny things out of habit. He reached the dark red brick building and could see her in the blackness coming steadily toward him. He pushed the hall door inward, easing himself into the small entrance hall. The

75

light was on, which was good because any bum could be hiding in a hallway like this. Not touching the brass knob of the door atop the flat steps, just pushing it with his shoulder, Murray felt an anger. The locks on these doors were always jammed. Someone should complain to the landlord, but a hell of a lot they cared about a young, beautiful girl coming home alone into a trap like this.

Murray's feet touched the tile floor of the long hallway so lightly he couldn't hear them himself. He narrowed his eyes in the dimness. That damn light over the sticky brass mail-boxes alongside the first staircase was flickering. Murray took out his handkerchief and touched the bulb. He could feel the heat of it even through the folds of cloth. Gently, he turned it. He took off his cap and, his eyes comfortable in darkness, he eased his glasses from his face, placed them inside his cap, which he set against the wall. He could smell the stale odor of dirty wet mops. Some great janitor they must have here, sloshing a filthy pail of water around.

Murray sucked his breath in, holding it now, feeling it in both of his lungs. He pulled his stomach in, hard and flat. He heard her open the door, heard her two hesitant steps, then she stopped. Christ, she was frightened by the darkness ahead of her. He didn't want her to be afraid. *He was there*. There was nothing to be afraid of.

He heard her short breathy sound, then heard her start toward the stairway, toward him. She could probably see that the lights were on further up the stairs and had decided to hurry past the dark place near the mailboxes.

Murray felt the fragrance of her preceding her, flowing from her, pressing down the odor of wet dirt, reaching out to him as he reached out for her, his arms silently, strongly, surely encircling her, one hand across her mouth, then his hand sliding away for his mouth to press on hers so completely that he could breathe into her and suck the sweetness of her into himself. She was so light. God, he had never realized that her beautifully limber body would be so light, but he hardly needed any strength at all to lift her to him, as though she were part of himself and he part of her, her body real and alive beneath him as he easily pressed her to the floor beneath him, carefully cradling the back of her head with his hand and forearm. And she, Carol, her hands unable to get to his chest, was digging at his back and her body was moving now beneath his and she rocked urgently on the hard floor beneath him, passionately and soundlessly beneath the great, unrelenting strength of his mouth, which never left hers, though her head rocked from side to side; his mouth clung to hers and his hand helped her because a man should remove a woman's clothing: only prostitutes, sitting there, glassy-eyed, pulled off their clothes. But when a man loved a girl, it was a thing a man did and he didn't want her to have to do anything, just to feel him there with her: loving her, giving pleasure to her, enjoying her, possessing her body with great joy, but not just taking, *giving*. She was so small beneath him: he could feel her heart thudding through the fragile rib cage hitting his own heart: it was as if they had just the one heart between them and his fingers could feel the great sound of exaltation rising along her throat and his fingers pressed the sound lovingly back: back into her so that she could savor it deep within herself as he did his astounding full, deep, anticipated and finally accomplished pleasure.

His mouth now lifting from hers, he gasped a lazy warm mouthful of air and the air was filled with Carol and he touched her lower lip with the tip of his tongue. Her mouth was relaxed and silent for she was at peace in the deep and beautiful sleep of his love.

Murray pressed his face into her hair, his tongue lightly touching at her earlobe, running down her cheek, along her parted lips, just skimming her teeth. He buried his face into that warm small place in the bend of her neck, wishing he could see her face in the blackness, but he knew she would be smiling, her eyes closed in that nice, happy, fantastic feeling which enveloped them both. And this canceled out all the other times: all those cold, mechanical, used bodies on which he had released the accumulations of nothing more than animal lust with a sense of despair and anger, his body juices being sucked from him absently as though he were alone on some filthy, paid-for bed, because this was Carol and he was now truly Murray and his body ached with a marvelous awareness of love and pleasure.

His voice was so soft it was almost as though he was thinking rather than speaking, but he spoke directly into her ear and he knew she heard him, because she lay so still: listening.

"Carol. Carol. I love you so much. I worry about you so much. You're so special, so special. Not like the little tramps in the candy store: they all wanted it, every one of them, anyone I picked out, taking it from me, but not giving me anything, just grabbing for it and then none of them even seeing me." Murray's eyes blinked against the darkness. He didn't want to think about that; letting his lips become still for a moment, he knew that none of it mattered, because he had given love and had received love and that was what counted. "Oh, Carol, you're so clean and so good." Then kissing her lips, nipping at them lightly, touching them with his fingertips, Murray knelt over her. "It's late. You rest for a while. I feel so good. I can't remember when I felt this good."

And then, Murray took a switchblade knife from his trouser pocket, letting the four-inch blade drop down. Lifting her head gently, so as not to disturb her sleep, carefully and surely his hands, steady and kind, gathered a small sweet thick lock of clean hair from that warm place at the nape of her neck. He cut the lock of Carol's hair, closing his fingers over that small part of her. He flicked the knife closed, replaced it in his trouser pocket, then unfolded his handkerchief, placed the hair into the center of it, carefully refolded it into a small square, placed it into the breast pocket of his shirt and patted it against himself like a treasure.

Smoothing her hair from her brow, he lightly touched her lips, then her forehead, with his lips and tongue, whispering to her, "Rest and sleep, Carol, and dream of me."

His hand went directly to his cap, his foot brushing against her leather satchel and pocketbook. He first put on his glasses and then his cap. Not knowing that her eyes were frozen open, he wished her sweet dreams and soundlessly, Murray Rogoff left the hallway, wedging his shoe into the partly opened door, prying it with his shoulder. He went

78

down the four flat steps, out through the opened street door, onto the cool black street.

Murray Rogoff walked the three blocks to the Grand Concourse, stood for a moment looking at the entrance to the Independent subway, then, holding the peak of his cap, he stretched his head upward to the sky. It was a great night: cool and clean and he felt so good. He turned and decided to walk a mile or two or maybe ten miles in the fresh clear air. He could take the subway somewhere farther down the line.

CHRISTIE OPARA sat in a leather and steel sling chair absorbing the black and white sterility of Dr. Sidney Ginsburg's waiting room. It was the kind of room that advised a prospective patient to expect extreme professional competency, if not sympathetic concern. A collection of pictures, placed on the ice colored walls with a mathematical precision, were either blackly indicated flowers against white backgrounds or whitely suggested figures impressed on black. A long narrow steel magazine rack hung low against one wall, and inserted in various-sized slots were celluloid-covered magazines: issues of everything from *Life* and *Look* to the *Partisan Review*. It wasn't what Christie had expected. Not from a cousin of Marty Ginsburg.

She hated to crush her cigarette into the gleaming black stone ashtray; it seemed a defilement. Marty's voice rumbled behind the black enameled door of the doctor's office, and in response, Christie could hear a low murmur of inaudible words. The door swung open and the face behind Marty's, belonging to the son of his father's brother, was narrow and pale, marked clearly and sharply by straight black eyebrows and a thin neat black mustache extending exactly the length of the thin lips. A crisp fresh odor of starch wafted from the cardboard-stiff jacket which covered a well-built, Sunday athlete's frame. Before Christie could extricate herself from the somewhat complicated chair, the door clicked shut and the voices began again. She exhaled a thin whistle of annoyed amusement. That nut, Marty Ginsburg, could never just *do* something: he had to build a plot around the simplest of things. Christie wondered what he was telling his wary-looking cousin.

Marty, leaning his bulk against the door, rested his hand heavily on the reluctant shoulder of his cousin. "There's nothing to worry about, Sidney, I'm telling you. This kid is okay now, honest. It's only when there's a lot of strange people around that she gets—you know." Marty nodded his head in a particular way. "Which is why I asked to come here on a Sunday night so there wouldn't be no patients around." His fingers pinched into the stiffness of his cousin's jacket. "And besides, like I said, there might be some of your patients who would recognize her: just because *you* don't read the papers don't mean that practically everyone else in the city don't know who this kid's father is." Marty shook his head at this possible danger. "That's all I'd need—for someone to spot her."

Dr. Ginsburg removed himself from Marty's grasp and traced his long slim fingertips along his mustache. "Marty, I don't see why you brought her here at all. Couldn't the District Attorney have arranged to have this done by one of your police surgeons?"

"A police surgeon? You're kidding. Police surgeons are the world's biggest blabbermouths. If the reporters ever got wise that the daughter of the . . ." Marty grabbed at his mouth, bunching his lips into a grotesque cupid's bow. "See? See, Sidney? Now see what you almost made me say? You almost made me say who she is and that would be very, very bad. My main job right now is to keep this girl under wraps." Marty's hand formed a barrier around his mouth, but his voice was still loud. "This whole thing is by way of a favor, Sidney. You know how these things work, huh?" He winked. "The D.A. does a very important man a favor and then the very important man can do a favor for the D.A. sometime." Marty recognized an alert gleam in his cousin's eye. "And of course both the VIP *and* the D.A. will know *who, exactly*"—his index finger dug into Sidney's chest—"is the man who really cooperated, you know?"

Dr. Ginsburg withdrew from any more of Marty's jabs and retreated toward the small examining room to the rear of his office. "All right, Marty, let's get this over with. I have everything ready for the cast."

"Okay, Sidney. But look, I got to go and talk to the girl for a minute. She's a little nervous, you know? Nothing I can't handle. See, she trusts me, which is why I'm the one brought her here. Anything Marty tells her, she does. Not even her old man could have talked her into this. You should have heard the story I had to tell her to get her to agree to this." Marty shook his head decisively; he couldn't tell Sidney any more.

This time when the black door opened, Marty seemed to fill the room. He motioned Christie beside him on the black leather couch but kept his eyes alertly on the door. "Poor old Sid. He's still nutty as a fruitcake."

Christie patiently asked the expected question. "What do you mean?"

Marty hunched himself closer to her. "Listen, Christie, my cousin, Sidney—well, he always *was* a little strange. You know." He smacked at his forehead. "But we always figured it was because he was so brilliant. A very brilliant man, my cousin, so I guess when you're a genius, you got to be a little crazy, you know, to balance things up."

Christie sighed. "Okay, Marty, let's hear the story."

Her tone did not affect the seriousness of Marty's words; he was very sincere. "Well, he'll make the cast for you all right. But Sid's got some weird ideas. He took one look at you and, don't ask me why, please don't ask me why, but he thinks you're the Mayor's daughter."

"The Mayor's daughter?" Christie lowered her voice in response to Marty's urgent expression. "The Mayor's daughter? Why would he think that?"

"Gee, I told you not to ask me, but okay, you asked me. See, Sidney is a real gossip column fanatic." Marty shook his head over his cousin's malady. "He reads all the gossip columns and he stores away all kinds of crazy information: especially about anybody in politics, and he goes to his district Reform Democratic Club every Tuesday night and he picks up little pieces of information and then he figures things out and he comes up with some real crazy stories. And he *really* believes them, which is the sad part. So, when he looked at you, he slams the door and he tells me, 'Marty, I know who that is. That is the Mayor's daughter and I know all about her.' Gee, I didn't know the Mayor had a daughter, did you?"

In a quietly rational, reconciled voice, Christie asked, "What about the Mayor's daughter?"

Marty shrugged. "Who knows? Sidney says she is a suicidal person."

Christie glanced at her wristwatch; this was taking more time than she had expected. "Marty, why are you playing games? Come on, just tell him who I am and let's get the cast made."

"I did, I did tell him, Christie, but he thinks I made it up as a cover story. See, he figures things out to suit his own theories, that's how some nuts are I guess." Marty nodded sympathetically at Christie's growing annoyance. "Okay, kid. Sidney says he knows—from little things planted in the columns and from his politician friends—that you, the Mayor's daughter, got involved in some kind of weird Oriental religious cult." He shrugged at her raised eyebrows. "Don't ask me. Sidney says, that's all I know. And that part of this religious cult is that you got to slash your left wrist and watch yourself bleed to death and while all this is going on, you got to recite certain prayers and that way you'll get into some kind of Oriental heaven." Admiringly, he said, "Gee, for a Jewish boy, Sidney knows a lot about non-kosher religions."

Flatly, Christie stated, "Marty, you're kidding."

"No honest, he's a Jew." Marty spoke rapidly, pulling Christie to her feet. "And that somehow the Mayor convinced you to keep your left arm in a cast for a while until he gets you over this whole business, and you have some kind of confidence in me, like I'm your trusted friend, so that's why you agreed to come along with me tonight." Marty lowered his voice to a warning whisper. "Listen, don't say nothing to him, nothing at all: you say anything, and right away, Tuesday night, he'll be telling all his pals at the club that the Mayor's daughter said this and that, you know."

Dr. Sidney Ginsburg opened the door, nodded briefly at Christie without meeting her eyes and led the way into his small examination room. She sat where he indicated, removed her wristwatch and placed her arm on the small cushion of clean lintless towels which Dr. Ginsburg had prepared on the table before her. With great care, quickly

83

and deftly, the doctor's long fingers removed a series of wide strips of gauze from the small steel bowl containing the plaster of paris solution. Christie noticed a beaded line of moisture forming over his thin mustache. His eyes were very small and very black and they darted from her arm to her face and when they met her eyes, they fled away again. She noted with admiration that not one drop of the wet solution touched anywhere but on his fingertips and her arm. Silently, he worked his way almost to her elbow.

"Isn't that a little high, Doctor?"

His hand leaped at the sound of her voice and for one split second, it seemed that he might drop the wet strip; instead, he carefully unwound the last layer, then with a damp cloth, he washed away all traces of the solution from the freed portion of her arm.

"Thank you," Christie said softly.

Dr. Ginsburg nodded and indicated another table where her arm was to repose under the purple glow of a lamp which, he informed them, quietly, would hasten the hardening process. Christie watched him as he moved rapidly, without a single wasted motion, cleaning up: scrubbing the little bowl spotless, winding up unused gauze, putting everything into little built-in compartments against the wall. She noticed that he had a tremor going near his left eye and a slight twitching at the corner of his lip which made his mustache look like a nervous, undernourished caterpillar. She dropped her eyes quickly when his beady black eyes met hers: Marty must have told him she was a subdued but unpredictable homicidal maniac.

She could feel a pulling all along the skin under the cast; it was hardening rapidly and she could feel the weight of it. Dr. Ginsburg ran his fingers lightly along the cast, turned off the purple lamp and held up an expanse of white cotton cloth which he folded deftly into a sling. Carefully, he rested Christie's arm along the length of it, then tied a knot behind her neck and asked if it was comfortable.

Her eyes glistened maliciously at Marty who stood like a bulky wall behind his cousin. "City Hall perfect, Doctor. My daddy will be pleased."

For one brief instant, the doctor studied her face furtively, as though trying to memorize her features. Christie gazed vacantly at Marty's shoulder, letting the doctor get his good look.

"Good, good, good, Doc," Marty said, slapping the starch down the center of his cousin's spine. "Wait for me outside, kid, will you? Be right with you."

Christie smiled brightly. "Anything you say, Marty. You know that."

Marty handed his cousin a wad of tissues. "Your forehead is all wet, Sidney. Sidney, I want to tell you something. You handled that really beautiful. Beautiful. I knew I could trust you. As you can see, this is a highly touchy situation." He leaned his face close, whispering, "You recognized her, of course?"

Dr. Ginsburg blotted his face, removed his coat and ran a single tissue inside his shirt collar. His face was very white. "My God," he said. "Yes. Yes I did. But don't worry about it Marty. I thought—I thought it was just one of your games." He shook his head. "Very sad." He flicked his dry tongue, almost touching the black line of hair over his lip. "The Secretary-General of the U.N.—he has other children besides the girl, doesn't he?"

Marty clamped a heavy hand over his cousin's mouth, glaring menacingly into the startled black eyes. "Swallow those words, Sidney Ginsburg! Swallow them down! Spit them out! Forget them!" he commanded.

The pale face squirmed free. "I will, I will. It's forgotten, Marty, believe me, it's forgotten!" The high shrill voice was comfortably familiar now: the voice of skinny little cousin Sidney with all the A's on his report card and all the whining complaints: Cousin Marty hit me; Cousin Marty spit in my orange soda.

Marty left his cousin washing his hands and face in cold water. Christie was standing before the magazine rack, wishing she had time to dig into a few of the new home-furnishings editions. Marty grabbed at her cast and steered her out of the office.

The outer door opened onto a small terrace two steps down from the sidewalk, lined on both sides by black and white wooden flower boxes filled with real looking artificial

white roses. Focusing on Marty's beaming face, Christie
demanded, "Come on, Marty. What was the game? What in
the world did you tell him?"

Marty's face pulled into a look of offended innocence and
he spread his hands, palms up. "He's a real nut, like I told
you. But you know, I got a theory," Marty said, and now he
smiled broadly over his own personal private joke which he
would not share with her. "Sidney's trouble is that he takes
life too serious. He don't know how to have a little fun once
in a while!"

9

BILL FERRANTI's voice on the telephone was pleasantly mild and somewhat puzzled by Christie's annoyance. "I don't know why, Christie. Stoney Martin called me around six this morning and told me to cancel out on the LSD."

"You mean *cancel out* or delay it, or what?" Christie's index finger could not reach high enough under the heavy cast to relieve the itchy spot.

"Cancel out altogether from what Stoner said. We're to report to the M.O. Apparently, they have something going and Mr. Reardon specifically wants you in this morning. Stoner said he'd explain when we get there."

The itch was tantalizingly close to the tip of her finger. She pressed the receiver between her cheek and shoulder and concentrated her efforts but to no avail. "You mean I won't need this cast?"

"I don't think so, Christie. I guess you could slip it off and leave it at home. See you in the office."

The cast had not been made to slip off or pry off: it would have to be hammered off and Mr. Reardon's directions had been to report to the M.O. forthwith which usually meant twenty minutes prior to whatever time you arrived.

There were more Squad members in the office than Christie had ever seen at one time. She correctly surmised that the gambling teams had made some kind of collar: they were rarely in the office and all six men were present now, holding quick conversations with each other, with Stoner Martin and with Casey Reardon who appeared briefly, then returned to his own office.

Detective Sam Farrell was a man who had been born clumsy and each year, as he had grown to his present large dimensions, his clumsiness had increased accordingly. Even standing absolutely still, his wide, nicely proportioned shoulders at ease, his large hands resting easily on his narrow hips, his broad flushed face looking at nothing in particular, Sam Farrell had the undeniable look of a clumsy man.

There was something in his manner that marked him as the man most likely to find the one existing crack in an otherwise smooth sidewalk: the man whose toe would find that crack, catch in it and send his body sprawling. When Sam Farrell crossed a room—any room—pieces of furniture seemed to reach out toward an unprotected thigh, smashing it. His kneecaps seemed drawn to low tables and his head was invariably the target of low-hanging lamps. He was the kind of man who did not walk across a room: he lurched, as though by moving in an almost galloping stride, he could thus avoid the unknown pitfalls which forever seemed to await him.

Bill and Christie watched Sam Farrell banging away, two fingers jabbing at the keys of the old Underwood. Christie grinned as Sam dug around in the top drawer for an eraser, then, hunched over the machine, he scrubbed furiously, stopping in surprise to regard the little hole he had made. He flipped the carbon paper from his copy, hoping to do a better job, and was confronted by a blank sheet of white paper. He had placed the carbons in the machine backwards.

Christie and Bill Ferranti moved in on Sam Farrell; Farrell was the man to speak to when you wanted confidential information.

"You fellows sure look busy, Sam."

He looked up, squinted, then his face stretched into a broad grin. "Hey, you guys really loused up on Friday, huh?"

Christie shrugged. "We'll make up for it."

"Oh, nobody told you yet, huh?" Sam shook his head. "Tough. Well, that's the breaks."

"Told us what?" Ferranti asked.

Sam Farrell hunched his shoulders forward and motioned them toward him. "Geez, Friday night the LSD blast went off and so did the kid. You know, the kid the whole thing was all about."

Christie felt the cast on her left arm get a few pounds heavier. "Which kid, Sam?"

"Gee, nobody told you, huh? Well, I don't know what kid it was exactly—some girl. Her uncle is a state senator, I think. From what I hear, the kid blasted off and is still revolving in outer space. Her family hustled her off to some upstate sanitarium." Sam snapped his fingers, as though he had just solved a problem. "That's right, you weren't here Saturday morning. Boy, did it ever hit the fan. Mr. Reardon got called upstairs to the old man. When he came down, well, it's just a good thing you weren't around. We were all in because of this round-up we got on and I heard him." Farrell laughed without malice. "I'm surprised you didn't hear him out where you live."

Christie ignored the itch inside the cast and kept her voice level. "What's going on here, Sam? What have you got?"

"Very hush-hush," Farrell said. "A little ordinary housewife, how do you like that?"

A female prisoner; that's why she was needed. They didn't have to ask Sam anything, he was telling them.

"Very confidential. She's part of a ring of little ordinary housewives. Been using her telephone for bets. She answered an ad in the paper—you know: 'make extra money at home'—that kind of thing." Sam had very round blue eyes which never remained still. "It reaches all over the place—very extensive. We'll be working in conjunction with Nassau and Suffolk police—even Westchester County."

Christie leaned over, turning the papers in Sam's typewriter. "You have the carbons in backwards, Sam."

Smacking his lips together, Sam muttered, "Boy, these machines are tricky, aren't they? I hate this old Underwood, it never works right."

Christie and Bill moved across the office. Christie leaned facing out of the window, while Bill kept his eyes on the activity. They deliberately avoided discussing the LSD case and in some desperation, Christie turned to him. "Sorry I can't tell you about all the goings on, but it's very hush-hush. You understand, don't you?"

Bill went along with her. "Please, don't tell me anything I'm not supposed to know: just tell me the confidential facts and we'll let it go at that."

Reardon's voice called her name and everyone heard it over the steady sound of conversation and irregular typewriter clatterings. "It's been nice knowing you," she said to Ferranti without looking at his face; his expression would be sad and she preferred not to see it.

Christie stood beside Reardon, waiting. She noted the quick, jerking nod, the impatience with which he set Stoney's comments into place with a few sharp questions. There was a kind of electricity emanating from him, touching everyone in the room with a distinct vitality: Reardon was a man who moved and who forced everyone around him to move.

His eyes circled the room restlessly, accounted for everyone present, then, satisfied with what he saw, he spoke to her without looking at her. "We have a woman in there, a Mrs. Lydia Ogden. She's been taking calls for a bookie ring: a little housewifely moonlighting." Now, his eyes rested on Christie; they were as clear as two amber stones. Without hesitating over a word, his eyes moved over her, stopped briefly, then flickered along the lines of her two-piece dress. Reardon's eyes had an expression completely removed from his words or business-like tone of voice. "We haven't had much luck with this dame. I thought she might need another woman to talk to. You know—girl talk." Then his voice and his eyes seemed to join forces as he looked at her body again. "You look more like a girl today."

"What will I be looking for, Mr. Reardon?"

"What I need is names; the more the merrier. We've handled her with kid gloves and that's how it has to be. She's a particularly beltable bitch and she knows we're being careful with her. She's important to this investigation. *Very important.* Think you can handle her?"

"Yes, sir."

Reardon's eyes narrowed, and, as though he had seen it for the first time, he reached out and tapped his knuckles against her cast. "You better get this damn thing off." His voice had that sharp irritable edge to it.

"Mr. Reardon, I heard what happened on Friday night and . . ."

"You want to go round on that again?" he demanded sharply.

"No, sir, but . . ."

"Then take the goddamn cast off."

"Mr. Reardon," she persisted, "I've made my contacts; we know who's involved. Couldn't we just play it for a while and . . ."

Reardon's face was angry and he shook his head and started to speak but then, for some reason, he changed his mind and just stood looking at her for a moment. "Ya never know," he said tersely, and walked toward his office. "Come on, Opara, come on, move."

Reardon turned unexpectedly at the door to his office and Christie slammed into him. "Take it easy, Opara, you'll knock the boss down."

Christie backed away. "Sorry. And, I can't take the cast off now. It has to be hammered off."

"I'd be happy to oblige but I left my sledge hammer at home." His voice wasn't angry now and he briefly told her about the circumstances leading up to the interrogation of Mrs. Ogden.

"Now look, I'm going to leave you on your own, okay? Got anything in mind?"

"I'll have to see her first, all right?"

Reardon studied her thoughtfully, then opened the door, and jerked his head for her to follow. He made a quick introduction, his hand still on the doorknob, then left the two women alone.

Mrs. Ogden was a small woman; small and round without being fat. She looked about a careful forty-two or forty-three years old. Her hair was held stiffly from her face and was coal black against the somewhat pale skin. She had small, sharp brown eyes, incongruously smeared with bright blue eyeshadow, a small nose and irregular lips which pulled downwards under the pearlized lipstick. Her short fingers bore a wide wedding band, encrusted with tiny diamonds, and the right hand, reaching for her throat as the door clicked shut, was decorated with a large cocktail ring of dull rubies and diamond chips.

Christie walked to the window and with effort managed to open it with one hand. "It's awfully hot in here, isn't it?" Christie rested the cast in her right palm, wrinkling her nose at it. "This darn thing itches like mad."

Mrs. Ogden stared at her; her eyes were frozen little dark spots in her face. She resembled, for no reason Christie could pinpoint, a tough little dog, warily watching a potential enemy.

"I broke my wrist playing baseball," Christie said easily, sitting in Reardon's chair, behind his desk. She wondered how he'd like that.

"Baseball?" Mrs. Ogden asked carefully.

Christie grinned. "Dopey, isn't it? Yes, I was playing with my little boy and some of his friends and I slipped and snap! There went the wrist."

Mrs. Ogden's head seemed to raise up a little, as though the stiff hair, acting as an antenna, was trying to catch some signals. "You have a little boy?"

"Yes. Mickey. He's just five."

The small arms folded themselves across her chest. The chin pointed upwards. Mrs. Ogden's voice, brittle and unpleasant, had the added quality now of righteousness. "Well, *I* have three children and *I* am at home with *my* kids. I'm there when they need me and it seems that the police should be worrying about untended children of working mothers. *They're* the ones who get in trouble, not children of mothers like me who stay home. Where they belong."

Christie let the words bounce against the particular shell she began forming around herself. Go right ahead, Mrs. Ogden, you fine and virtuous little mother, get good and angry at me and tell me exactly what you think of me: because, lady, in a million years, I won't tell you exactly what I think of you.

"Tell me about your job, Mrs. Ogden. Mr. Reardon didn't really fill me in on what this is all about. What's the story?"

"The story," the woman said coldly, "is that I am a decent woman, just trying to help my husband out a little." Her mouth twisted down again and Christie felt a twinge of sympathy for the man who had to face that mouth each day. "I answered this ad in the *Journal*—you'd think I was a criminal—I just answered an ad, that's all!"

"What did the ad say?" Christie asked, ignoring the nasty, impatient tone.

"An ad—an ad. How can I remember what it said? It was a few weeks ago. You know, 'Housewives, earn extra money in your spare time. *At home.*' That kind of thing."

"I see. Did it give a phone number for you to call?"

The small hands flew to the teased hair, catching an imaginary strand and pressing it back into place. "Yes, some phone number, don't ask me what it was, I wouldn't know. And I called and spoke to Mr. Somebody or other—some guinea name."

Another tiny piece fell into place; expressionless, Christie nodded the woman on.

"So he told me that all I had to do was to call at least five or six people a day and give them this sales pitch about magazines. They were selling a whole group of magazines, and he sent me all the information: like you could get five years of the *Ladies' Home Journal* and three years of the *Saturday Evening Post* and two out of a list of fifteen other magazines for a flat payment, which brought each copy, over a period of five years, down to about 13 cents a copy."

"Uh-huh. And then what?"

The small brown eyes hid beneath the bright blue lids for a moment, while the pearly lips pushed into a pout. The lids unrolled and Mrs. Ogden fingered her cocktail ring, turning it so Christie could enjoy the small rubies. "So, I made my calls every day, taking names out of the phone book. In one whole week, I sold only one subscription. To some kike in the Bronx." The mouth went down in a smile. "You know—Abie could never resist a bargain!" The laugh was a hard sound.

Christie's eyes revealed nothing and her voice was flat and soft. "But then, you called them back, right, the number from the ad?"

"Yeah. All I had was the one subscription and the ad had said I could earn up to seventy-five bucks a week. Some seventy-five. So I called, and then this guinea—whatever his name was—he told me that a lot of housewives did make a lot of money that way, but some didn't. And that he worked for an agency that handles phone calls for a lot of clients— an answering service for people who can't be around when their phones ring, you know? So he said I seemed reliable and intelligent"—the small body preened—"so I said, sure, why not? So he told me to take down messages every day between ten and twelve for a Mr. Stowe and that Mr. Stowe would call me at twelve-thirty and I should give him the messages. And that was all I did." She held her arms out, palms turned toward the ceiling, her eyes rolling back and up. "That's all I did and I'm here, like a criminal or something."

"Mrs. Ogden, do you know any other women who took messages?"

The eyes, which had innocently beseeched the ceiling, now glared at Christie. "I already told that loudmouth redhead in there and I'm telling you now: that's all. That's it. I don't know anything more about it."

"Didn't you consider the messages peculiar? The names of horses and the numbers of races? Didn't that seem odd to you?"

"I took the calls when the kids were in school. I had things on my mind—like lunch and cleaning the house and going to the store and taking care of my kids. I took down whatever the people said and when Mr. Stowe called, I read off the messages and goodbye! I had my home and family on my mind, not a bunch of phone messages."

Christie leaned back in Reardon's chair, responding to the shadow and the tap at the door. "Come on in."

Stoney Martin crossed to Reardon's desk, an amused expression directed at Christie. "Excuse me, but Mr. Reardon asked me to get this file—yes, here, this is the one."

Christie nodded, but she was watching Mrs. Ogden; the viciousness broke through the makeup, cracking her face like old glass. Her small eyes watched Stoney's dark hand reach for the folder, watched his tall, lithe body cross the office and leave. Her eyes on the door, her face twisting down, she asked, "That nigger—he's a cop?"

Christie played her fingers along the edge of her cast for a moment. She rose, came alongside Mrs. Ogden, sat tentatively beside the woman, meeting her eyes. Slowly, she shook her head. "No, he's not a cop, Mrs. Ogden." Christie paused, the words reaching her mouth almost before her brain thought them out. "He's an F.B.I. agent."

The face before her screwed into a look of bewilderment. "F.B.I.?"

"Yes. Apparently, no one has bothered to explain this whole situation to you." Mrs. Ogden shifted her weight; Christie felt the cushions moving and her voice was soft and she was amazed at how kind, how concerned she sounded. "Let me try and explain it to you. You see, the 'agency' you were working for—and taking bets for—is a very large syndicate: interstate. New York, New Jersey, Connecticut. Now, you live up on 175th Street in Manhattan, I believe? That means you're part of the Manhattan operation."

"*The Manhattan operation?* What the hell does that mean?" The woman's voice was not as tough as she tried to make it sound. There was just the merest breaking quiver beginning; Christie noted it with small pleasure.

Christie let words come automatically from her lips, gauging their impact by the woman's face. "The F.B.I. and the *Treasury* agents are involved in this as well. The F.B.I. because it's an interstate operation and the Treasury men, of course, because of the *income tax* angle."

Mrs. Ogden leaped from the couch as though she had been touched by a live wire. Christie hadn't noticed the high spiked-heel shoes before. "Taxes? Income taxes? What do you mean? I'll file on my income when the time comes!"

Christie's voice was deliberately calm; it made Mrs. Ogden sound even shriller. "But on what amount? Sixty, seventy dollars a week?"

"That's all I made! I swear to God, that's all I made!"

"Mrs. Ogden, sit down and let me explain your situation a little better." Christie didn't give herself time to think, didn't plan or calculate the words, just took her cue from the tense, rigid body on the edge of the couch beside her. "You see, the way these gambling syndicates operate is pretty standard. Let's say a particular operation—upper Manhattan, your area—pulls an operation averaging approximately one hundred thousand dollars a week."

The black eyebrows shot up to the hairline, the mouth dropped opened in protest. Christie held her hand up. "Don't get excited, now, just listen. Standard operating expenses for 'message-takers' or 'relay-people' like you are set at a flat 5 percent for each area." The words, unquestioned by Mrs. Ogden, came from some unexpected reservoir within her; Christie felt a small trickle of perspiration streaming between her shoulder blades and she spoke rapidly, for if she stopped, was interrupted, was questioned, she might not be able to continue. "So, the amount involved would be about five thousand dollars a week, right? Therefore, the F.B.I. and the Treasury men, who of course know *exactly* how an operation is set up and know *exactly* how much money is spread around to people like you, however innocently you became involved, aren't really interested in *you* or in your 'innocent-involvement.' They just want to know who got what money, so the government can get the amount it is entitled to."

Christie stood up, moved silently to Reardon's desk, sat in the tilting chair, swiveled to face the woman. She caught the steadily growing panic that crept through the woman, working into her eyes and cheeks and down along her mouth, through her shoulders and into her suddenly busy hands which locked and unlocked one into the other. "So you see, Mrs. Ogden, if they don't come up with more names—*they always have you.*"

"That's all I got, seventy-five a week. *That's all I got.*" The voice was an empty chant, then the woman looked at her and there was some new emotion now, clearly evident, unhidden and terrible: fear. "Could they do that, miss? I mean, you're a detective, you'd know. Could they *really* do that?"

"Yes," Christie said, a logical answer to a logical question, without emotion of any kind, "they *really* could."

Mrs. Ogden walked to the window. Christie could see the rapid calculation, the profile frozen with decision. Mrs. Ogden turned, her hands nervously plucking words out of the air. "My sister, she took calls. And two of my cousins. And a few of my neighbors; some other girls, too." Then, trying to qualify the betrayal, "They didn't know either what it was—no more than me. I mean, I don't want *them* to get into any trouble, they didn't know either."

"Uh-huh."

Christie opened Reardon's top drawer, her fingers playing

among a collection of broken pens and pointless pencils and stray Life Savers and gum. She found one ball point that seemed to work; testing it on a white legal pad, Christie tore off the sheet. "Here, Mrs. Ogden. Write down the names, addresses and phone numbers of all the people you know who took phone calls the way you did."

The woman snatched at the pad and pen, curling herself in one corner of the couch. Christie, hearing the frantic scratchings the woman was making on the pad, felt a cold and angry pleasure at the sound, but the sight of the woman, revealed now beneath the destroyed surface smugness, filled her with contempt and revulsion and she avoided looking at her. She took a stick of half-wrapped gum from the top drawer, absently curled it into a roll, dropped the tiny piece of wrapping back into the drawer and pressed the gum between her back teeth. She reached for the double-framed photograph, leaning back in the chair.

Mrs. Casey Reardon wasn't what she had expected, although it would have been difficult to say exactly what she had expected. She really hadn't given any thought to Reardon's wife. The face, at first glance, was surprisingly young and pleasantly pretty, the smile just a little aware of the camera. The eyes, a clear cornflower blue, were startling against pale skin and black hair, which had a few becoming streaks of pure silver. The bright blue at her neckline was probably a favorite color: it did a lot for her eyes. Christie regarded the eyes thoughtfully. They seemed to convey a vague sadness. They did not match the expression of the lips, which now seemed mechanical.

She shifted her attention to the two young faces in the opposite side of the frame: the same dark hair and blue eyes and small features and pointed chins, each girl indistinguishable from her twin. Their young faces were clear and earnest, unsmiling: younger versions of their mother. Yet not exactly. The girl on the right could have been her mother in an earlier photograph: no slightest trace of Casey was contained in her delicate face. It was odd: her twin, though identical, had something about her that was familiar, something of Casey's, some hint, maybe in the slight tilt of the chin or the set of the mouth.

She hadn't heard Casey Reardon at the door and as he approached his desk, she felt the silver frame stick to her hands like some personal correspondence she had been caught reading. Deliberately, her eyes on the desk, she carefully replaced the frame in its proper location. His questioning look, however, was not directed at her actions but at Mrs. Ogden. Christie said quietly, "Mrs. Ogden just remembered some of the other ladies who took those phone calls."

His eyes, appraising the woman who kept her head bent over her pad, returned to Christie, questioning. *Why did he always seem so surprised when she accomplished what she had been assigned to do?* His hand signaled her. "You'll excuse us for a moment, Mrs. Ogden?" The woman's head moved without her face showing itself.

In the hallway, Reardon looked at Christie with a kind of amused admiration. "How the hell did you do it?"

Christie told him the story she had made up as Reardon covered his eyes, shaking his head. "Where in God's name," he asked, "did you ever hear anything like that? About the percentage of operation set aside for 'message-takers'?"

Not sure if she had to defend herself, Christie said carefully, "I thought I heard it somewhere." Then, seeing the grinning wonder on his face, she shrugged. "Maybe I just made it up as I went along. It just seemed to be the right thing to hit her with."

"Stoney," he called, "come over here a minute. Opara, tell him what you just told me."

Christie repeated her explanation of how she had gotten Mrs. Ogden to "cooperate." Stoner Martin's mouth dropped open and he filled the hallway with a soft, low, musical voice. "Great God in the morning. You've never been to Gamblers Course at Detective School, that's for sure. Casey, I think we could use Christie to give a few lectures!"

Reardon's voice was hard and sharp, but his eyes, on hers, acknowledged what she had done. "Well, it worked this time because that bitch in there is an idiot. But you try that story on a sharper operator and she'd laugh you right out of the room. Remind me to have someone educate Opara on gambling operations."

"But it *did* work, *didn't* it?" she asked him triumphantly.

Reardon rubbed his chin. "Beginner's luck," he said shortly. "Well, Stoney, you're an F.B.I. man—let's make Sammy Farrell our Treasury agent."

"Sam would make a fine Treasury man, boss. Just picture him making a casual tour of the mint one day: Washington on a dollar bill with two unexplainable heads."

Reardon jabbed a finger into Stoney's shoulder. "You leave Sam alone. He's working his fingers off on that two-paragraph report for me, and you can stake your life on the fact that he won't leave here today until that report is done, complete."

Christie accepted Reardon's needling without resentment. She knew she had accomplished something that would become part of the Squad legend: one of those implausible, unlikely, one-in-a-million, spur-of-the-moment, impossible-to-preplan con jobs that were in the realm of the unteachable part of police work: the intuitive chance-taking of being a good police officer.

The Squad worked late, the teams breaking into small busy huddles, dividing the long list of names among them, knowing that each woman interviewed the next day would, in turn, realize that she had to protect herself, and provide them with equally long lists. Calls were made to other Squad detectives who would become involved, to county police, notifying them of the new development, checking on their progress in other parts of the investigation.

Casey read over Christie's report, scanning the last page while it was still in the typewriter. "Good, good. You and Ferranti will get up to the Bronx early tomorrow and hit this Ogden's sister, Mrs. Phyliss Lynn." Christie tried to interrupt him, but Reardon kept talking, giving his directions, his suggestions, his eyes all around the room, checking on what was happening, who was in action. Finally, they returned to Christie and the dark red brows shot up. "What's the matter? What's your problem?"

"Mr. Reardon, I have court tomorrow—it's Tuesday."

"Court? What the hell for?"

"You know—Rogoff?"

"*Who?*"

"The 1140 I collared on Friday."

There was an expression of annoyance, a quick rubbing of his face with the palm of his right hand. "Swell," he said tersely. "Wait here a minute." He searched out Stoney, spoke rapidly to him while looking steadily at Christie, then he signaled her toward him. "Stoney's going to make a call first thing in the morning to have your case put on top of the calendar. Ferranti, you meet Opara in Felony Court, then get going up to the Bronx, right? You got wheels?"

"Yes, sir," Ferranti answered.

Reardon held Christie's cast and pulled her toward him. "Get this thing off your arm."

"Yes, sir."

"Oh, and Opara: you looked pretty good sitting in the boss's chair, but don't get any ideas. You ain't big enough to fill it."

The voice was tough and grating, but Christie was getting to know Reardon, learning to gauge what he said against when and how he said it. There was something in his eyes: an amusement but also a respect.

Christie shrugged her arm free, imitating his voice and tone perfectly. *"Ya never know!"*

Reardon's lips turned into a short smile, then he shook his head slightly. "You are fresh, Opara, really fresh."

10

FRANK SANTINO nodded his head and grunted a few sounds in reply to the bits of court gossip being offered to him by one of his less distinguished colleagues. But his eyes, though seeming to rest responsively on the face of the speaker, darted across the corridor to where the Rogoff brothers stood.

Frankie Santino was—if nothing else—a quick and good judge of a situation and from the moment he spotted Murray and David Rogoff standing silent and nearly rigid in the lobby of the Criminal Courts Building, Frankie knew he had better rush this thing through: cop Murray out and get it over and done with.

At least, Davey had gotten his brother cleaned up. Frankie couldn't help but admire the build on Murray Rogoff. The guy still had that lean hard look the girls used to climb all over. But from the neck up: Christ. Like something out of his kids' horror comic books. And now, Murray-the-Norseman had to ride around subway trains, waving it at women.

There was no doubt in Frank Santino's mind that Murray was a psycho: but he wasn't going to suggest mental tests. Hell, he had acted on an intuition that was the major reason why Frankie Santino rarely was done out of a fee: something had warned him that David Rogoff wasn't going to stay with it: not for too long. So Frankie had made a phone call Friday afternoon and had the case waived to Special Sessions for pleading. It wasn't a phone call *anybody* could have made; Frankie knew how to do favors and when to collect on favors done. And neither of the brothers even realized that he had done something special for them. They both just stood there when he told them they didn't have to return to Felony Court, like he had said it was a sunny day. What the hell, they didn't know the difference. But Frankie was going to make sure David Rogoff didn't

101

chicken out. Davey didn't have to be present for sentencing and Frank would have his fee before then. As for Murray, he acted like he didn't know what the hell was going on: and he wasn't faking. Frankie knew all the tricks, and Murray was really living inside some kind of fog. He should really be psychoed, but what the hell. That wasn't his responsibility.

Frankie glanced at his wristwatch at the same moment that his friend consulted his, and with a quick exchange of shoulder slappings both men headed toward their clients.

"Okay, boys," Frankie said, taking Murray by the arm and smacking David with his briefcase, "we better get upstairs now. When they call the case, Murray, we just move up to the front of the court and the judge'll ask you how you plead, and you'll just say 'guilty'—like we decided, okay, kid?"

Murray nodded.

"And then what?" David asked, looking straight ahead.

Dropping Murray's arm, Frank turned his full attention to David. "That's it. You see, Murray is on bail and the judge'll continue it, and set a sentencing date." Quickly, he added, "You don't have to be there, Dave, I'll be with him, right Murray?" Frankie looked around, then put his hand over his lips. "I can practically *guarantee* a suspended sentence. Of course, it took a little doing, but what the hell is a friend for?" The way Murray batted his eyes under those weird glasses was terrible, like he was trying to make out exactly who you were. Frank guided David's elbow, negotiating a turn. "Here we are, boys."

Murray and David sat on the bench in the courtroom. They waited, wordlessly, for Frankie to return from some mission which he assured them was very important to their interests. It was a small room, wider than it was long. It had an air of definite purpose about it. Everyone present knew his role now: defendants knew what was expected of them, for they had been guided and briefed by attorneys. Members of families sat, not less nervously than in the hugeness of Felony Court, but less distraught; a period of days had given them a certain heavy resignation. There was less directionless commotion; only those whose names were called moved forward, accompanied by lawyers who invariably made some physical contact with their clients: a touch on the back, a hand brushing along a sleeve.

Frankie's hands rested on a shoulder of each of the brothers and he leaned his face between them from the row of benches behind them. "Okay, kid, we're being called next. Come on, Murray. Take it easy, Davey—this'll take a few minutes."

David sat rigidly watching Frankie Santino walk easily up to the front of the room, looking like some sharp little bookie. Five hundred bucks. The schmuck. The schmuck. Five hundred dollars. David let his breath out slowly, closing his eyes for a moment. Okay, so pay the man and that's it. That's all of it.

Murray stood beside Frankie Santino and when Frankie poked him, Murray looked straight ahead and in a low voice said, "Guilty". He stood uncertainly until guided by Frank's hand, which led him across the room to a desk, where he sat beside some graying Negro with glasses, who wrote down his name and address and occupation on a printed form. He did not answer any of the questions: Frankie spoke for him and then, finally, Frankie pressed the man's shoulder and clamped Murray's arm and led him around the fenced-in section of the courtroom, waving David toward them, and they went out into the hallway.

Murray's eyes were burning and dry and he closed them tightly, screwing up his face against the aching throb inside his head. This was a hot place and he wanted to be out of here. He accepted the slip of paper Frankie pressed into his hand without looking at it, not listening to the words Frankie was saying, but nodding. Murray closed his eyes again feeling within him a great, familiar pit of emptiness like a hole swallowing him up. When he opened his eyes, they rested directly on the face of some girl who had come up to Frankie. Murray stopped blinking so that he could see her better. There was something familiar about her.

"Mr. Santino," Christie Opara said angrily, "why wasn't I notified that you had waived to Sessions?"

103

DOROTHY UHNAK

Frankie smiled easily. "Why, hello, Detective Opara, honey. This here is Mr. Davey Rogoff, brother of Murray, who you already know."

Christie glanced at David who kept his eyes fixed at some point past her head, then at Murray who looked different, dressed in a suit and tie. She shrugged off Frank Santino's hand, moving just a slight step backwards, but she couldn't shake off his lewd little eyes which skimmed her body without subtlety.

"Can you believe that this little girl with those big round eyes is a cop?" Frankie asked no one in particular. David wasn't looking at him and Murray seemed a million miles away, lost behind his glasses. He leaned close to Christie, "Honey, you can lock me up anytime."

"I might have to one day," Christie said coldly. "Mr. Santino, can you give me the sentencing date?"

"Sure, sure, but you won't have to be there."

"I know that."

Frank poked David. "You bet she does. This little cookie knows all there is to know, don't you, Christie Opara?"

Christie bit the inside of her cheeks, her eyes narrowing contemptuously at the small, stocky man. She had met Santino in court many times; had been subjected to his crude insinuations and raised eyebrows and booming voice and had responded with controlled anger, keeping her poise and scoring convictions against him. "Never mind, Mr. Santino, I have to write up my report for the probation officer, anyway. I'll get the date from him."

Frankie's smile stayed on his lips but he watched the girl walk into the courtroom with a tightness in his throat. The little bitch. One day, he would get her on that witness stand and that cold, smug sureness would fall apart: he would shred it apart into little ripped up pieces.

Murray Rogoff reached his arm into the barrel, and the cold cleanness of the water seemed to extend through his body. He could feel the thudding of the strong dark bodies as the carp churned themselves in small circles against his arm. For a moment he let his arm hang there, then his fingers seized a tail and in one quick motion, the cool water

104

running along the inside of his arm, he held the fish up before the squinting eyes of the customer. The customers were all alike: the old women with colorless eyes and lumpy bodies who could measure and calculate to the ounce how much they were getting for their money.

"Nah, nah, nah," the old woman wailed, rocking her head from side to side.

His father's voice, whining, insistent, argued with the customer and the exchange, in Yiddish, was rapid and to the anticipated conclusion. "Cut him up, Murray," his father said and Murray slammed the cold body onto the butcher's block, his free hand reaching for the sharp knife. Deftly, he severed the head, turned the quivering body flat on its side, slashed it open and in the next movement, his fingers, bloody and wet, entered the body and gathered the yellowish guts, which he threw into the pail at his feet. The old woman, watching closely, began arguing and Murray's father reached down, grabbed up the mess in both his hands, and held it before the woman's face. She shrugged: it was hers. It was part of the fish. What business of his was it what she did with it? It was hers.

Murray reached for two clean sheets of newspaper from the stack against the wall and carefully spread them out on the small marble counter beside the chopping block. He wiped his hands down the front of his solidly stained apron and squinted at the headlines: "Dancer Strangled in Bronx Apartment House." There was a picture of some girl in a white blouse, her hair pulled back in a pony tail. She was smiling and directly under her picture were smaller words which said, "Third Victim in Three Months." After that, there was a paragraph in regular size newsprint which Murray found hard to read: "Carol Logan, age 23, was found strangled early this morning behind a stairway in her Bronx apartment house. Police believe she is the third victim of a rapist-murderer responsible for the March murder of career girl Jody Lane in Greenwich Village and music student Agnes Lichtenberg of Riverside Drive last month. Story page three."

Murray felt a sudden confusion staring at the paper: it was dated Saturday, May 7, 1966. It was strange. Something

105

was wrong. Ignoring the old woman who tried to hurry him along, Murray thought about it for a moment, then his face relaxed and it was no longer a problem.

His father, who always observed the Sabbath from Friday evening through Saturday sundown, would never have purchased the *Daily News* on a Saturday. The colored boy who delivered ice to them Monday morning had probably taken it from the truck and tossed it onto the stack of newspapers.

Murray added another sheet of paper so that the gummy guts wouldn't leak through. His eyes were bothering him again. He wanted to take the glasses off and smash them against the floor: why were they always so smudgy? Murray wrapped the fish into a neat package which he then slid into a brown paper bag. The old women wouldn't put the newspaper package into their string bags: they wanted what they paid for and a brown paper bag was included in the price.

Murray turned and plunged his arms into the barrel; the water felt good. He sloshed the coolness over his neck, then took off his glasses and rinsed his face. He didn't listen to his father who told him it looked funny for him to wash in the fish barrel and that he should go into the back of the store if he wanted to clean up that bad. He didn't listen to his mother either. Her voice so like his father's with that same whining sound and all the words running together and always the same things, over and over: Murray, why don't you and Murray, why won't you and Murray you must and Murray you should and Murray and Murray.

"I'm going up now," Murray said. He ignored their combined voices which pursued him into the hot street, telling him that he had started so late in the day, he should at least work with them until supper time, but Murray didn't want to work until supper time and he left the shop, as he always did whenever he felt he had to and they couldn't stop him from leaving any more than they could stop him from leaving the hot string of rooms on the top floor whenever he wanted to, their words and questions just part of their breath and of no meaning to him.

Murray was tired and he didn't know how tired he was until his body hit the hard mattress and then he knew he was very tired. Murray was too tired to sleep and he pressed his face into the pillow, rubbing his eyes against the coarseness of the pillow-case, trying to burrow into some dark place where it was cool, where there would be dreams that were not dreams, but real. He lay, not moving for a long time, seeking sleep, and then he bunched the soft pillow in his large hands, as though that was the obstacle to rest and he tossed it across the small airless room. He rolled onto his back, stretching his body so that his head touched the metal headboard and his feet were over the edge of the mattress. He strained his eyes, sketching figures among the cracks on the ceiling, and Murray felt a deep sense of uneasiness, as if there was something wrong: something he should remember but couldn't. Or *someone* he should remember, but couldn't.

And then, Murray felt his body relax: felt the odd and welcome and good feeling of not trying to remember at all, because it all came to him now and he knew he could sleep deeply and soundly because everything would be all right.

Murray closed his eyes and smiled. His hands wandered down his body, lightly touching the smoothness of his thighs, then resting on the center of his being were he could feel the life of him rising, hard and strong and vital.

"Christie Opara," Murray Rogoff said softly, letting himself drift off into a good, safe, relaxing sleep.

11

THE HOT WATER of the shower hit the center of Christie's spine and she leaned forward so that the water ran down her body. She straightened, turning her face upward so that her cheeks tingled. Slowly, she adjusted the hot water faucet so that the temperature of the water changed gradually. Finally, taking a deep breath, clenching her teeth against the shock, she stood in the ice-cold water for the count of ten before exhaling, letting the pores of her body close in the clean coldness. She reached out blindly for the towel, patting her face and letting her body feel cool in contrast to the steamy air.

It had been a long day, even though she had learned not to measure a working day in terms of hours. The job was not an eight-hour deal which you walk away from until nine the next morning. You took the people, with their grating voices and tight lips and calculating eyes, home with you, into the shower with you, trying to scrub them out of your skin. But they stayed there, no matter how much hot water you used to open up your flesh, no matter how hard you scrubbed with a stiff, invigorating bathbrush. When you closed yourself up with icy water, the cleanness was only a fleeting sensation: they were still there, inside of you.

Mrs. Ogden's sister had been a somewhat younger replica of the woman Christie had tricked, her eyes the same alert little holes watching her from under heavy eyeshadow over a small sharp nose and a mouth that twisted in protest and indignation. And the two cousins: not at all alike. The one with a high, hysterically shrill voice and bony fingers that kept working frantically along the housedress and throat at the realization that seventy-five dollars for taking phone messages at home was to be something less than a profitable pastime. The other, a young, placid, poker-faced woman, encased in heavy layers of flesh, all squeezed and overflowing from beneath a tight electric yellow shift, her brows blatantly drawn heavy black lines over each eye, her mouth a wild orange slash in her large bland face.

More than anything else, it was the greed they had revealed which ground into Christie. The women she had spoken to all afternoon and well into the night were not poverty-stricken. They had overly furnished, tasteless homes, husbands who could pay all outstanding bills, children who were overfed and well supplied with bikes and games and outdoor gym equipment. The money had been for the extra day at the beauty parlor, the mink stole and beaded sweaters and cocktail dresses with satin shoes dyed to match which could be flaunted, smugly and matter-of-factly, before the neighbors. And the sneering, insistently repetitious justification: *I'm at home with my children.*

Mickey, of course, had been asleep when Christie finally arrived home, after two final hours devoted to typing up reports. He had been just sleepily awake when she had left for court in the morning and that was how she would see him tomorrow morning. Christie, standing in her light cotton pajamas, watched her small son, sleeping, the breath steady and even and moistly warm. The young forehead was drawn into a frown and the pink lips were working over some words, then pulled upwards into a smile of triumph. Whatever the battle he had been fighting, he had just won. She stroked her fingers lightly through his thick dark hair and automatically, in sleep as in consciousness, the strong little hand roughly placed the hair back on his forehead. Christie leaned her face close against her son's and whispered softly in his ear—not because she had read once in a psychology class a long time ago that whispered words registered, were recorded in a sleeper's brain and became part of the sleeper's memory—but because she felt a great surge of loneliness for her child: "I love you, Michael-Mickey, my little Mickey." Her lips touched his brow and the quick hand raised in protest but she ducked away before he could push her.

All right, my little toughie; but I'm still going to think you're a beautiful boy with your hard little body so removed from me now and I'm still going to think you have the most fantastic clear blue eyes in the world. And I *will* stick to my

109

resolve to keep my mouth shut about all of that, at least to
you, but it's hard.

Christie watched the small body suddenly fight off the
light cover which she had just tucked under the mattress;
the legs bent at the knees, then the feet were thrown into
the air and the summer blanket went flying. Mickey
stiffened his back, his arms reaching over his head, every
part of him enjoying the pleasurable stretch of growth.
Then, he turned on his side, his face toward the wall, his
knees tucked up. He looked so small. Christie put her lips
against the back of his head for a last quick kiss then put
the top sheet over him and for once he didn't fight it off.

In bare feet, she went down the carpeted steps, through
the hall and into the kitchen where she had left the small
stove light on. She foraged without appetite in the refrigerator. Nora had asked her what she had eaten for supper and
she couldn't remember. There wasn't a regular meal sched-
ule when you were working on something: you had a sandwich sometime during the day and again sometime during
the night, not when it was a normally designated mealtime,
not even when hunger demanded it. You ate when you could
find a minute or when someone had a chance to run down
to the luncheonette and bring back a box of sandwiches and
cardboard-flavored tea or coffee or tinny canned soda.

Christie saw the remains of Nora's lasagna in the Corning
Ware; at one-fifteen in the morning, though there was an
emptiness inside of her, Christie rejected it with distaste.
She filled a glass to the brim with cold milk and drank
it too fast. She filled the glass again, drinking like a child,
interested only in quenching her thirst. She rinsed the glass,
turned off the light, letting her eyes get accustomed to the
darkness. She should have left the small lamp in her room
on. Groping for the banister, her feet found the steps and
then the landing, but her shin smashed into the small table
leg in the upstairs hallway and Christie bit down on her lip,
her fingers rubbing the unexpected pain. She listened for a
moment, assured that she hadn't disturbed Nora or Mickey,
then, hands extended before her, feeling for the doorway,
she entered her own room.

The room was so dark that she could not pick out any of

110

the familiar forms: not the dresser or the oiled walnut rocker by the window or the table by her bed. Christie eased herself onto her bed, lying with her hands folded beneath her head, her eyes able to make out the small phosphorous dots and slashes on the alarm clock on the dresser—1:25. She counted: 2:25, 3:25, 4:25, ticking off the number of hours she could sleep, if she fell asleep right now. The alarm was set for 6:30.

Stop counting; stop wasting sleep time. Christie's eyes closed, she shifted her arm so that it rested lightly across her forehead, her mind became slowly enveloped in the blackness, growing more and more relaxed and freed from words and images.

The sudden shattering sound caught Christie somewhere in her throat, racing down her body like a shock wave. Instinctively, without solid thought of any kind, she responded with two different actions, each independent of the other and both independent of her conscious mind. Her right hand reached up over her head and twisted the light switch and her left hand reached and lifted the receiver to her ear.

"Hello," she said clearly, as though the loudness of her voice would convince her that she was fully awake. Then again, into the silence, her eyes staring, giving the room shape and the moment reality, "Hello?"

There was a soft, breathing sound in her ear and Christie could feel a pounding within herself: the reaction of her heart startled into quicker action than it had been prepared for. Listening intently, straining for some voice, some word, Christie asked, "Who is this?"

The voice was not familiar. "Is this Christie Opara?"

"Yes, who is this?" Pressing the phone harder against her ear, straining to catch the voice, for no reason she could explain, she asked, "Marty? Is that you?"

"Hello, Christie Opara."

Steadying her voice, lowering it, she asked again, "All right, who is this?"

Softly, familiarly, almost pleasantly, the voice, not answering her demand, repeated, "Hello, Christie."

That was all the voice said and then there was a click in

her ear and a dead, toneless silence. Stupidly jiggling her finger on the button twice, not really expecting to hear the voice, which had cut itself off, she said into the steady hum of the dial tone, "Hello? Hello?" and then she placed the phone in place.

Nora emerged in the doorway, her face puzzled by sleep. "Did the phone ring, Christie, or did I dream it?"

Christie pretended annoyance. "Wrong number, Nora. Go on back to bed. I'll leave my light on until you get to your room."

She heard Nora muttering about people who dial wrong numbers in the middle of the night, heard her enter her room, then heard her settle on the bed.

Wrong number. Christie switched off the light, lay back on her pillow. She could feel the tenseness of her body, the tight expectancy, the unwillingness to be caught off guard again, to be stabbed in the dark by the shock of unexpected sound. Consciously, she began a relaxing of her body, starting at her feet, wiggling her toes, flexing the muscles of her legs and thighs, her shoulders and arms and fingers and neck, but her stomach, filled only with milk, felt cold and knotted.

Christie stared into the darkness. Wrong number. She closed her eyes, pushing the faceless voice away. "Hello, Christie Opara. Hello, Christie." No image formed, no face, just a hollow repetition of her name. She put her arm across her forehead again, lying very still.

Some wrong number.

12

WHY WAS IT that the one particular key that didn't work in the Underwood was always the one particular letter that seemed to appear in every single word? Christie smashed the "o," jamming it onto the skipped spot. Ferranti sat alongside of her, consulting his notes as she sat, hands poised, listening to him, then, holding her hand up, she quickly rephrased the information and her fingers raced over the keyboard. Except when they reached for the letter "o."

Christie grumbled to herself, glaring at the irregular line of typing, and in sudden resolve, she ripped the half-page of work from the machine, crumpled it into a ball and tossed it to the wastebasket. Bill Ferranti offered to do the typing; he was slow, but steady.

She shook her head. "It's this bomb of a machine. You'd think the People of the City of New York could afford to supply decent typewriters. Or at least send a capable repairman."

Casey Reardon, leaning against the long table in the front of the room, instructing his driver, Third-Grade Detective Tom Dell, hadn't heard Christie's complaints but he had observed her annoyed balling up of her work (carbons and all) and the angry set of her head. He walked over to the desk where she was working. She glanced up at him, then slammed the "o."

"What's your problem?"

"My problem," she said shortly, as though he were somehow responsible, "is this typewriter. That's my problem. The so-called repairman fixed the 'k' but he broke the 'o.'"

"Well, you do the best you can," Reardon said softly. "I need all reports completed by 12:30. You have plenty of time, even allowing for the insurmountable problem of the 'o.'"

Christie failed to anticipate the stuck key and the typewriter skipped a space. She tapped her clenched hand on the stack of clean papers and he could tell she was turning something over in her mind; her mouth pulled down for a moment. He knew she would say whatever it was: she always did.

"Mr. Reardon, is it true that we're turning all of our information over to the Nassau County authorities? That we're dropping the investigation?"

"That's right. Why?"

Christie shrugged; Ferranti was thumbing through his notebook, his head down.

"Why?"

She looked at him steadily, her words bitter and, it seemed to Reardon, bordering on some accusation. "Then none of the 'ladies' we've been interviewing for the last two weeks—none of the 'at-home-housewives-earning-money' are going to be prosecuted?"

His eyes, a glinting reddish now, never left hers. "That's right. They're cooperative witnesses. You don't prosecute cooperative witnesses when they're essential to the successful completion of an investigation."

"Swell." Christie backspaced, ignored Reardon, hit the wrong key, but didn't reach for an eraser. She'd wait until Reardon left.

Aware that he had been dismissed, Reardon still stared down at her. "Why?" he demanded, noting the deep, slow breath, the deliberate way in which she lifted her fingers from the keys and placed them on the edge of the desk.

"Because I think that someone should throw the book at them. Or even maybe a page of the book at them."

"Is that what *you* think?"

Ignoring the slight pressure of Ferranti's shoe on the tip of her foot, warning her, Christie said, "Yes. That's what I think."

Reardon smiled. He turned away without another word: what Christie Opara thought was not particularly important. He heard her resume her sporadic typing, stopping— probably for the 'o'—as he entered his office. Sitting at his desk now, Reardon rapidly scanned the pile of material submitted by the teams of investigators. He absorbed the

114

information while at the same time allowing some part of his mind to engage the problem of Christie Opara. Very quickly, that particularly annoying problem engaged a greater portion of his attention. He removed his glasses, tapped them on the edge of his desk, then dug his thumb and index finger into his eyes.

Was it the pinch? The fact that no one in the Squad—particularly not Detective Christie Opara—was going to make an arrest on this case? He knew she had worked hard the last few weeks—hell, they all worked hard on this. He didn't like handing over his Squad's work any better than his people did, but it was one of those things. A cooperative effort had a way of being repaid in the future. The jurisdiction with the strongest evidence was the logical location for prosecution. He certainly didn't owe *her* any explanation.

The expression on her face: Reardon had seen it the first time he had prosecuted a case when she was the arresting officer, a few years ago, when he was in Special Sessions. What was it?—a bag opener. She had testified during direct in that steady, confident way, stating the facts, then had handled the cross-examination capably, if almost defiantly. It was just a routine bag opener and the decision was acquittal, two-to-one. They had both done their job properly, and then it was up to the three judges and no longer his or Opara's responsibility. Reardon had gone into the briefing room with a young uniformed cop, and was listening to a recitation of the facts involved in his next case when, absently scanning the room, he had noticed her scowling over her acquittal report as though she were the only police officer in the world who had ever lost a case, and as he observed her, she looked up and glared at him coldly. Reardon grinned, remembering the anger in that look and the way she dismissed him with a deliberate blinking of her eyes.

She had been neither surprised nor disturbed when he excused himself from the cop, walked to her and asked, *"What's your problem?"*

He had caught the momentary hesitation, the determination to frame exactly the right answer in exactly the right tone. "Doesn't it bother you—in the slightest—that a guilty man was just set free?"

115

He had shaken his head nonchalantly, amused, annoyed, yet somehow touched by the realness of her anger. "No, not in the slightest. Win one—lose one. Why does it bother you?"

She hadn't hesitated that time, blurting it out at him, "If you don't know, I doubt if I could explain it."

Fresh little bastard, he had thought then, and thought it now: fresh little bastard. But the words contained a strong element of respect. She cared. *She really cared* and God knows that was rare enough. Reardon's finger reached for the intercom button, he played with it for a moment, then pushed it down. "Detective Opara, come into my office."

Reardon knew what it was about her that made her attractive. Her figure was neat—a little thin and wiry, but she moved well with a confident, easy grace. But that wasn't it. Nor her face: that was pretty in a cute way, the clean-cut all-American girl, showing every feeling with too much honesty. It was something else, something he didn't think she was aware of, or if she was aware of it, wouldn't realize it was a point of attraction: *her intensity*. There was a vitality about Christie Opara; it was interesting and curious and somewhat mystifying. He let her sit there for a minute; he knew the tricks she used to relax herself—at least outwardly. A few deep, silent breaths, a conscious flexing and unflexing of her fingers, then forcing them to rest on the arms of the chair.

He ran his thumb across his lip, then closed the folder and raised his head. Reardon didn't think there was a woman alive who didn't look good in pink: deep, vibrant pink. Opara was no exception. "Now," he said, pacing his words so that they were not just a repetition of what he had asked before, "what-exactly-is-your-problem?"

He could see that she was making some decision and in the four or five seconds it took, she bit the corner of her lip, blinked twice without looking at him, then, resolved, met his eyes.

"I have been getting some phone calls."

He responded without any inflection of surprise. "What kind of phone calls?"

She shrugged.

"Obscene phone calls?"

She shook her head. "No. It's crazy, I guess. Not obscene phone calls. Just—phone calls. Late at night. Just some voice getting on and saying, 'Hello, Christie Opara—how are you?'—things like that."

No turn in any conversation, no information unexpectedly revealed ever rattled or detoured the neat, precise workings of Reardon's mind. His courtroom experience served him under any and all circumstances and the questions rose, one after the other, in logical sequence, to track down the needed information.

"When did they start?"

"Couple of weeks ago."

"How many have you received?"

She looked at the ceiling for a moment. "Two in a row— then none for a few nights—then one every night for a week. Last one—last night."

"At what time?"

"Between midnight and about 1:45 A.M. The first one was the latest, then the time varied. Last night was just after midnight."

"Recognize the voice?"

She hesitated. "No. Not really."

"What does *not really* mean?"

She took one of those steadying breaths. Then, firmly, "No, I don't recognize the voice."

Reardon considered his glasses for a moment, then, annoyed, asked, "Why the hell are you listed in the phone book?"

"I'm not," she shot back, then, softer, "but my mother-in-law is."

"Uh-huh. And how many other 'Oparas' are listed in the Queens directory? Or in any of the five boroughs?"

"Not many," she said weakly. "In Queens, only Nora. My mother-in-law."

"You ever get anonymous calls before?"

"A few times. Obscene—routine nut calls."

"Did they rattle you?" His sarcasm has been building slowly.

Not as much as you do, Reardon. Not realizing it showed

117

on her face, she carefully adjusted her voice. "It is a little—disturbing—to lie there in the middle of the night, knowing that somewhere, some man has nothing better to do than to dial your number and ask you how you are." She added, without intending to, "It's upsetting."

"What have you done about it?"

The question was sharp and logical and she answered it without a word: her blank expression told him what he wanted to know and set the cutting edge to his voice. "So, you just lie awake every night waiting for the phone to ring and then it does and this anonymous caller asks how you are, and then when he's sure you're fine, you can get to sleep?"

"Mr. Reardon, I don't think it's a very funny situation."

Tapping his glasses against his chin, his eyes the color of honey held to light, he said, "Neither do I. What do you think you can *do* about it?"

Impatiently, she said, "Oh, I know, I know. I could get the number changed and keep it unlisted or leave the phone off the hook or put a pillow over it or something but . . ." She stopped, biting her lip.

"But what?"

She was silent, not looking up until he repeated his last two words insistently. "I don't know. There's something more to it. Something I can't quite put my finger on." She shook her head, puzzling thoughtfully. "There's 'something' way in the back of my mind and when I hear that voice, I feel like any minute it'll come to me. It sounds stupid, I know."

"Then, in effect, you're willing to take the phone calls and wait it out to see if the 'something' materializes?"

"Yes, I guess so. In a way."

Reardon ran his hand over his face, then scratched the small red hairs at the back of his neck. She knew that sign: it always preceded the softly, steadily building verbal assault. "So, you're up half the night waiting for some nut to call and ask how you are and then you get a few hours sleep and come in here and bitch about the Underwood and bitch about not getting the chance to lock up some cooperating,

118

vital witnesses, and mope around like a sullen kid when your real problem is that you need some more *sleep* which you're not getting because instead of taking some definite, logical action to stop these phone calls, you're waiting them out because of some 'feeling' of some kind or other which you can't explain. *Right?*"

"*Right*," she snapped, matching his tone exactly.

They held it between them for a long time, neither of them moving, but she dropped her eyes first, because she could feel the redness, the damn, stupid, uncontrollable blushing, and she knew he had seen it because the grin was pulling at the corners of his mouth. Not only did he think she was stupid, he thought she was amusing.

"Well," he said slowly, "why don't you dig up your copy of the penal law and maybe you can find a loophole in the area of annoying, obscene phone calls? Maybe there's a special subdivision that makes it a violation of law for someone to call you to ask how you are, Christie Opara." He knew she didn't trust her voice to answer him. He leaned back, locking his fingers over his stomach. "Christie Opara," he repeated softly. "What the hell kind of a name is Opara anyway?"

"Pronounced *properly*," she said coldly, "it is '*O*-per-uh': not Op*a*ra. It is a Czech name." As you damn well know.

"*O*para. What was your maiden name?"

"Choriopoulous." Which you damn well know.

He raised his brows, two dark red indications of surprise. "Greek? A fair-haired, green-eyed Greek?"

"My mother was Swedish." As you *probably* know. All this is in my personnel folder; plus whatever other information, private and official, you wanted to know about me from the day I was born right up to and including this very minute. *Right*, Reardon?

Reardon shook his head. "A Swedish-Greek with a Czech name that comes out Irish."

"And my mother-in-law *is* Irish, so that adds a little to the stew."

"It does indeed. Well, Opara"—he purposely reverted to the Irish pronunciation, which nearly everyone used—"if

119

you come up with anything exciting, you know, anything worthwhile, on these phone calls, you be sure to let me know. Maybe the whole Squad can get in on it."

"I'll do that, Mr. Reardon."

"In the meantime, Detective Opara, regardless of your sleepless nights, you see if you can't shake yourself out a little and get your work done without so much glaring and cussing and wasting of taxpayers' stationery."

"I don't swear, Mr. Reardon. I am as careful with my language as I expect the people I work with to be."

"You can outcuss me any day, tiger. Remember, I told you I can read you right through those green eyes and I wouldn't ever want to hear you say out loud what you're saying with your eyes right now. Go on, beat it and get that report typed up."

Reardon knew the report would be typed up quickly and accurately in spite of the delinquent "o," and with all facts explicitly and concisely stated. Whatever she did, she did well. He reached for Sam Farrell's report, filled with near holes and poorly disguised strikeovers, but containing all necessary information somewhere in the wandering, ungrammatical statements.

There was something about that kid that aroused an odd combination of responses within him. There was some kind of a continuous battle going on between them and it was irritating and annoying and yet, something more, leading to something other than sharp, biting word duels. For a moment, he thought about the phone calls and, more importantly, her reaction to them. She was too sharp to let just the normal, female reaction to the situation disturb her that much. He trusted her intuition to a great extent: she was a real pro and he'd let her ride with it for a while. Then, he filed the entire matter, including Christie Opara, into some neat chamber of his brain for future reference, and turned his full attention to Farrell's sloppy but informative report.

13

CHRISTIE CLIMBED the broad flat steps of the Fifth Avenue
entrance to the 42nd Street Library, stepping around the
midtown sunbathers who were trying to reinforce their
weekend tans on late lunch hours. In her hand was the slip
of paper Mr. Reardon had given her, covered on both sides
with his cryptic notes: "Gerardo Const. Co—Alf. Gerardo
—connect. w/Cong. Littlejohn-R—Feb. 64 (?) any n.g.
info. (Times—Trib.)." Which meant that she had to spend
the better part of the day squinting at the library's microfilm: endless columns of print dating back, probably, to
1963 and possibly up to the present date, since when Mr.
Reardon indicated a date of February 1964 he meant
"maybe" and from having done some previous research for
him, "maybe" covered a long area of possibility.

She was beginning to feel the full force of her usual
springtime blues and some of her growing uneasiness and
restlessness related directly to her job. She didn't like jump-
ing from assignment to assignment—still not having a
definite partner—still not following through an investigation
from its initiation to an arrest, trial and conviction. She
didn't like to have loose ends dangling, never knowing if
what she had worked on two days ago was merely some
curious whim of Reardon's or part of a larger whole, which
she would never know about anyway. There was a lack of
satisfaction, a lack of accomplishment in her work now.

None of the other Squad members seemed to raise these
objections. Not even when Reardon wasn't around. They
did some small piecework: that's what it was. Christie's
mind seized on it: piecework, like in a factory. I turn the
screw to the left and pass it on to the next man; he slips a
band around it and the next man tightens the band, then
after a while we change places, each of us attending to one
small detail, handing it on to Reardon who accepts it without a word and hands you some other small item.

121

"Boy, whatever it is, it sure has you sore!"

Christie, startled, squinted into the high strong sun, but the voice was as familiar as the crushing handshake, from which she had to remove Reardon's crumpled bit of paper. "Hey, Johnnie, how are you?"

Detective John Devereaux was a Homicide man and the imprint of his profession, while stamped clearly and permanently on his face, had not touched his voice, which was musically soft and light. He was a bulky man with broad shoulders and a huge barrel of a torso carried on legs that were much too short for the rest of his body so that, sitting down, he gave the appearance of great height, while standing up, he seemed to be in a hole. Not that he was short, just that he looked like a man who, somehow, should be taller.

"The D.A. got you doing research, Christie?"

Christie made a face, indicating exactly what she thought of the D.A. and she let Johnnie steer her, with a large and heavy hand, so that she was turned about and heading in his direction. "Got time for coffee and? I been in that mausoleum for two and a half hours. Boy, this sun is hard to take; let's find some nice dark, cool spot."

Leading her through the crowds that surged businesslike across the broad expanse of Fifth Avenue during the brief "Walk" signal, which blinked "Don't Walk" almost before their feet hit the warm tar, Johnnie pulled her along. Christie winced. This was Johnnie's friendly grasp; she hated to think what his official in-custody hold was like. He more or less wrenched her into a small bar on Madison Avenue just off 42nd Street. He was apparently known here, for he just held up his finger at the bartender who appeared with a tall highball.

Christie asked for a Coke, checking the clock on the wall. She'd tackle Reardon's research in a half hour.

Johnnie took his hat off in concession to Christie for he was always a gentleman when confronted by what he defined as a lady and he had known Christie for some four years, having met her when he was on his first assignment with Homicide and the corpse was female—white—age 35—suicide by gas—and the policewoman assigned in uni-

122

form was Christie Opara, twenty-two, arriving from the Bureau to search her third corpse, which she did quickly, and finding nothing, had swallowed dryly, told him "Nothing," then gratefully accepted his cigarette. He had taken solace from her whitened face and tenseness: it eased his own because in Homicide, as he had learned through the years, you never knew what to expect.

Sipping his Scotch and soda, his eyes adjusting to the dimness easily, Johnnie looked around. "Nice place, this. Lot of advertising people." Johnnie Devereaux had a fantastic acquaintance with people in all areas of the city. He could talk intelligently with anyone in politics, clothing manufacturing, advertising, construction, waterfront activities, labor negotiations, religious movements, education, any large industrial or small commercial business. He could blink his eyes and tell in which section of the city, which small, hidden, unknown pocket, you could find a particular group of people, what the ethnic makeup was three blocks to the west or one block to the east. Where to eat authentic Cantonese food, not the American chop suey junk; where to get real Northern Italian cooking or non-commercial, absolutely pure Kosher meals like someone's Grandma used to put in front of someone's Grandpa. People and their strange quirks of behavior and their fascinating customs and remnants of blood-culture were Johnnie's hobby and a knowledge he enjoyed sharing.

"What has Homicide got their ace looking up in the Library?"

Johnnie wiped his mouth with the back of his hand and his voice was sad. "Ah, these murders. These girls: three in three months." He ticked off the months and the murders with his fingers. "February, March, beginning of this month."

Christie recalled the most recent, then remembered the other two only because they had been referred to in the newspapers as being linked to the most recent. "Is there really any connection, John, or is that just a newspaper gimmick?"

"Well, you know the papers: what sells is what they print. They discover some drab little mouse got bumped off and they print it that way—no sales. So they change her into a

bright, blowsy blond and jazz it up like that and it sells
papers." His face was deeply troubled and he shook his
head. "But there was no jazzing up these girls, Christie.
Nice kids, you know. Clean, really clean, hard-working,
good girls. No fooling around, no long lists of boyfriends to
check out. All in their early twenties. This last one, the kid
in the Bronx: a *nice* kid."

That said it all for Johnnie Devereaux. It was the best
word there was for describing a female: *nice.*

"But is there a real connection? I mean, there's a murder
every hour somewhere, every day." She closed her eyes,
recalling the newspaper accounts. "First one in Greenwich
Village, second, Riverside Drive and third—this last girl, in
the Bronx." She thought a moment, then asked, "Any *real*
connection? Or is it possible that there are three murderers
—you know, the first case setting some other psycho into
motion, the second giving another fellow the same idea?"

His voice was cautious; Johnnie Devereaux did not give
information relative to his work away freely. "Same age,
same type; none of them knew each other, if that's what you
mean, no friends or acquaintances in common. All three
were raped and strangled."

Christie yawned, excused herself and then, filled with the
weariness of her sleepless, interrupted nights, she absently
asked, "Any of them get any anonymous phone calls?"

Johnnie Devereaux was a swarthy man, the darkness of his
face making the paleness of his light gray eyes even more
startling. They narrowed into bright slits and his voice
changed: alert, sharp, demanding. Pure Homicide. *"Why?"*

Christie grinned at his reaction. "Why is it that a cop
always answers a question with a question?"

Johnnie's face relaxed. "Yeah, how come about that?" He
held the cold glass between his hands, turning it slowly between his palms. "I wonder how many women in New York
City get anonymous phone calls every day of the week."

Christie started to speak but her words were held back by
the thoughtful expression as Johnnie Devereaux looked up at
her again. "Two of the kids got phone calls," he said. "The
third kid, we don't know—that was the first girl murdered.

She was a loner, didn't confide in anybody." He shook his head. "Funny calls, too. Not the usual, you know, not obscene. The second girl and the last girl told their friends they had been getting calls, pretty regularly, for a couple of weeks. Some guy would get on, just—you know, talk to them—as if he knew them."

With great effort, Christie kept her voice normal; she spoke with nothing more than professional interest. "You mean, just conversational phone calls: hello, how are you, how've you been? That kind of thing?"

Devereaux leaned his shoulders forward and his voice was low and clear. "Yeah. We kept that out of the papers. Christ, imagine the wave of hysteria that would set off. Every woman in New York City would be sure that any wrong number or 'funny' phone call was our murderer setting her up."

Christie swallowed some Coke and nodded; she was glad she hadn't told Johnnie about the phone calls which had kept her awake every night for the last few weeks. "The newspapers kept playing it up as if the three girls were definitely the victims of the same man. Is that because it sells papers, Johnnie, or do you think so too?"

"It's the same guy," he said flatly. "There's something the papers haven't got hold of. Each one of these kids had a lock of hair hacked from her head." His fingers reached into his own head, which was scantily covered by the dark remnants of what had once been thick curls. "From the back of her head"—he held his index finger and thumb before her eyes—"just about an inch or two hacked off."

"*Hacked off?*"

"Coroner said probably with a knife. He could tell by the way it was cut." He smiled, admiringly. "That old Doc Mendel, he must be over seventy, but he spotted it with the first girl. What an autopsy that guy does; a real pro. So, of course, we alerted the other coroners to look out for that— hacked hair—on any female homicide of any kind, under any circumstances—anywhere in the city. And sure enough, these two kids: same thing, lived alone, raped, strangled, and the hair cut."

125

The bright glaring sunshine stung Christie's eyes right through the green sunglasses as she walked rapidly back to the Library. The unseasonably hot temperature made the marble corridor seem air-conditioned and Christie felt a shudder right down to the small of her back. She glanced absently into a glass-enclosed phone booth set against a marble pillar, then watched, fascinated, as a man deposited his dime, waited, then dialed a number.

Anybody with a dime. It could be anybody with a dime.

Peering into the viewer in the quiet of the library, where it was darkly cool, Christie didn't know if she were relieved or not to see the words neatly and precisely encased inside the machine: "Representative Littlejohn Recommends Addition to State Capitol Building." And the date, she noted with sour triumph: *October 17, 1963*. She copied down the pertinent facts, then noted the small items relative to sealed bids being accepted and then, some nine months later, the small blurb, on page 36 of the New York *Times* relative to the Gerardo Construction Company being awarded the bid.

She asked the librarian, a weary woman who kept breaking into an accommodating smile, if she could look through the 1961–1962 files, and starting in 1961, Christie peered her way through column after column until a small item appeared: "Builder Cleared of Fraud." The builder's name was Alfred Gerardo. He had been charged with fraudulently padding his bill on the construction of a city-owned powerplant by indicating items which, in fact, had not been used in the construction. His attorney was Ralph F. Littlejohn.

Christie's neck ached and her eyes were moist and her fingers were numb. She hoped she'd be able to read her notes later; they seemed to be getting smaller and smaller and were running off the lines of her notebook. She pressed her hand over her eyes, but she could still see the sharp tiny print behind her lids. She should continue checking back to the time the fraud charges were initiated. She should. But she would do it tomorrow, after giving Reardon her report up to date. Collecting the microfilm, snapping her pen closed, putting the notebook into her pocketbook, Christie pictured Reardon's face in response to her explanation that the job wasn't completed: Oh. I see. The *rest* of the information I need is still in the library. Well, at least it's in a nice safe place, right?

Grinding her teeth at Reardon, Christie abruptly thrust the microfilm at the librarian, who looked wounded when there was no smile returned. She quickly muttered, "Thank you very much, ma'am," and the librarian's tired smile reappeared briefly.

Littlejohn-Gerardo-Gerardo-Littlejohn-fraud or whatever. Maybe if she knew *why* she was looking for something, she would be able to find *what* she was looking for and maybe if she knew *what* she was looking for she'd . . .

Christie stopped suddenly in the vastness of the Library's marble corridor. Her mind was cleared of all the tiny printed words. She leaned against the smooth wall and closed her eyes tightly, forcing herself to slow down: to let all the sounds fill her brain, the low, murmuring voices, the muted echoing footsteps, and then, the voice, soft and intimate, entered her brain in the darkness behind her eyelids, "Hello, Christie Opara. How are you, Christie Opara?" But she did not hear the *sound* of the voice as she had strained to hear it, to define it, to identify it, night after night. She heard the *pronunciation* of her name.

Silently, Christie's lips formed her name and she opened her eyes and saw another place: the corridor outside of Special Sessions and Frank Santino with his lewd little eyes and she heard Frank Santino say her name with his particular, lazy slurring of the syllables so that it came out sounding neither Irish nor Czech, but like the word "opera." But it was not Frank Santino who called her every night. It was not Frank Santino's voice, it was a voice she had never heard before, coming from a man who knew her and who knew how to pronounce her name because he had heard Frank Santino say it.

Christie bit down hard on her index finger; the sharp pain intensified her sudden, complete awareness: Murray Rogoff.

Murray Rogoff had called those three girls and raped them and murdered them and hacked off pieces of their hair.

And now he's calling me.

14

MARTY GINSBURG haggled his way down Delancey Street. Haggling is a most joyous thing when done properly and with the whole heart. But there are stringent rules and requirements that must be met in order to fully pursue this ancient, complicated and respectable method of dealing with a fellow human being. The first essential is a loud voice and the second essential is a deaf ear and the third essential is a glass eye.

With these essentials, the bargainer can outshout his opponent (who does his best to outshout you); let his words of protest bounce unheard right back at him (as he does with yours); and his facial expressions, which range from cunningness to outrage, go unseen (while your expressions are similarly ignored). Of course, haggling ends at the logical, sought-for conclusion: you pay the price you originally had in mind (though well concealed) and your opponent accepts the price he originally decided upon (but would have died before revealing when the contest began). Then, each ignoring the other's moans of bitterness: Robber, thief, crook, stealing money for inferior merchandise—Depriver of my family, food from my children's mouths, roof from my family's head—the package, containing a length of multi-colored material, or sandals for a child's feet or aprons for a wife's ample middle or a hundred multi-sized screws and nails, is transferred from the seller to the buyer with glares of mutual hostility but feelings of mutual satisfaction.

Haggling is a most joyous thing and it hardly exists in its purest form any more. That was one of the reasons Marty Ginsburg loved the East Side: the old East Side which still did exist, but only in smaller and smaller areas, closing in about a tighter and tighter nucleus, hemmed and edged and encroached upon by coffee shops and art supply shops and sandal-makers and copper jewelry craftsmen pushed up from Greenwich Village and twenty-story, terraced and patioed high-rental red brick buildings, gaunt and out of place amid the colorlessness of the honest, old tenements.

Further up Delancey Street and off on the side streets, the haggling was done more and more in Spanish, furiously delivered by black-eyed, dark-skinned Puerto Ricans who were small and sharp-boned, their shrill voices indignant and righteous. Marty regretted this change with a sense of loss and deprivation. How could he possibly hope to get in on it, when the language was alien to his ear?

It felt good to dig out the childhood Yiddish, for nothing could sound as full and rich and furiously angry as bellowing at some old man, who, hawk-eyed, bellowed right back at you, snatching the piece of yard goods between you, each waiting the other out, each stomping away, then turning at just the right moment: a matter of precise timing was involved, then each confronting the other again with continued accusations and with the feigned regret of having to relent a little to the thief before him, but that was life and, God, what else could a man do.

Slowly he made his way along Delancey, then turned down Sheriff Street. Marty inhaled the warm and heavy air with all the childhood memories filling his large lungs. Not that he had ever lived on the Lower East Side. He hadn't. But the streets of his childhood Greenpoint, that pocket of Brooklyn, were the same streets after all. Marty sighed nostalgically. His kids, his four sons, were missing a hell of a lot growing up in a five-room apartment in an elevated building in Forest Hills with trees crushing them in and nothing but the sounds of jets from Kennedy and LaGuardia and all prices marked clearly on everything and no daily encounters to grow with, to learn from, to measure themselves by.

Ambling along to Rivington Street, Marty was confronted by a sight that took his breath away and called forth his spirit of challenge. The entire street was lined, on both sides, with cartons containing all manner of things: bargains! Left and right, wary old men and squinty old women alertly guarded their treasures, flexing their voices and strong tough hands against the possibility of customers. Marty advanced steadily, not letting his eyes rest too heavily or with too great an interest on any particular item for they watched your eyes and your eyes could give you away.

He walked past a display of bright material, ignoring the old woman who glared at him, stopped at a box of handkerchiefs (ten-for-a-dollar-pure-linen). He fingered the handkerchiefs, shrugged at the owner, who snarled at him, then cautiously, Marty worked his way back the few feet to where the yards of bright material, the flowers and color pulling at him, were watched over by a shapeless old woman whose skull was outlined by a safety-pinned kerchief. It was the red material with the blue and green palm trees that pulled at him, so of course, he lifted the corner of the white material with the green and yellow and pink polka dots, narrowing his eyes at it, pulling his mouth down at it, making an unpleasant sound at its lack of quality and beauty. Marty did this to several bolts of material, aware of the beginning rumbles from deep within the old woman's throat, until his hand rested lightly on his target, his face screwing into a look of disdain, his hand dropping the material quickly, passing on to the next bolt, then returning again to the target bolt, his mouth now asking, disinterestedly: "How much?"

The haggling began in earnest and the old woman was a good fighter. Suddenly, she called forth an obscenity of such pure and precise and fantastic clarity that Marty's blood was warmed and delighted by a surge of half-forgotten memories, and he surrendered for that reason alone. The old woman, suspicious and somewhat flustered, bundled the length of material, folding it at crazy angles, into a used brown paper bag, thrusting it at him and taking his money without respect. She had expected better of him.

Marty stopped before the glass case which faced onto the street, regarding the rows of fish which lay in an even row on the crushed ice, their eyes like clear buttons staring back at his. Overhead was a large folding door so that at the end of the day, the wooden stand, dripping with the debris of the fast-melting ice, the glass case on its rusty wheels, the old tin scale balanced precariously on a milk box, could all be slid into the small recess of the store, the door unfolded and chained into place so that no one could make off with any of these items during the night.

The aroma of the store permeated the street for at least twenty feet in each direction and was no stronger inside the cool, yellow-lighted cubicle than outside. Detective Martin Ginsburg of the District Attorney's Squad had fused into Marty Ginsburg the glorious haggler now, and the two personalities, melded into the large, package-clutching form, entered the store and his heavy, free hand reached into the barrel within and caught the tail of a perch. He held it distastefully in the air, then dropped it back with a splash.

"These fresh this morning?" he asked the old man who was barely tall enough to see over the small counter.

"From the mountain lakes they were taken at four o'clock this morning and from Fulton Street I purchased them at five A.M. and into that barrel I placed them at five-fifteen A.M.," the old man recited. "Fresh they are."

"Yeah? They don't look so fresh to me."

"So go catch them yourself, they ain't fresh enough?"

With his free hand, Marty jiggled the barrel, peering into the dark water. "How do I know they haven't been swimming around in there since last week?"

The old voice was sharp and hissing, beside him now. "They ain't swimming around. They been dead for a month. A little motor inside keeps them moving."

"I believe it," Marty stated, grasping another tail, studying an unblinking eye.

"So don't handle the merchandise if you ain't going to buy."

"Aw, what the hell. This one looks like he's going to croak from old age, so I'll let you do a mercy killing—it will be a kindness. How much?"

"By the pound," the old man rasped. "A set price—by the pound."

They haggled just a little, eliminating the weight of the head and tail but including the weight of the guts, and the old man took the fish from Marty and handed it to his son who stood silently at his chopping board.

Marty watched the strong smooth arms rather than the bloody hands which quickly and expertly divided the fish into pieces. Hell, the guy was a giant: the muscles on his shoulders and across his back and arms were like something in one of those body-building magazines over which his oldest boy, a chubby twelve-year-old, sweated and groaned.

"Can you bone it?" Marty asked, directing his question at Murray Rogoff, but the old man, turning from the front of the store, whined, "You want boned, you buy at the A and P."

A small dark girl came into the shop, cautiously watching and cautiously watched. She was short and black-eyed, her figure showing through the bright sheerness of her yellow blouse: the breasts high and pointed and sharply divided; her waist, tiny, pulled in with a wide plastic yellow belt clutching the short black skirt under which, as she turned, it was apparent she wore very little. Marty's eyes rested pleasurably on the girl's backside and he nudged a friendly elbow into Murray's side. God, the guy felt like a rock.

Murray looked up, puzzled, then followed Marty's stare for a moment, then when Marty turned for his reaction, Rogoff's mouth pulled down and his eyes, or at least the glasses (you couldn't find his eyes behind those crazy glasses), went back to the fish.

Murray's father didn't haggle with the little Puerto Rican: he told her the price, it didn't please her and she left.

"What a pair on that broad, huh?" Marty said. The only response was a noncommittal grunt. "How'd you like to get that against the ice? Turn it into boiling water in about two minutes."

The large naked head shook. "Not my type."

"Not your type?" Marty asked in disbelief. "You're kidding. Man, that's anybody's type."

"No," Rogoff said. "That's dreck. That's for anybody with two bits. That's nothing. *Nothing.*"

"Well that *nothing* sure as hell did *something* to me." Marty looked at the spot where the girl had stood.

"That's garbage," Rogoff said quietly as he folded the newspaper package into a brown paper bag. "*Dirt.*" Marty could see his eyes now, batting rapidly behind the dirty, goggle-like glasses. They were pale and small and round and lashless: like a fish.

133

"Hell, nothing wrong with a little garbage now and then," Ginsburg said, smiling lewdly. "Not when it looks like that."

"I wouldn't touch it with a ten-foot pole." There was a strange smile on the smooth face now, a thoughtful look.

Marty cursed in a friendly way, using the marvelous obscenity the old woman had recalled to his vocabulary, adding, "I would."

"No class," Rogoff said. "Who wants what anybody can have?"

"Who don't?"

"Me. I don't." Murray handed the brown paper bag to the stocky, dark-haired customer, then added in a low voice, "Not with what I got. What I got, brother, you couldn't get near."

Marty raised his eyebrows, licked his lips. "Yeah? You got something good? Around here?"

Rogoff smiled. He measured the stocky figure, comparing the hefty stomach and flabby arms against his own hardness: the little runt. "Forget it, pal. Not for you. Not when you go for *that* type."

"Me—I go for any type, so long as it got the equipment, pal."

Murray shook his head. "Uh-uh. What I got is one-of-a-kind, friend. Clean and nice. The one-man kind." His hand, closing into a fist around the money extended for the fish, pressed against his own chest. "*This man.*"

Marty accepted his change, readjusted his packages against his chest and grinned. "Well, it takes all kinds. Me —I like all kinds, just so long as they're broads, that suits me."

It would, Rogoff thought. He stood watching the heavyset figure in the bright-flowered shirt leave the store, looking up and down the street: looking. Murray took the dull edge of his sharp butcher knife and ran it over the wooden block, scraping the sticky remnants of guts and flesh off the edge and into the slop bucket beneath the table.

That slob. What would he know. What would *he* know about a girl like Christie. Christie Opara.

15

CHRISTIE OPARA typed rapidly on the Underwood without even realizing that since Stoner Martin was in the field she could have used the Royal. She copied her notes verbatim, mindlessly letting her fingers find the keys without translating the words into meaning.

Marty Ginsburg left the office shortly after she arrived, indicating the few telephone messages he had taken for Mr. Reardon while banging over his particular report. Marty had seemed oddly quiet: no jokes, no wisecracks, not commenting, of course, on his assignment, but still unusually tight-mouthed for Marty. He seemed in a hurry to leave, ducking into Reardon's empty office, leaving his report on the boss's desk and asking Christie to notify Reardon of that fact when he arrived.

She lifted her fingers to her face for a moment: she would notify Reardon of a fact today all right. She didn't plan what she was going to say: she couldn't. It would just have to come to her at the moment. She understood herself well enough to realize that if she tried to phrase it now, it would come out wrong then. If she tried to anticipate the sharp questions he would ask, she would not be able to find the instinctive answers that were somewhere inside of her, waiting.

The voice—*Rogoff's—she knew*—had taken to speaking a little more now: "Is this Christie Opara? How are you, Christie? Are you all right? Why do you work so late? Take care of yourself. I worry about you." And then, last night, before the sharp, disconnecting click, "I love you, Christie Opara."

And her own voice, after asking, "Who is this?" had responded to his questions carefully, "I am fine. Don't worry about me. Thanks for calling." Resisting the temptation to say it, breathing it down, "How are you, Murray Rogoff?"

135

because she didn't know what would happen then and she didn't want to take the chance, because this was more than phone calls in the night and was heading somewhere else and it had begun and she had to ride it out to the end.

She typed another paragraph, then flexed her fingers and kneaded her wrists, her right wrist aching in a peculiar, sympathetic pain: Poor Mickey, breaking his wrist. Just leaping down the two steps in front of the house in joy at being invited by the neighborhood kids to full partnership in their lemonade stand (I was going to bring the sugar, Mom) and his sneakered foot catching and his hands shooting out and his wrist cracking. Nora, feeling just the way she could be expected to feel: when it's your own child, it's bad enough, but when it's your grandchild, it's worse. And Christie, comforting Nora: but it could have happened anytime, if I were there or not, you know that. Kids run and kids jump and kids twist and kids fall. And kids break their wrists.

Christie wanted to be home, right now home, with Mickey, she needed to see his bright daytime face. Knowing he was comfortable, knowing he was busy and happy and not complaining over his games and coloring books wasn't enough: his voice on the telephone wasn't enough. She wanted to be home with him, not here, finishing this completely senseless report, preparing to confront Reardon with her completely senseless, yet absolute, definite, positive conclusions on this other matter. This Rogoff matter.

Christie felt both a relief and a tensing when Tom Dell entered the office. That meant Reardon was around.

"Hi, Tom. Boss back?"

Dell pushed his hat back from his forehead. He was a dapper man and always looked as though he'd just had a shower, suit press and shoeshine. He never gave out any information about his boss's comings, goings, appointments, conversations or overheard remarks, but the question of whether or not Reardon was about to appear was legitimate so he answered, "Yeah, he's talking to some guy in the hallway." He moved his head to the side. "Ah, the mighty footsteps are approaching."

Dell carefully placed his hat on the aluminum rack, took

out his report form and began transferring the mileage and gas information from his notebook to the official, required form.

Reardon scanned the room. "Empty house?"

"Not quite," Christie said. "I'm completing this report, Mr. Reardon. I think this will wrap it up." Then, anticipating him, she added quickly, "For now."

Reardon smiled: she was learning. "Good."

"Marty Ginsburg left a report on your desk—and asked me to give you these telephone messages."

"Right."

Christie checked her completed report carefully, stapled the sets of papers together, read it over, giving Reardon time to attend to the matters on his desk and herself time to think how she would begin but no words came, just the soft voice: "Hello, Christie Opara," but maybe that was enough.

She tapped lightly on his door, taking the grunting sound from within as permission to enter. She took one long full breath, holding it until she sat in the chair before his desk, releasing it slowly as he reached for her report then looked at her, still sitting there, in some surprise.

"I'd like to talk to you for a moment, Mr. Reardon, if you're not too busy."

She caught the impatient glance as he consulted his watch, but he said, "I'm busy, but go ahead. What's the problem?"

It didn't start to come, not yet. She searched for a moment, trying to find the right words and she was startled when he asked, directly, "Is it about the phone calls?"

"Yes." She nodded at him; there was a hollowness in her throat and she bit down hard on her teeth.

"Let's have it."

Christie ran her hand over her eyes feeling the silence around her. She had wanted her voice to come out strong and certain, not trembling; hating the sound of her words, she said, "I know who it is."

"Who?"

"Murray Rogoff." She added, "The 1140 I locked up a few weeks ago. You remember?"

137

There was no biting wisecrack, no caustic, "Yeah, how could I forget?" Reardon just nodded at her.

"Murray Rogoff," she repeated softly, and saying his name aloud, to Reardon now, not just inside her own brain where it had been echoing around for nearly a week, released the hidden words. She leaned forward, her fingers grasping the edge of his desk. "Mr. Reardon, I want to say something now that you can probably cut into ribbons with a few questions, but I'm going to say it anyway."

"Go ahead. Say what you want to say."

She raised her face to his and her voice was steady and unshaken and certain. "Murray Rogoff murdered those three girls." Her fingers shot up, ticking them off. "The one in Greenwich Village last February, the one on Riverside Drive in March, the one in the Bronx this month."

Reardon watched the paling of her face, aware that she was saying something now that had been eluding her the way the solution to a game-puzzle eludes your brain: all the facts present, the answer contained in your knowledge yet your mind not able to cut through the extraneous matter to the logical words, then all at once, the answer standing there, inside your head: clear and undeniable. She hadn't said: I *think* or he *might* be or *possibly* is. She had said *Murray Rogoff murdered those three girls.*

"You sound positive."

"I am positive."

Considering her for a moment, he tapped his pen against his teeth, then, with no challenge in his voice, just a logical question, he asked, "Court positive?"

She wavered, shook her head, her voice lower, but her eyes not leaving his. "No. Not *court* positive. But *positive.*"

She waited for his barrage of questions, for his fine, precise legal mind to destroy her certainty, but he just told her to go on and spell it out for him and Christie told him about her conversation with Johnnie Devereaux; about the victims' phone calls; about the scraps of hair, and then about the pronunciation of her name.

"Do you recognize his voice when he calls?"

Impatiently, Christie shook her head. "No. The voice is

138

what got me hung up; I tried too hard with the voice. I never heard Rogoff speak; he was silent when I locked him up and silent in court. I missed the pronunciation of my name completely, but it was there all the time—just the way Santino says it."

Reardon walked from his desk to the window, the silence broken by his clicking some coins together in his trouser pocket. He stood for a long time, then turned, walked to his desk and removed a folder from the bottom drawer.

"Here," he said, tossing the folder at her, "read this."

Frowning, puzzled, waiting for some hard laughter, some nasty comment, she took the folder, opened it absently, her eyes racing without comprehension over the typed words. She looked at him blankly.

"It's a background report that Stoney prepared for me last week. *On Murray Rogoff*. Christ, Opara, close your mouth." He picked up Marty's report, shoving it across the desk at her. "When you finish reading Stoney's investigation, read Ginsburg's. He made an observation on Rogoff yesterday." Reardon ran his hand over his face, down, then up, then back through the thick red hair, then rubbed his knuckles under his chin. His voice seemed irritable but at the same time weary. "You know, Opara, you really knock me out. I mean, it really never even *occurred* to you that possibly, *just possibly*, by some miracle maybe or even by some long years of experience, out of habit, your old boss might have sat quietly one afternoon and given just some slight thought to the problem of your phone calls, et cetera." He smiled tightly and held his hand up. "Oh, not because I was interested on *your* behalf, or *concerned* or anything like that— hell, no. More likely because I felt I'd better do something to stop your sleepless nights since you've been goofing off during working hours—carrying over assignments that should be completed in one day." He leaned his chin on his hands, pressing his elbows on the desk. "So, giving me some credit for my long years in this business, let's say that the possibilities went through my mind, and that one of the possibilities was Rogoff."

Reardon stopped speaking and dug a coin from his trouser pocket. His eyes still on Christie, he spun the dime on his desk, then abruptly slammed the palm of his hand over it and leaned forward. His voice forced her eyes from his hand back to his face. "Approximately ten million people have access to your phone number every day in New York City. When you begin with ten million possibilities, you have to narrow it down a little, right? Rogoff was the only collar you've made since you've been in the Squad and Rogoff is a degenerate and he was the first possibility." He leaned back, slipped the dime into his pocket and watched her closely. "Do you want me to spell out in detail the various reasons I felt a run-down on Rogoff should be done?" His voice was patronizing now and he ignored her terse "no." "Hell, I'd be glad to lay it all out for you; even tell you what I was planning to do if we hit a blank wall with Murray."

She still had that incredulous, half-comprehending expression on her face and Reardon felt anger or pride, or whatever the hell it was, rising to his lips. "Tell me something, Opara," he said sharply, "what the hell impresses you?"

"Competence," she said evenly. "Professional competence."

The anger, unexplained, forced the words from him. "Then why is it that you seem to feel you're the only one around here with the slightest amount of professional competence?" Stopping himself, not needing her acknowledgment, yet oddly annoyed at her lack of recognition, he irritably gestured at her, "Go on—go on, read!"

Dropping her eyes to the papers on her lap, Christie said, "Yes sir."

Her eyes raced over the words, then deliberately slowed down, picking out the meanings. She gnawed on her pinky absently, reading Stoney's precise background report which took the infant Murray Rogoff home from Bellevue Hospital Maternity Ward, where he had been born on February 1, 1930, son of Hyman and Gilda (maiden name: Posner) Rogoff; weight: 8 lbs. 6 ounces; 21 inches long; other children: 1; father's occupation: fish store owner; mother's occupation: housewife.

Education: elementary school, where he had been an

average student; junior high school, where he had been an average student, but excelled at sports. Into high school, where he had been a low-average student, but had developed into a star athlete. And then the school records stopped after he had completed his third year of high school.

The medical record picked up where the school record left off and copied verbatim from the Medical Records-Bellevue Emergency was the following: August 2, 1946; 12:45 A.M.; Murray Rogoff; 136 Rivington Street, N.Y.C.; place of occurrence: Delancey Street, in front of Loew's Delancey; nature of injury: patient in comatose state; possible skull fracture; witnesses to accident: David Rogoff (bro.), same address; Sol Weissman, 138 Rivington Street, N.Y.C. Notations: patient, male, white, 16 yrs., removed from scene of accident by ambulance; remains in comatose state; apparently well-nourished, good physical condition; no evidence alcohol. Patient's brother states patient slipped while engaging in "horseplay" at location of accident. Dr. J. Gonzalez-ambulance attendant; patient removed to Intensive Care Rm.—Dr. Fogel supervising.

The Aided Card: prepared by Patrolman K. Nugent, Shield #130567, officer not on scene when accident occurred, containing a terse account as stated above.

Notation: August 5, 1946—patient semi-comatose, complaining of intense headache across forehead. August 6, 1946, patient fully conscious, removed to Ward 6; taking food and medication well. X ray reveals hairline fracture, lower cranium. Patient comfortable, uncomplaining, resting well. August 12, 1946, patient complaining of severe pain in eyes; examined by Dr. J. Gold, ophthalmologist who removed several lashes from each of patient's eyes; patient reported to supervising physician some significant hair loss from head and pubic area; August 13, 1946, patient examined by Dr. Leonardi, neurologist, who reports no significant findings. August 18, 1946, patient considered physically fit for discharge, but noticeably disturbed by continuing hair loss. Seen this date by Dr. Loeb, psychiatrist.

Stoner's report continued: undersigned spoke this date with Dr. Loeb who reported that all information contained in his interviews with subject was considered privileged and confidential. Then, without further notation or explanation, Stoney's report continued, spelling out the "privileged and confidential" information he had obtained—somehow—from Dr. Loeb.

Dr. Loeb first saw subject, Murray Rogoff, on August 18, 1946, date subject was due to be discharged from hospital. He described subject, a boy of 16, as a very well-developed physical specimen, apparently in excellent health, but very agitated by the significant loss of hair he was experiencing. Dr. Loeb advised subject to leave hospital and remain on Out-Patient basis; further scheduled tests to determine cause and possible cure of said condition. It was noted that a "differential diagnosis" was recorded on subject's medical file. [Then, in parentheses, Stoner Martin, knowing Reardon's impatience and unwillingness to consult the Medical Dictionary, had spelled out] this means that cause of subject's hair loss had not been determined and a series of tests was scheduled to eliminate possible causes and hopefully to arrive at a definite cause; subject continued under supervisory care of Dr. Loeb, returning to Out-Patient Department three times a week for tests given by Neurology Department and Department of Internal Medicine.

September 1, 1946: patient fitted with special moisture glasses to protect his eyes, which are now devoid of lashes; apparent damage to tear ducts; eyes tearless, burning, dry.

Dr. Loeb noted that patient seemed more hostile and uncommunicative at each visit; very agitated and angry at inability of doctors to pinpoint cause of hair loss. Though it was explained to patient that the injury he suffered did not seem instrumental in causing this hair loss, patient feels that skull injury was motivating force. Patient bitterly disturbed by loss of status within his social group; at first visit, patient bragged considerably about his female conquests, now describes all females as "dirty, filthy." Patient seems unable to accept what has happened to him and is building a wall of protective hostility and resentment around himself.

Patient last seen on October 15, 1946, after missing three previously scheduled appointments; physical changes in subject are evident in his carriage and uncertain manner; he wore a cap which he refused to remove; holds his head down; mumbles; patient completely hairless now; informs he has quit school; spends his time working with his father in his fish store; sleeping; "just walking around"; when queried as to his sexual activities, patient became highly agitated, used obscene language and said "that's my business." Patient failed to keep any subsequent appointments, though patient's brother was seen once, on November 3, 1946. Brother reports patient is most disturbed and abusive to him, his parents and customers in the store, yet refuses to return for any counseling.

When Dr. Loeb was asked by undersigned [Stoney's report continued] if such a patient might, at some future time, resort to acts of sexual violence, Dr. Loeb said he could not, with any accuracy, based on his knowledge of subject, make such a prediction but that the possibility could not be eliminated from any prognosis.

Christie placed the report face down on Reardon's desk and reached for Marty's report without looking up at Reardon.

Detective Ginsburg's report was brief but informative: "Subject expressed no interest in female customer who entered store while undersigned was present. Undersigned engaged subject in conversation relative to types of females who are of interest to him and it is the conclusion of undersigned that subject has one particular female in mind, such conclusion being based upon subject's saying to undersigned, 'What I got, friend, is one of a kind. Clean and nice.'

143

(The word jumped out at Christie as though it were typed in capital letters.) 'The one-man kind.' Then subject indicated himself, saying, 'This man.'

"It is the opinion of undersigned," Marty's report informed her, "that subject is not interested in the females abroad in streets of his resident neighborhood but that subject has another female in mind, and is possibly involved with this female or had some contact with her, although there is the possibility that this female is all in subject's mind, since he is a very weird-looking person."

Reardon spoke the moment she finished reading Marty's report. "Marty isn't eloquent but he is sharp. By the way," he said slowly, "I didn't tell Marty *why* or *what*. I just told him to go down and strike up a conversation with Rogoff and see how he feels about girls in general." He watched her face; Christ, he could see right into her. She *had* been sore when he sent her out for information without telling her why. "You see," he continued, his eyes darkening, "when you know *what* you're looking for, you tend to find it. You tend to steer in that particular direction. This way, when I get a report, it's more or less objective and unbiased: *I* know what I have—even if *you* don't know *why*." Raising his chin slightly, he said pointedly, "Not that you deserve any explanation, Opara. I just threw that in gratis." He admired the fact that she didn't pretend, just nodded. Her face reddened though. She had been put in her place and she sat there, defenseless, acknowledging it. There is something about this girl, Reardon thought, but not letting it show. His face could be any kind of mask he wanted it to be and he wanted nothing but professional authority to show now.

"Okay, Christie, spell it out for me. What have we got?" He leaned back, motionless in his chair, watching the hesitation. Not doubt, just a careful search for the right words.

"Rogoff. We got Rogoff."

Wordlessly, he shook his head.

"All right: not yet. But we are going to get him." She leaned her hands on the desk and her words were defiant. *"I am going to get him."*

144

His first impulse was to cut her down. He could, of course, with a swift change of expression, a few sharp, probing questions. But he didn't respond to her tone, just watched her face, and a different feeling came to him now because the tense firmness and certainty with which she had spoken revealed something else. She was so goddamn vulnerable, like a little kid who sees something wrong and without hesitation or self-doubt, knowing that it must be made right, simply says: here's what must be done and *I* must do it.

"How?"

She pulled in her lower lip, bit down on it, then pushed it out. "I'm not sure yet, but . . ."

He cut her off rapidly. "Well, hey, I'm glad to hear that there is still at least a question of *method* in your mind. You're so damn sure of everything else, it's nice to know you do have at least a little doubt."

"Not about Rogoff," she shot back, "not about him."

"All right. Let's run over what we have. Three murdered girls: they are a fact. Raped and strangled and no witnesses, no fingerprints, no tangible evidence at the scene to link any suspect to them, right?"

"Right."

"A murderer: unknown." He saw her mouth begin to move, but she remained silent. "Repeat: *unknown*. He is a fact, right?"

"Right."

"Okay. Now, we got Rogoff: a known degenerate. You locked him up as an exhibitionist, but he has no previous record."

"That doesn't mean anything—that just means it was the first time he was caught."

His eyes searched the ceiling, his voice not containing his anger. "You going to teach me something or are we going to discuss the situation?"

"Sorry."

"Damn it. All right. The murderer is in one way or another a sexual deviate; there have been arguments both ways relative to the progressive acts of exhibitionists: some

145

say he turns rapist or molester, some say not. Now, we have the phone calls, which began shortly after you locked up Rogoff. You think it's Rogoff calling . . ."

"*I know.*"

"Will you just shut up, Opara?" Reardon stood up, walked to the couch, eased himself the length of the green leather, his head and feet propped on opposite armrests, his hand resting lightly over his eyes. "Just keep quiet, all right? Now, let's *assume* that your caller *is* Rogoff. His calls aren't obscene or threatening. He just asks how you are, et cetera. *Assuming* it's Rogoff and assuming we could prove it's him, what have we got?" He waited for a moment, then answered his own question, "Nothing, right?"

Grudgingly, she said, "Right, but . . ."

"No *buts.*" He uncovered his eyes, raising his head. "*Nothing.* Even if the calls take a nasty turn and we bag him on an obscenity charge, that would be it, right? There's no physical evidence, no nail scrapings, nothing from the murder scenes." He eased himself up, so that he was resting on his elbows. "So where are we?"

The totally unexpected coldness of her voice forced him into a rigid alertness. "I think you know where we are as well as I do, Mr. Reardon."

"No," he said, unmoving, "you tell me."

"We have to bait a trap," she said, "and you are looking at the bait." Her chin rose slightly and she seemed devoid of any emotion. "Rogoff selected me. Okay. Let's set it up."

He knew she had spoken with the clear, professional logic of a good police officer: yet, why was it, Reardon wondered, that every time she opened her mouth, every word hit him as some kind of a personal challenge? Controlling his voice so that he would not engage her, he asked, "What did you have in mind?"

She frowned. "I really hadn't thought it through. Just that it seems the only way." She held her hand up, practically into his face, and Reardon, resisting the urge to grab that hand (and do what?) jammed his fists into his pockets, standing now, half leaning against the desk before her. But she wasn't watching him; she was digging inside her mind, recalling whatever facts she felt she had to have. "Last night, he said something he's never said before. He—he said that he loved me."

"I can't imagine why."

Her eyes did a slow stare, then a deliberate blink, dismissing his remark.

The fresh little bastard.

Ignoring his closeness, yet speaking to him, she said, "I don't respond to anything he says." Then altering that quickly, "I mean, I do answer, but nothing that would lead him on. That wouldn't be right—that would be entrapment."

Reardon nodded solemnly. "Oh, absolutely, that wouldn't be right." They were talking about a suspect in three rape-murders. Reardon ran his tongue over his front teeth.

"He's been watching me somehow, so he knows . . ."

"*Watching you?* You never said anything about that before." The District Attorney's voice accused the witness of withholding vital information.

Christie shook her head impatiently. "No, no, I haven't spotted him or anything. But he *has* to be watching me, because he always calls just about thirty or forty minutes after I get home." Her eyes narrowed and she was speaking more to herself than to him. "He must be somewhere around the subway station because there aren't any phone booths near my house. He probably gives me about ten minutes to get home, then time to shower and . . . et cetera."

"Has he ever called when you weren't there?"

"Yes, twice. Nora, my mother-in-law, answered. One night, Marty drove me home, one night Bill Ferranti dropped me off." She snapped her fingers. "That must be it. He watches the subway station. He didn't see me come home, so he called."

"Did he speak to Nora?"

"Yes—asked if I were home. She just said I was out." Reardon's brows went up, questioningly. "Nora knows about the calls. I told her to just put him off without any further conversation. He thanked her both times and hung up, but didn't call me back."

Christie closed her eyes, completely unaware of him,

147

standing there so close that the fabric of her dress, a light nylon jersey paisley print of wildly contrasting pinks and oranges, brushed against his knee as she moved, shifting in the chair. Observing the concentration, Reardon had the oddest feeling: as if they were two little kids and that any moment she would open her eyes and instruct him: "and then you must be the daddy, and when you come home from work, I'll say . . ." But her eyes snapped open and she told him, "We could use Nora. She could give him a message."

"Like what?"

It rushed from her fully conceived. "Well, that I moved. We could stake out a place. I did some research at the library on the other murders. The one in the Village and the one in upper Manhattan. Each girl lived alone in a ground floor apartment and entry had been through a back window."

His voice was lightly taunting. "Did you research on *my* time?"

Earnestly, she shook her head. "No, sir. *After* I did my assignment."

"I bet. Go on, don't let me stop you."

"We could stake out a place. Ground floor, back window, then when he calls, Nora could tell him that I moved and give him the address and apartment number." She seemed to have run out of breath and words at the same time.

"Yeah? Then what?"

"Then," she said, slowed down and steadied by reality, "it would be up to him."

Reardon, eyes on his shoes, watched his feet move from the desk, watched the shiny black leather tips stop alongside the radiator which was built into the windowsill. He raised his head, vacantly looking down to the street.

Christie didn't break the silence, but sat waiting, suddenly certain that he was standing there, gathering ammunition, that he would whirl around now, his face set into an angry grin, his voice nasty and sharp as steel, and his words would tear everything but her knowledge into useless little pieces. But he turned around, finally, slowly, and his face was thoughtful.

"I'll think about it," he said.

That was even worse than his sarcasm because that was a way of dismissing it, that was absolutely nowhere. She wondered why he added sharply, "I didn't say *no*. I said I'll think about it. There is a matter of communication involved."

"Communication? With who?" she demanded.

"Did you ever hear of Homicide? Or did you intend to handle this whole thing single-o?"

"Do *they* have to get into it?" She regretted the question before it was completed, regretted it more, as he sat, his eyes glowing at her like darts.

He flung words at her like accusations. "Homicide's business is homicide. We're not looking to take over anybody's case." Her lips moved, but he spoke too quickly for her. "Don't say a *word*, Opara, don't even open your mouth. Relax—nobody's going to take anything away from you. *If,* after a conference with the other people involved in this, I decide to pursue this case along the lines we've discussed, you're in it." You're damn right: that's what she was saying, with her mouth set and tight and her eyes blazing back at him. Reardon's finger jabbed the air. "But as part of a team. You got that? *As part of a team!*"

"*Right!*" She threw *his* word, in *his* tone, into his face. Reardon curled his fingers tightly; he wanted, more than anything in the world at that particular moment, to walk around the desk and grab her by her shoulders and shake her until her teeth rattled. Or something. He glanced, unseeing, at his watch, then snatched up some papers, his head bent down, then raised his eyes to her.

"You still here?" Blush; go ahead, damn it. Yes, I *do* see it; that kills you doesn't it? He watched her hesitate at the door. "Yeah? You got something *else* on your mind?"

He could see the struggle and he knew she would say whatever it was even though she knew she should just keep her mouth shut and keep going.

One long deep breath drawn in and carefully released, then her voice a little thin, but with no tremor, "Mr. Reardon, whatever happens in this case," a pause, then her words an undeniable demand, "*Rogoff is mine!*"

149

Reardon let the papers fall flatly before him, his words
and reactions catching in his throat, then unnecessary
because he could see that, wordless, he had given his
message and she could probably still feel his eyes reaching
after her behind the closed door, down the corridor to
whatever section of the Squad office she had retreated to.

His eyes remained fixed on the door, as though Christie
were still standing there telling him: telling *him* how it was
going to be. Reardon whistled angrily through his teeth,
then cursed softly and steadily, pulled open the bottom
drawer, swept all the papers from his desk in haphazard
disarray, then kicked the drawer closed.

That fresh little bitch might very well get herself raped
and murdered. If not by Murray Rogoff maybe by Casey
Reardon.

16

NORA OPARA was the damnedest grandmother Casey Reardon had ever met. He was momentarily taken off guard by the stunningly bright appearance of the small figure and at first had the impression of a faceless mannikin dressed in a slacks set of unbelievable color combinations. Reardon's taste was not sophisticated enough to accept bold, jagged squares of clear greens and yellows against pure deep pink, but focusing on the woman's face, it was evident that the colors could not overwhelm her. Everything about her was vivid and clearly defined: the eyes, so definite a blue as to make any other blue eyes slightly questionable, the hair a pure white with no hint or trace of what the original color had been, the nose, short and finely shaped, and the bright, healthy pink of her skin were memorable.

Her hand, when he introduced himself, gave his a good firm grasp and she led him quickly into the living room. At first glance, the room might seem to be disordered or untended, but as Nora bent down, rolling up a long narrow mat, Reardon could see that it was, rather, a lived-in room. Without apology, she told him, "This is my yoga mat. Ever stand on your head, Casey?"

She used his first name casually and naturally as though they were well acquainted. Reardon grinned. "Last time, Nora, I think I was about twelve years old. I remember that it made me dizzy."

She held the mat under her arm and told him, "That passes in a few minutes; it's great for the circulation. And for brain power, fills all the cells with blood." She leaned over the couch and called, "Mickey, look up from your picture for a minute and say hello to Mr. Reardon."

She motioned Reardon beside her and he looked down at the small boy, who was stretched on his stomach, paintbrush over a large sheet of paper on the carpeted floor.

"*That's* Mr. Reardon?"

His voice was so innocently revealing and Nora's reaction to it was so natural that Reardon felt delighted by them. Her hand shot up to her forehead, covered her eyes and then she said softly, "*Tact*: yes, we have to add that to the list of things." Then to the boy, "Mickey, remind me to add the word 'tact' to the list of things you and I have to discuss in private."

Reardon caught the quick half-grin and nod the boy gave his grandmother. He cleared his throat and said softly, "I get the very definite impression that someone in this house has much maligned my good name."

Although he didn't understand the words, the boy sensed that his grandmother and the redhaired man seemed to be friendly toward each other. Mickey stood up after carefully placing his paintbrush in the jar of blackish water and accepted the large hand that was offered to him.

"Well, how do you do, Mickey Opara."

The child corrected the pronunciation of his name, and Reardon, serious and polite, repeated the name properly. He noted the firm grip of the small left hand. "How'd you break your arm, Mickey?"

The boy watched Reardon closely, trying to measure the angry, overheard remarks of his mother against this smiling man. Standing his ground firmly, his feet wide apart, the large light blue eyes an exact replica of his grandmother's, Reardon noted, the boy drew in his bottom lip for a moment, then pushed it out. It was a deliberate pause before speaking and it was familiar to Reardon: not a hesitation, just a consideration.

"The step tripped me," the child said.

Reardon didn't smile. "Hey, that was a mean thing for it to do. It must be tough to paint left-handed. Can I have a look at your picture?"

Nora noted that he hadn't fallen into the typical adult mistake of trying to interpret what the boy was painting; he just squatted down and admired the colors without being patronizing. Reardon glanced up at Nora and nodded just once, a very quick movement of his head which indicated his approval not of the picture but of what he had sensed and observed between the two of them.

152

"How do you like your Scotch, Casey?" Nora asked, expecting his answer.

"On the rocks, please," Reardon told her, enjoying the opportunity to look openly around the room. The atmosphere was not what he had expected from two widows living with one small boy. There was no overpowering femininity, nothing that clearly marked the absence of a man. The room was long and wide and bright: the walls stark white (very different from the soft beiges and golds of Reardon's own, more formal home). The unexpected hot colors didn't lurch out: the plaid sofa facing him, a bright orange and pink, covered with an assortment of pillows, wasn't the kind of furnishing he would have chosen, yet, set in this room, it seemed right and pleasing. The chair he sat in was a deep burnt orange and the tables, holding large wood and iron lamps, were of dark Spanish carved wood. Bookshelves ranged along the long wall, from floor to ceiling, holding a large collection of books of all kinds. Casey's eyes skimmed titles and subject matter: from popular novels to classics to history to current events. There was a large group of art books and, without being told, he knew those were Nora's as were the paintings grouped over the low bench on which was set a portable TV. He could see the small but clear signature in the lower right-hand corner: "Nora '64"; "Nora '63"; "Nora '66". And then, unexpectedly, "Christie '64." He rose, came closer to Christie's painting: it was an ocean scene; the strokes were firm and strong and somehow angry at their inability to draw the energy from beneath the waves which crashed against a sunlit boulder.

"Your mother paints, too?" he asked. Mickey nodded wordlessly. Reardon studied the small collection of photographs on the brick mantel of the fireplace. Mickey, small and sturdy, staring into the camera, apparently disturbed at play. Mickey, standing thigh-high against Christie whose legs were deeply tanned against the white shorts. Reardon reached out, taking the photograph of a young patrolman from the mantel. It was Mickey's face, fixed in manhood; the eyes wide and steady, the jaw square and strong, the mouth smiling just a bit. Reardon glanced down at the boy and replaced the only evident photograph of his father. He

153

DOROTHY UHNAK

had his father's dark hair, too; nothing, physically, of his mother; yet, looking at him, catching the concentration, the hard pressing of his lips together, and then meeting the questioning glance of the child, catching the slowly changing look of challenge crossing the boy's face, there was no mistaking Christie's son. The boy, hearing a car horn blast twice, leaped to his feet, his face now exploding into a smile.

"That's Uncle Pete," he explained, dashing from the room. Nora came, handing Casey his drink, carrying a highball for herself. There was a loud burst of sound from the hallway, moving into the living room. Mickey was enthroned perilously on the shoulders of one of the handsomest men Reardon had ever seen. He moved easily and with an athlete's grace, extending his hand to Reardon as Nora introduced them. The black eyes, smiling along with the wide mouth, told Reardon Christie's brother had never heard of him. Whatever was discussed in this house stayed in this house.

Mickey's uncle bent down easily, letting the boy scoop up his small overnight case. They left in a roar of masculine joking which echoed back into the house until the car pulled away.

"No family resemblance there at all," Reardon commented, his head tilted toward the door, "between Christie and her brother."

"You should see Christopher Choriopoulous: he and Christie are ringers. Two Swedes and two Greeks," Nora said. "That's what Christie's father used to call them—his Swedes and his Greeks."

"Interesting combination; two fair and two dark."

Nora sipped at her drink, then put it carefully on the cocktail table before the couch, and without preliminary she said, "Christie was born on Grand Central Parkway. The family was coming back from Jones Beach one hot summer evening. They were all tired and happy; Christie wasn't due for about three weeks." Nora regarded the glass thoughtfully, then looked into Reardon's face, her eyes pure and intent. "An old man, well over seventy, lost control of his

154

car. Heart attack, probably. There was a head-on collision and Christie's father delivered his only daughter in the back of the family's station wagon." She hesitated a moment, then added, "Her mother died before they reached the hospital. Never even saw Christie. The doctors were surprised that the delivery went as well as it did, but Christie was a tough little character; right from the start."

Reardon, holding the cold wide glass between his palms, his face serious and not showing any question, sat listening: and waiting.

"Christie's told me about this case, of course, and about what is involved in the stake-out. I guess you know how she feels about doing this job."

Reardon's hands moved, rolling the glass. "She's been sweating it out for this past week, I know that. There were a lot of conferences, a lot of arrangements to be made. I know she's anxious to get this done, if that's what you mean."

There was something in Nora's voice that made Reardon lean forward just slightly, his mind sharply alerted for the information he sensed she would convey. She nodded her head. "Yes, she's anxious to get it done. Christie has a *need* to finish what she's started." Nora's small hands hugged the back of her neck, and she leaned her head back for a moment; then, her head came forward, her eyes closed as she began speaking, her voice oddly flat, as though this needed telling and there was just one way to tell it, she said, directly, "Mickey never saw his father. He was conceived the night before my son, Mike, was killed—in the line of duty, as I'm sure you know." Her blue eyes were wide now, dry and wide. "It was two months before Christie even knew she was pregnant. That was when we decided to join forces, so to speak: I had this house—it's where Mike was raised. We talked it over and decided to take the chance." She smiled. "And it was a chancy thing no matter how you look at it, but it worked. We've made a life here for the three of us, and Mickey gets his share of masculine company, what with three uncles all the size of Pete—he does pretty well."

"I'm sure he does," Reardon said. He knew he would be

155

surprised by nothing Nora said; she was a completely honest woman and used to speaking her mind. "Go on, Nora. You haven't reached it yet, have you?"

The blue eyes narrowed, showing the only lines on her face: the crinkling laugh lines. "Okay, Casey Reardon: Christie *has* to go through this case, even if it involves considerable risk." She glanced at her hands for a moment, then back at him, moving her legs under her now, *"Particularly* if it involves risk."

"I'm not too sure I understand what that means."

"Relax, Casey; she isn't *looking* for unnecessary risk; not that." Her eyes searched somewhere over his head for a moment. "Let me try and explain it: Christie's life began with the death of her mother; that was a loss she didn't really experience in the true sense. She never had a mother, so she couldn't really conceive of a *loss*. But," she said softly, "there *was* a loss. Mike's death was a true loss, the worst kind for a woman. Two years ago, Christie's father was killed. He was a construction crew chief and he was killed on the job."

She was getting closer to it now, but still not stating it; Reardon put his drink on the table beside him, his voice quiet and patient. "Spell it out for me, Nora—the point."

"The point: Christie lost three people—all in premature ways, all more or less through violence. Now, Christie has to face it for herself; it involves her personally and she has to be there and prove to herself that she can beat it. *Death,* Casey, *violent death."*

He visualized the tense young face, defiant, angry, demanding: *Murray Rogoff is mine.* He had known there was something deeper, something more personal involved than an arrest. He had known it was something more important to her than the arguments he had advanced when the Chief of Detectives told him to keep her out of it (you don't need a dame lousing things up if the action gets rough). He had taken two definite approaches with the Chief: first, pointing out that as a Squad member, she had the right to follow up on what was essentially *her* case. Then, realizing that the Chief of Detectives was not interested in a Squad member's right, Reardon hit on the case itself: unless Opara was there, in the room, they would be in a position to nail Rogoff for nothing more than breaking and entering: her presence was essential to the case they were trying to build. Yet, all during that particular discussion, Reardon himself did not fully understand why it was so essential to Christie that she be there. Quietly, he said, "Yes, Nora. Yes, I think you're right."

Nora took a long, slow drink, then held the cold glass against her forehead. For the first time, an expression of concern drew her dark brows down. "You won't let anything happen to her, will you, Casey?"

"Hell, no," he said rapidly, "that would make some publicity for the Squad: 'lady cop raped and murdered on official stake-out'!"

His hard laughter joined hers and she told him, "With that remark, Casey Reardon, I now believe *everything* I have been told about you."

It was not a thoughtless remark, blurted out; it was an indication of Nora Opara's honesty and the fact that she expected the same from him. Reardon tipped his glass toward her, swallowed, then consulted his wristwatch at the melodious chiming which filled the room. "That will be Sam Farrell. Twenty minutes late."

Nora stopped by his chair before going to the door and her face, though smiling, was somehow serious. "I just wanted you to know, Casey: Christie is someone *very special.*"

Reardon said, "I know that." His voice was light again, "A little fresh, but special."

Farrell filled the living room with heavy breathing and noise, rocking his head in despair over the flat tire he had had to deal with en route from the Bronx. "Second flat in a week, Mr. Reardon, and the car is only six months old. I think I ought to go back to the dealer, I mean, I don't think two flats should happen to a car that new, you know?"

While Nora went to get Farrell some coffee, Reardon briskly went over his instructions. "Now, Sam, as soon as the phone rings, Mrs. Opara will take the call upstairs and you lift the receiver in here. You know how to set up the tape recorder, don't you?" A heavy doubt, somewhere in the pit of his stomach, prompted the question, but it was dispelled, not by Farrell's prompt reassurances but by the remembered words of Stoner Martin (he's a little clumsy, boss, but you can count on Sam). "Okay, Sam, now you record *everything*. Now, *if* and *when* the call comes from our suspect, you have the phone number up at the stake-out, right?" Farrell dug into his pockets, coming up with a slip of paper. "Keep that right by the phone; when you get the call we're expecting, dial right away, give the word to Stoney or Ginsburg or Ferranti, then play back the conversation for them and that's it, right?"

"Yes, sir, Mr. Reardon. Hey, you want to listen a minute, I'll play back what we just said."

In surprise, Reardon heard his own voice and Farrell's and he was pleased because he hadn't even noticed that Farrell had set the compact tape recorder on the table beside the telephone.

"Good," he said briskly, "but make sure you hook it up to the phone. You know how, don't you?"

Patiently, Farrell set the plug into place, dialed for weather information, then played it back for Reardon. "Good. Okay, Sam, you're in business." Farrell nodded silently, bringing the cup of coffee Nora had given him to the table: Reardon would have bet that Sam Farrell, during the course of the next ten or twelve hours if need be, would not be farther away from that telephone than his arm could reach.

Reardon, preceding Nora through the hallway, tripped over a large, gray animal lying stretched across the white tile floor. Recoiling in mock horror, he asked, "What the hell is *that thing?*"

Nora reached down, taking the large cat in her arms; its heavy paws sprawled unconcerned, the eyes locked in undisturbed sleep. "This is Sweet William," she said, nuzzling the fur against her cheek.

"It would be: My God—*Sweet William*." He stared at the cat, who opened two large vacant green eyes, then snapped them shut again.

She walked with Reardon onto the patio, which was cheerfully furnished with white wicker chairs and table and stone pots of red geraniums, and deposited the cat onto one of the chairs, where he promptly stretched, rolled on his back and continued sleeping. Tom Dell, patiently sitting behind the wheel of the black Pontiac, without turning his head toward them, automatically reached his hand to the key, tuning the engine.

"Nora"—Reardon reached out, placed her hand in both of his—"Thanks for going along with us. I have every confidence that you'll handle your part without any problem. You've done a damn good job with that little guy, by the way."

"Christie and I go fifty-fifty where Mickey is concerned —credit and blame."

He added that to his collection of impressions about Nora Opara, turned toward the car, but her fingers pulled lightly at his sleeve and he turned, surprised.

"There's just one more thing I want to say, Casey." Her eyes were steady and the blue was not paled by the brightness of the late sun. "This is a little difficult."

Reardon grinned. "But you're going to say it anyway, so go ahead."

"Christie isn't as tough as she likes to think. She's really pretty soft and she feels very deeply about things. About *people*." Nora's eyes didn't waver. "She could get hurt," she said, not talking about the stake-out now.

Reardon's face tightened slightly; they stood measuring each other for a moment, then he said softly, "Okay. Don't worry about her, right?"

She watched him walk to the car and returned his brisk wave.

Reardon slumped in the seat beside Dell, his eyes staring through the spotless windshield. This Nora Opara was indeed a very shrewd little lady. He wondered if Christie realized that Nora had read something more than anger or annoyance into her complaints about him or if Christie herself even knew there *had* been anything else.

Reardon smiled and closed his eyes. He didn't think so.

159

17

CHRISTIE FOLLOWED Bill Ferranti as he led her about the tiny apartment which was not really an apartment, just a compartmentalized room with a separate bathroom. The diagramed floor plan she had studied in the office did not translate into this small, hot sticky room; there was a kitchen unit contained in a half-walled alcove, consisting of a waist-high refrigerator, lined up flush with a small sink which was wedged against a narrow, four-burner stove.

Each ugly, alien piece of furniture in the room had been shifted to a location calculated to meet their needs: the heavy stuffed flowered armchair had been pushed alongside the door. This was where Stoner Martin would crouch, giving him coverage for either of the two possibilities: that Rogoff would enter the apartment via the hallway door or that Rogoff would enter through the bathroom window. The lumpy couch bed had been moved from its location against the wall and centered on the short wall so that there was free space on either side of its length: this way, Christie could follow her instructions which were, "The minute the lights go on, baby, you roll to the left, hit the deck and stay down until ole Stoney says otherwise!" The scarred and loose-legged wooden table had been moved off center in the small kitchen alcove for two reasons: first, that it would not pose a stumbling block for Rogoff who would enter in the darkness, and secondly, that it would not interfere with Ferranti's movements as he emerged from his hiding place behind the half-arched alcove.

Her mind automatically rearranged the ugly furnishings, trying to get some measure of balance. Christie made a determined effort to accept this room, to let its dimensions and narrow passageways have meaning and necessity. The bathroom was another matter: everything stationary, everything exact in the range of its requirements.

160

Stoner Martin signaled them all into the long, narrow chipped and dirty bathroom and they all stood, Christie and Ginsburg and Ferranti, their eyes following Stoner's to the bathroom window: the all-important rectangle on which it all depended.

"Now, this, as we have discussed, would seem to be the logical place." Leaning across the tub, his muscles straining slightly, his fingertips gently slid the smoked glass window up, soundlessly, then back into place. Stoney stepped into the tub, turned to face them, his eyes shut tight. "Now, we will assume that this is point of entry and it is dark now." His hands extended before him, his feet carefully moved, measuring the edge of the tub; he bent over, his hands on the side of the tub, and they stepped back clearing a pathway as he walked like a blind man, his fingers tracing the tile wall, guiding him toward the opened door, his hands moving lightly in the air, finding the dimensions of the doorway.

"Now, by this point, his eyes will have become somewhat accustomed to the darkness of the room," and then to Christie, his eyes opening, "we did this last night in the dark, Marty and the boss and I, and we noticed that if we left the toaster out there, on top of the stove, it picks up a glint of light and you can tell that's the kitchen area." Moving into the room now, eyes closed again, he pointed, "So, if I know that the kitchen area is to my left, I know that the bed will be to my right." His hand circled quickly and Christie passed him, sliding her body on the bed, her eyes on his approaching figure, edging closer to her, his knees lightly hitting the bed, his body bending, leaning toward her, but she spun quickly, so that when he opened his eyes, the bed was empty.

"Where'd she go?" he asked playfully. "I know she's here someplace!"

Christie propped her head on her arms along the edge of the bed. "Try down here," she said, trying to match his voice.

"Good. Only you slide yourself way down *under* the bed and you don't come out until I say."

"Right."

"Hey, Stoney old boss man, can we eat now?" Marty clicked the handle of the refrigerator impatiently.

Stoney's eyes glided about the room in despair. "We better let this man set a table or he'll be hollering all night and we don't want any hollering herein. Go ahead, Marty."

Marty filled the table with paper cartons of corned beef and pastrami and pickles and potato salad and coleslaw, then reached for a half-gallon bottle of milk, ignoring the groans. "Milk is good for you, good for you," he insisted.

Christie folded a piece of rye bread around a few slices of corned beef, eating without taste. Only Marty ate with any appetite, insulted that the others refused the milk. Christie put up a pot of water, grateful that Marty had remembered tea bags and instant coffee.

She wondered where Johnnie Devereaux was at that moment: or more exactly, where Murray Rogoff was, since wherever Rogoff was, Devereaux, tailing him since early afternoon, was close by. This last week of telephone calls had been the worst, the voice more and more intimate, more and more familiar, whispering in her ear, reaching into her, the image of the sixteen-year-old hairless boy forming: an image of horrible despair and panic. She had forced her own voice into a casual, conversational level: "Yes, this is Christie. Yes, I am fine. Yes, I am safe. Yes, thank you for calling, goodbye." God. Oh dear God, not saying anything more, the words shrieking through every part of her, but not saying anything.

"Say there, Christie." Stoney's voice was quiet but pulled at her, making her jaws work over the dry piece of sandwich she hadn't realized was between her teeth. "Did any of the fellows tell you about the 'particular problem' we have always had in our Squad?"

She shook her head. "What particular problem?"

"Well," Stoney said, "this is not generally known or discussed, as you will understand, but among the members of our Squad, there is not one real marksman. In fact, you might say, among the members of our Squad, there is hardly a qualified target-shooter."

Marty jammed a huge bite of pastrami sandwich between his jaws, wiped his mouth with a flowered paper napkin, and shook his head heavily at her. "Hey, Stoney, don't tell her about that now."

"Well, I think she has a right to know. Bill, what do you think?"

Seriously, carefully, Bill Ferranti said, "Well, *I'd* want to know."

She knew what they were doing: all of them. Pulling her and each other and themselves into the room, into the reality of the place, forcing the wandering complicated thoughts out and away: starting the easy, joking, relaxing story-telling which would put them here, aware of each other. Christie made herself respond, her voice mock-serious. "Well, I think somebody better tell me if it's something I should know."

Stoney's hand moved toward Bill Ferranti. Bill fingered his horn-rimmed glasses, "Well, I never can line up those little ridges in my gun sighting. In fact, last shooting cycle, I put two holes in Stoney's target, and he was *two* booths to my right."

"Yes," Stoney said sadly, "and those two holes were only in the five ring and didn't help me much." He extended his long brown arm across the table and his fingers trembled. He regarded them, clicking his tongue. "My hand shakes. Just a little. But just enough to throw me off."

They all waited for Marty to swallow his cold milk. "And me," he said, smearing a milk mustache on his paper napkin, "every time I go down to the range, my hand jumps in *anticipation* of the shot. I'm very sensitive to noise, you know, so just expecting the noise, before the shot is off, I get bugged and my shot always drops down to the left." He moved his arm in an arc. "Eight o'clock."

Becoming part of it, part of them, Christie's voice struck just the right note. "Well, gentlemen, that is all *very* reassuring to me. I'll tell you what—you're all going to be on *this* side of the room." Her hand pointed toward the bed, her index finger extending from her fist like the barrel of a gun. "And *I'm* going to be on that side of the room. And if there's going to be shooting, *that's* where the bullets will go. Now, how about we all reverse sides? *I'm* a good shot: no glasses, no tremors, no eight o'clocks!"

163

"Well, now, Christie, just because none of us are very good, that's not saying we can't hit *something*, right, fellas?"

Stoney's head twisted toward Marty and his voice was sharp, yet it was part of the game; Stoney was following Marty's cue. "Shut up about that, Marty."

"Yes," Ferranti said, "let's not discuss *that*, Marty."

Christie looked from face to face, admiring them; this was all by-play, yet it was essential. An establishing of lines of communication, of reading and responding. No one really knew what story Marty was about to tell, yet each would help him, filling in, building on it. It was more than time-passing, it was an interacting on a light and unimportant level: it was a rehearsal.

"I think there's something else I should know," she said.

"Well, if it was *me*, I'd want to know," Marty grumbled. "You tell her, Stoney."

Stoney smiled, blinked, settled back in the rickety wooden chair and began. They were like kids at a campfire, passing fragments of a story around. "Well now, you ever hear of a fella named Phil Jones?"

She shook her head. Marty sighed and covered his forehead. Bill clicked his tongue. "Well, old Phil," Stoney continued, ignoring Marty's "may-he-rest-in-peace," "was a member of our Squad some years ago. Well, we were all on a stake-out, similar to this, but of course the circumstances were different, but anyway, it was one of these things." His hands indicated the room. "Without going into detail . . ."

"No, don't go into detail," Bill said almost fervently, joined by Marty's voice, "No, don't."

"Well, old Phil, at any rate, took two." Stoney's hand touched the center of his forehead and then his heart.

"Two bullets? He was killed?"

"Honey," Marty said, "one in the head and one in the ticker. He was killed dead."

"And," Stoney said, "only Marty and Bill and I had guns. Our suspect, upon apprehension and further investigation was as they say 'clean.' "

The three men silently stared at their hands, all clasped and motionless on the table before them. "Well, what happened?" Christie asked.

164

Marty's head popped up. "We gave him an inspector's funeral, of course."

"And you know, Christie," Bill said in his quiet, humorless way, "I know that at times you've been annoyed at Mr. Reardon, but he does take care of his own. Right, Stoney?"

"He does indeed, Bill. Tell her."

It was Bill's part now. "Well, he knew how badly we all felt. Anyone would—after all, our own man. Mr. Reardon ordered the inspector's funeral *immediately*. He wouldn't let an autopsy be performed. Boy, he did some fast talking to get that pushed through."

"Yeah," Marty picked up on it. "After all, how the hell would old Stoney feel, knowing he had killed his own partner?"

"Me?" Stoney bellowed. "Why you ingrate: all these years the boss and I have been protecting you from that terrible knowledge, and now you try to put it on me!"

"Not me." Marty shook his heavy head. "Everyone knows I can't hit the broad side of a barn."

"But Phil wasn't a barn," Bill said quietly.

Marty began collecting the paper plates, finishing off odd pieces of food. "Not me, Stoney, but hell, if it makes you feel better, it's okay with me." He leaned across the table to Christie, whispering loudly, "It would be too tough for him to admit: hell, he was partners with the guy for six years."

"Well, fellows, I appreciate your complete honesty and I really think, under the circumstances, Stoney, you should let me keep my gun under the pillow. I'd only shoot if you got me first."

"Oh no, no," Stoney said. "Absolutely not. If one Squad member gets shot, we can cover, but if two of us got hit, it would look real bad. Bad for the Squad image!"

"Gee," Christie said, her voice young. "I wouldn't want to hurt the Squad image. I'm sorry, I wasn't thinking."

At seven P.M. there was an impatient thud at the door and a muffled, familiar voice. "Reardon," it said, and Ferranti opened the door. Reardon barreled in, sniffing, wrinkling his short nose. "Smells like a delicatessen in here! My God, Ginsburg, you eating pickles and drinking milk?"

Marty innocently held up his glass. "Milk is very good for

165

you, Mr. Reardon. They even give it to babies nowadays."

"Stoney, you better have a good talk with that guy. Remind me to issue an order relative to meeting Squad regulations re height and weight. Marty, you are putting on too much weight."

"I know, Mr. Reardon," Marty said sadly, "and it worries me, so when I worry I eat. It's a syndrome or something."

Christie watched him and began to feel cold now and still and aware: it was not a game. Reardon moved rapidly about the room, squatting down behind a chair, his head cocked to one side, easing himself into the position where Ferranti would be, placing himself inside the small closet. "You sure Ginsburg will fit in here?"

"Yeah, but I'm not too sure if he'll be able to get out."

"I'll get out, Stoney, don't worry, I'll get out."

Reardon crossed to the bed, sat beside Christie who let the magazine fall opened on her lap. He bounced lightly. "Feels pretty comfortable. Don't fall asleep on us, Opara."

"I'll be awake, Mr. Reardon."

He stood up, looked down at her, then asked Stoney, "Hey, how come you got Opara dressed up like a little boy again? I can't see anyone busting into a room after her in those dungarees and—Opara, at least tuck your shirttail in!"

"She'll be hitting the deck, boss, and I think she'd do it better not having to worry about a dress riding up and all."

"Umm, I guess." He strode into the bathroom, and she could hear the window sliding up and down and then he was back, standing in the center of the room, and they all watched him. The bantering tones had left his voice which was flatly informative now. "I just gave Jimmy O'Neill a wave: he's at his post—you know where. Right, Stoney?"

Stoner Martin nodded. "Two windows up and three across; in the building directly across from us."

"Right. Now, the two other Homicide men are three doors down the hallway. They're not going to move until"—he corrected himself—"*unless* they hear action in here." He moved to the door, checking. "Good, leave this on the latch in case our boy decides to use the door, but I don't think he will." His eyes, and theirs, turned toward the bathroom. "He'll come in the window if he comes at all."

He will, Christie told him silently, and Reardon's eyes, on hers, saw it and she knew he saw it. *He will.*

"Sam Farrell will call you in about"—he consulted his watch—"in about ten minutes just for a check ring. Now, after that check call and for the remainder of this assignment, no one will use that telephone to make a call." Their eyes were now all on the strangely old-fashioned black telephone on the small combination lamp and table placed near Stoney's hand, against the plush chair. "Here's what to anticipate after the check call: *if* suspect calls Opara's house, as soon as that call is completed, Farrell will ring here and play back the tape. Devereaux is on Rogoff right now. As soon as suspect makes his call, you'll get the relay, then I'll get it. I'll be in my car, which is parked across the street from access to the alley. If suspect—and we are assuming he'll make his call from Queens—if suspect then heads toward Manhattan, Devereaux, if he can, will give me a blast on my car telephone; as soon as I get the word, I'll call here and let you know." They all listened silently, their faces solemn and still, their eyes between Reardon and the telephone, none of them looking at each other. "*Then*"— Casey paused, his eyes turning to the phone now—"when and if suspect hits this block—and I'm located where I can see both entrance to the alley and entrance to the building, I will give you just one blast on the telephone. Don't answer it—that's the signal that he is in the immediate vicinity. Any questions?"

Marty opened his mouth, saw Casey's eyes, changed his mind and shook his head.

"Now, this is important: under *no* circumstances is anyone to make a call. There will be a lack of communication. I realize that, but we will all be waiting it out and if it goes through the night, it goes through the night. Nothing might happen, no calls at all." He shrugged. "Ya never know, right?"

They all nodded. He put his hand lightly on Stoney's shoulder, but he was speaking directly to Christie now. "Stoney is in charge, he is the boss here."

"Right," Stoney said, "I am the boss!"

Reardon shoved him, his voice a growl. "Not with me in the room, you're not, buddy!"

"Well, then, Mr. Reardon, sir, how come you don't leave and let me be boss now?"

"Well, I got one problem that I didn't want to mention, but I'd better tell you, fellas." Reardon lowered his voice including them all in his bantering confidence. "This is one helluva building; I mean, there is P.D. brass all over the place, across the street, up and down the block, practically breathing down our necks, and this building is a trap for an honest man. See, there's a little blonde down the hall there." He looked over his shoulder. "I was given an unmistakable set of little signals when I came into the building." Pulling his mouth down, Reardon said, "I don't want any of *that*, naturally, so, Stoney, since you're in charge, will you assign Opara to give me a safe escort to the front door?"

Stoner's tongue clicked. "Age finally takes its toll; never thought the day would come when Casey Reardon needed the protective escort of a policewoman against the advances of a blonde!"

Smoothly slipping in his punchline, Reardon said, "The blond is a *fella!*"

Not joining the easy, relaxed laughter, Reardon gestured impatiently to Christie. "C'mon, come on, Opara, I have to move." He grasped her arm, then stopped for a moment, his eyes meeting each man in turn, locking for one split moment of communicated but unstated concern. "It's all yours now, fellas; stay loose."

She didn't know whether he was kidding, but Reardon pulled her into the hallway with him, pushed her against the wall, then he glanced over his shoulder for a moment. His fingers pressed her arm and he leaned his face to her ear. "There, the bastard," he whispered, "see the crack in that door? He wriggles in and out." His thumb jerked behind him. "Tell you what, Opara, let's straighten him out about me, okay?" He pulled her toward him, pressing his lips lightly on hers, then moved away, his eyes not on hers. "Is he looking?"

Christie tried to see Reardon's face in the yellow-lit

darkness of the hallway; she moved back but her shoulders were against the wall. She raised herself on her toes, trying to see some face behind the small crack in the door. Reardon's face, half hidden in the dimness, seemed serious. "I think he's watching. Yes, he just ducked back behind the door, but he is watching."

"Well, we ought to fool him, huh?" Reardon's lips were against her ear and his breath was warm. "Hey, did you shrink or what? You weren't always this short, were you?" Still gripping on her arm he took a step back. "Oh, yeah, you got your sneakers on again. For pete's sake, you're not very tall at all, are you?"

She started to answer, but his face was suddenly against hers again and he asked, earnestly, "He looking again? I heard the door move!"

Not understanding his concern, but caught up in his seriousness, she stretched her neck, tilted her face up, then her eyes came back to his and she had some vague impression that he was making fun of her. "Why are you so worried that some little mixed-up blond wrong-o might get the wrong impression about you?"

He grinned at the fresh, mocking tone and his hands moved along her shoulders to her neck. "Hell, I'm always concerned about creating a wrong impression. I like to keep the image intact. At all times."

"What image?" she asked, and his lips pressed against hers again, only slightly harder this time, taking a little longer to withdraw, and when he moved his face back, his eyes seemed almost red.

"Relax, Opara, relax. You don't think that was for you, do you? That was for cutie, behind me," he whispered.

Christie smiled now, released from the pressure of his mouth, released from whatever had held back the words that could match and top him; her voice was firm and clear and loud in the narrow corridor. "Okay, Dad, and you tell Mom I'm all settled in and I'll be just fine here."

Reardon's eyes narrowed and his voice was tough and low. "You little wise-guy, you have to have the last word, don't you?" Then, his hands reached behind her head, his fingers plunged roughly through her short, thick light hair.

"Okay, honey," he said, "we'll give cutie in there something that'll send him running to his Freud books," and now Reardon's mouth was on hers, firmly, strongly, surprisingly full and warm, and Christie, not expecting it, anticipating another light, teasing, playful kiss, accepted it, then, startled, tried to turn away, then stood, motionless, her hands hanging limply, but not really motionless: participating, but not really participating, surprised again by the gently affectionate touch of his hand along her earlobe, the quick caressing of her cheek and chin as he withdrew from her and walked briskly down the length of the hallway. Reardon turned for just a moment before leaving and called to her, "So long, Daughter. I'll tell Mom you're just fine, yes sir, just fine!"

Christie heard a small, harsh gasp and the sharp closing of an apartment door and the fumbling of a chain lock being slid into place but her eyes stayed down the length of the hallway. She touched her lips lightly with her fingers, closing her eyes for a moment. Her heart was pounding and she wasn't quite sure how she felt: amused? angry? what?

At 9:32 P.M., the telephone rang. It wasn't a particularly loud ring: it didn't blast through an intense silence, for they had been story-telling, reminiscing, teasing, joking, arguing. Yet the sound cut through their cross-conversations as clearly and shockingly as the spattering of a live electric wire tossed suddenly in their midst and three masculine hands lunged, simultaneously, for the instrument as though it were somehow vital that it not be permitted to ring again.

"I got it, I got it," Stoney said in the voice of an outfielder warding off unwanted assistance. The eyes of the others fixed on Stoney's face and they moved toward him.

"Yeah, Sam, Stoney here." He glanced at his watch, nodding. "Yeah, yeah, go ahead and play it." Then, his hand over the receiver, "The call came."

Stoney held the receiver slightly away from his ear, but the voices were so clearly familiar that Christie would have heard them had her head been buried beneath sand.

"Hello?" Nora. Friendly and pleasant.

170

"Hello, Christie? Is this Christie Opara?" The voice went through her body like a needle: the faceless nighttime voice. They were all watching her now, dropping their eyes as she met theirs.

"No, Christie isn't here." Quickly. Nora said it quickly, not giving him time to continue the pacing of his own conversation, stopping him, forcing him to *listen*.

There was a silence now lasting a full five seconds and Marty groaned as the same thought flashed through everyone: Sam Farrell had loused it up. But Stoney's hand impatiently kept them quiet.

And then, "I want to talk to Christie Opara." The voice was hoarsely insistent.

No pause. "Christie moved away from here, you see. She moved out this morning, to a place of her own." Nora, sounding so cheerful and reasonable.

Again a pause, a little longer this time. Their minds held the singular thought: the caller would hang up.

But the voice again, different, a strange quality, somewhere between anger and panic. "Where did she move to?"

No one in the room breathed. Nora's voice, easy, relaxed, "Do you have a pencil? I'll give you her address."

Quickly, "I want her phone number."

"No, she hasn't had a phone installed yet." Don't say that, Nora; don't say *yet!* He'll hang up and call back tomorrow for the number; oh God, Nora, that was a mistake.

But the voice, "Yes. I have paper. Wait a minute." A muffled, digging around sound, a heavy sigh. "Okay."

Listening to Nora's voice, carefully spelling out the address, giving the apartment number, Christie felt the sense of unreality bearing down on her; the pleasant casual insignificant conversation was so out of keeping with her surroundings, with the circumstances. She studied the faces of the men, huddled in a small semi-circle around Stoney; nothing around her balanced. The two voices speaking from the telephone, asking for and giving information, the normal, polite exchange of goodbyes, the clicking of the two receivers yet the call not disconnected and now, Sam Farrell's voice, normal, familiar. "That's it, Stoney. I hung up and dialed your number as soon as he disconnected."

"Right," Stoney said. "You did fine, Sam." And now Sam was out of it; staying beside Nora until ordered to leave, but out of it, finished and done with it.

Stoney's hand still rested on the telephone. "Marty, you spoke with Rogoff. What do you say? Recognize the voice?"

Marty shrugged. "Hard to say; yes and no."

"It is Rogoff." They all turned, no one questioning the cold hard certainty in Christie's voice.

At 9:42 P.M. the telephone rang again. It seemed less sharp, less insistent this time, but Stoner Martin grabbed it midway in the first ring. "Martin here. Right. Right, Casey."

He replaced the receiver on the cradle and said softly, "Devereaux just called Casey from the subway station; they're waiting for a Manhattan-bound IRT." Stoney lit a new cigarette from the inch-long glow between his fingers, smashed out the stub, blew smoke around his head. "Devereaux and Rogoff," he said quietly.

"Of course Rogoff," Christie said to no one in particular. "Who'd you think it would be, Devereaux and Santa Claus?"

Stoney said evenly, "Now the next time, it will be a one-ring blast and then it should be a matter of minutes. Marty, take a run around the corner and alert Jimmy O'Neill that his partner is close on suspect and that they are on their way, then tap on the door down the hall and tell the other Homicide men." Stoney picked up a magazine, slumping into the upholstered chair, his long legs dangling over the arm.

Ferranti adjusted the gas higher under the glass pot of water, spooning instant coffee into a mug. He stood watching the odd shapes of the orange fire under the tall, transparent, slightly roiling water. It was like a flower with long bright tentacles reaching out from a blue center. He poured boiling water into his cup and adjusted the flame so that Marty could have a cup of coffee when he returned.

Christie walked into the bathroom, shutting the door behind her. For a moment, she stood in the darkness, then switched on the light, gazing without recognition at her reflection in the small scarred mirror over the sink. Her cheeks seemed drawn in, her mouth was tight. She ran the cold water full strength, cupping it into her hands, sloshing the coolness over her face, but it seemed to turn warm on contact with her skin. She filled her mouth from her hands then let the water run back into the sink, finally swallowing a mouthful, but it did not slake her thirst nor the dryness that was not only in her mouth but deep inside her throat. Not reaching yet for one of the paper towels on the roller directly under the mirror, Christie turned sideways, holding her dripping hands out before her. No tremor: not the slightest tremble. She regulated her breath, remembering one of Nora's endless yoga exercises: empty the lungs completely, force out the air even though there doesn't seem to be anything left because there is some stale pocketful of air stagnating inside. Feeling emptied to the point of suffocation, Christie slowly drew new breath into her but the air was heavy and unclean and gave no sense of purification or revitalization. She ran the water again, on the insides of her wrists, then blotted her face and hands on the scratchy paper towels, but, stopped by the eyes in the mirror, she could see that her face was wet again, sprinkled with small drops of perspiration. She felt the damp clinging all along her back: the lightweight cotton shirt glued to her body. She pushed the tail-ends into her dungarees which had become part of her skin. She ran her fingers through her hair, then across her neck, stretched her face, pulling her lips back into an exaggerated smile, then let them ease back into a normal expression.

Switching off the light, Christie carefully stepped into the bathtub, raised the window an inch or so, hunched down so that her eyes could scan the darkness of the small, common courtyard formed by the arrangements of tenement houses, back to back on a square block of city street; her eyes found the alleyway and her lips said quietly into the emptiness: *"I'm ready for you; I'm ready."* Her eyes closed now, she carefully slid the window to exactly the location Stoney had placed it, her fingers measuring the distance. Then she went back into the room.

Marty broke into their silence, his eyes glowing. "Man,

you should see what Jimmy O'Neill's got going for him up there!" His hands traced voluptuous forms in the air.

"Knock it off, Marty," Bill Ferranti said, his voice unexpectedly angry.

"Not me," Marty said innocently, "but hell, if Jimmy up there don't knock it off, he's crazy!"

Bill's voice was tight and unfamiliar and he stood up, putting his cup of coffee on the edge of the table. "Watch that kind of talk, Marty." His chin jutted toward Christie and she blinked at him.

"Don't shush him on my account, Bill. Frankly, I wasn't listening. I didn't even hear what he said."

"Well, what I said was . . ."

Stoney steered Marty to the stove, taking control now. "Have your cuppa and fill your mouth with a few pickles, Marty. It's too hot to get tense." Stoney poured the steaming water into a cup, then carefully closed the marbleized black and white tin cover over the burners, then placed the toaster, a shining, aluminum four-slicer, in place. "Little old toaster," he intoned, "you are an important part of this here little old plan and if you do your job properly and guide our suspect well, we will reward you handsomely by eating anything—regardless of condition—that pops out of you."

"Except raisin toast," Marty said, his eyes on the toaster. "Because with raisin toast, unless you count carefully before the bread goes down, you never *really* know if any of the raisins are actually bugs when the toast pops up!"

They all had casually positioned themselves about the room now, Stoner Martin leaning against the arm of the chair, Marty squatting beside the closet, Ferranti taking his half-empty cup with him as he eased himself to the top of the waist-high refrigerator.

Christie sat stiffly on the edge of the bed, her back straight, her hands over her knees. The denim clung heavily to her thighs and constricted her movements. There were no sounds in the room except for the occasional swallowing, as the men finished their tepid coffee.

"I think," Stoner Martin said, "that we will turn out the lights now and maintain a modicum of silence." His hand reached out, clicked the yellow circle of light over his head.

Ferranti pushed the silent button over the refrigerator, obliterating the purplish cast from the fluorescent tube.

"I can see the toaster," Christie said from the bed. "It does pick up a glint of light."

"Into the closet, Martin, and do not fall asleep." But Marty was already in the closet as Ferranti was already settled behind the half-wall of the alcove and Stoney was down now, behind the chair, and Christie was stretched full length on the creaking bed.

"Stoney?" Marty's voice was different in the dark now; serious, no more joking. "Question."

"Yeah?"

"When the lights go on, won't we be blinded from all this darkness? I mean, hell, how will we see good enough?"

There was a silence as they all visualized the stabbing glare of sudden light. Then, Stoney, softly, "This little light here is pretty dim. We'll do the best we can: we'll be fine."

[18]

MURRAY ROGOFF sat huddled on the wicker seat of the slow-moving IRT train, his arms wrapped around his knees, his chin pressed into his locked hands. The train came to a hesitant, not-quite-completed halt, then lurched forward a few feet, then picked up speed steadily until it was careening through the black tunnel, but Murray Rogoff was too filled with other things to notice the irregular movements of the train. His eyes, opened wide behind the enclosure of his glasses, saw no further than the smudge marks.

He had known there was something wrong. All day, working in the store, he had felt it, known it. His hands closed even tighter against each other. His teeth moved hard, grinding the words inside his mouth: What kind of a mother was that woman? What kind of a mother? To let a girl like Christie move to a place like the Village. What kind of mother was she?

He had kept his voice steady; he had kept all the anger and fury from his voice and from his words but not from inside himself; it grew surely and fully when the calm voice told him, "Christie moved out this morning." Moved out: as though the woman had no idea what kind of place her daughter had moved to. Murray's eyes remembered the woman: small and crisp and clean and taking the little boy by the hand, carefully fussing over him, smiling at him. *That was it!* She wanted to be alone with her little son. That was why she had made Christie move out, made her leave that safe, good brick house, attached to all those other nice houses, all lined up neat with small flower gardens and patios on one side of the street and the old wooden houses facing them. God, it had been so hard to find the place where Christie lived; so hard to make sure it was a safe place with all those sharp-eyed old women who had nothing better to do than watch anyone who walked past their houses. But he had been careful: Murray knew how to watch without being seen.

Everything had been so hard: how could he keep watch over Christie when she worked at some crazy job with some crazy hours? Coming home every night at a different time: it was wrong for a girl like Christie, walking those long dark blocks in Queens. They seemed to think it was way out in the country, all safe and quiet, but they didn't know what could happen. Murray's mind whirled with images and pieces of things that did not fall into place and he closed his eyes against all the things he could not understand.

What had Christie to do with Frankie Santino? Then, Murray smiled behind his hands: she knew how to talk to pigs like Frankie Santino. That day in the hallway of the court building, she had cut Frankie dead like so much gutter dirt, which is what Frankie Santino was and always had been and always would be. He remembered her face and her voice: the kind of face a girl like Christie always turned to a bum like Frankie and the kind of voice she saved for punks like that.

The tormenting, puzzling mystery of *why* Christie had been there that day no longer bothered him, because Murray knew the important thing was that she *had* been there and that he had seen her and she had seen him and that they had looked at each other. His smile widened and Murray felt good, yet the nagging worry bit into his happiness forcing him to remember that something was wrong and that Christie was not living at home anymore with her mother and little brother but had moved to some dump in the Village and that he had to find her.

Murray Rogoff walked along the narrow Greenwich Village street deliberately slamming his hard body into all the queers who tried to block his way, leaving behind him a trail of shrieking insults. He knew they would love nothing better than for him to turn back, rough them up a little: touch them again. His hands deep in the pockets of his chinos, Murray walked with long steps, seeing only the sidewalk before him, using his wide shoulders to sweep a path for himself. His eyes saw the net stockings and spike heels of the whores, heard the dirty low voices of the pimps, but his eyes never met theirs. He walked through them with one terrible knowledge: this is where Christie must walk now, through them. They could reach out and touch her. God. Oh God. What kind of mother?

He stood now leaning his large arm on the sticky counter of an orangeade stand, his lungs filling with the sour smells of pizza and juice. He watched pale liquid slosh around and up and over within the dirty glass bubble of the juice machine; he pointed to it, accepted the glass from the pimply boy who bounced his dime change at him, absently put the coin in his pocket. His eyes saw none of the bodies around him, and they, realizing that whatever it was he sought did not include them, shrugged. Nothing about the giant of a man interested them: not the odd-shaped skull which continued from beneath the plaid cap into the collar of his white knit shirt; not the strange welder-goggles which hid half his face nor the massively muscled arms. His eyes discounted them and they, intent on searches of their own needs, discounted him.

Rogoff's eyes were fixed on the tenement building directly across the street. A four-story tenement, surrounded up and down the block by identical structures, each opening directly onto the street. The hall would be long and narrow and badly lit. In one long gulp, Murray let the cold and tasteless liquid run down his throat, feeling it plunge into his chest with a coldness that did not cool him, but merely created a passing sensation of pain.

Without hesitation, without consulting the slip of paper in his pants pocket, Rogoff strode across the street, pushed the door open with his rubber-soled shoe. These doors were never locked; the hallway, too, was what he had expected: nothing surprised him. The two electric bulbs on the high ceiling glowed yellow in small circles which did not penetrate the darkness. Not stopping, going directly to the long, narrow stairway, Murray Rogoff took the steps easily, two at a time. Three long flights were nothing; he stopped at the top landing, pushed his cap back, then leaned his face close to the door of the apartment nearest to him, his fingers rubbing, searching for something. The lettering had long since been obliterated; he moved to the next door and it was the right one: 4-C—directly in line. Rogoff took the next flight of stairs soundlessly, pushing against the sticking door with his shoulder, feeling a sudden rush of air against his face. But it was only breeze caused by the pressure of the door opening suddenly onto the roof, for the night air was still and heavy and breathless as Murray, walking with some strange and quiet shrewdness, rolled his feet on the tarpaper surface. He stood motionless: no bodies lying against chimneys, no whispers or laughter. The roof was deserted.

Crouching now, Murray moved carefully, sliding himself to the edge of the unprotected roof, and looked down, his mind holding his purpose to the exclusion of all other thought: there was a little courtyard below and the windows of the apartments in the "C" line opened onto that little courtyard and that was what Murray needed to know. His eyes, seeing well in the darkness, studied it like a road map all sketched out for him: the narrow alley cutting between the buildings like a path, leading into the courtyard, leading like a beam of light to the window four stories down, directly beneath where he now lay. Counting, he calculated exactly where the street location of the opening to the alley was and, this firmly in his mind, Murray stood up, inhaled with a gasp, for the air seemed to contain no oxygen, seemed to be choking him and his head ached and his eyes burned and for the moment, he had the strangest feeling: as if he had just fallen from the roof into the courtyard below, or that his body, rocking forward now, was going to fall.

Rogoff had to get away from this place: had to get on the street again. He spun around looking for direction, then, no longer concerned about sound or footsteps, he ran heavily across the seemingly endless series of roofs until his eyes picked out a structure and he lunged his body against the door which didn't move and then he pulled at it and thudded down the long flight of narrow stairs. He sucked the night air into his lungs and walked with rapid, heavy strides along the safety of the sidewalk.

Johnnie Devereaux, standing in the darkness, pressed his body against the crumbling brick structure of a chimney and felt unavoidable reality race through him like an uneven pulse. His lips moved silently over the words that he could taste inside his mouth: Jesus, Mary and Joseph, I've lost him. Jesus, Mary and Joseph, I've lost him.

But the desperation was checked immediately by that calmer voice which took over instinctively, as he knew it would. Okay. So you lost him for a minute or two. So he took off into another building. Did you expect him to drop pebbles for you? There's only one place he'd head for now: the alley.

Detective Jimmy O'Neill's legs were aching. Kneeling on the hard floor, his long torso made it necessary for him to bend down in order for his eyes to be level with the two inches of space between the shade and the window sill. He couldn't adjust the shade to better advantage because he knew that then his head would be outlined, darker against the darkness of the opened window.

To keep his vision certain, he had to glance away periodically from the two figures on the roof across the alley and he had found a fantastic contrast for his vigil: on the fourth floor of the building adjacent to the stake-out there was an orange-headed girl, and for the life of him, Jimmy O'Neill couldn't figure what the hell she was doing, but Christ, whatever it was, she sure was doing it great. There were no shades on her window, which was thrown open, and she would appear suddenly across the rectangle, gyrating to some music, then disappear into the recesses of her room.

But Jimmy O'Neill, who had watched the odd, continuing movements steadily for the last hour, glanced there now only as a necessary part of his job: to keep his eyes sharp. From the moment he had heard the one piercing ring of the telephone, clearly reaching him from across the courtyard, the orange-haired girl aroused no feelings whatever within him. His interest was directed solely on the two figures who moved about the roofs across from him. Figure number one was suspect: Christ, even from this distance, outlined against the gray sky, Jimmy could see he was tremendous. Devereaux was harder to spot and probably the only reason

180

O'Neill knew there was a second figure was because he had worked as Devereaux's partner for four years.

This bastard is shrewd as hell, O'Neill thought with grudging admiration. Reconnoitering: placing the apartment, then the alleyway, then leaving the roof via a different route; it was tough on John. Tough to do a close tail job under the circumstances. The long even line of roofs was deserted now and Jimmy O'Neill let his eyes rest for a few moments; the orange head flashed by, then her body spun around: Christ! She was stripped from the waist up! A flash of breast moved past the window, then disappeared. Jimmy O'Neill dug his long bony fingers into his watering eyes, then with great determination, he concentrated on the concrete courtyard two stories below him, becoming familiar with its dimensions and shapes and shadows. That's where the next action would be.

John Devereaux entered the alley like a phantom: without sound and without form. He let his body blend with shadows, moving only against that part of the wall where no dim light from some window touched, crossing with a short step whenever necessary so that he stayed part of the darkness.

John Devereaux didn't breathe because automatically he stopped breathing at moments like this. He had learned long ago that there are times when a man can go for a very considerable period of time without drawing in or letting out breath. His eyes narrowed, darting rapidly around the small yard, first to the particular window, which had not yet been raised, then to all the corners, into all the shadows and all the dimly lighted places.

John Devereaux softly exhaled all the stagnant air and soundlessly drew in another portion, moving carefully against the wall of a building. Once again, the words filled him and his lips twitched: *Jesus, Mary and Joseph. I've lost the bastard!*

Casey Reardon slumped in the front seat of the black Pontiac, his knees digging into the dashboard, his arms folded across his chest. He licked the beads of sweat which collected over his lip, glanced again at his watch, which registered a minute more than the last time he had consulted it, which was twenty minutes from the moment he had dialed the telephone, letting it ring once to indicate subject was in the area. Though Casey had been silent for all the intervening time, Dell spoke now as though in response to him.

"Want me to check it out, boss?"

Reardon hesitated, shook his head. He wondered how Dell could look so cool and uninvolved, because he *knew* Dell was keyed up too. "We wait," Reardon said, his eyes watching the alleyway, trying to figure out why Devereaux had gone in but Rogoff had not.

Christie felt her left arm growing numb and carefully trying to prevent the grating noises caused by the slightest movement on the bed, she raised her head. She had to lift her deadened arm with her right hand, biting her lip against the sudden assault of pain as feeling returned in aching waves of pins and needles.

Her mouth fell open as though that would help her to hear: her eyes sought the direction of the sound. A slight, bumping sound from the kitchen area. Or was it from the bathroom?

In a whisper so light it was hardly heard, "Sorry. That was me." Ferranti.

She couldn't hear the release of breath, but she knew Marty and Stoney had resumed breathing as well as she. How long had it been since that single crashing ring of the telephone? It was impossible to measure time now and there was no slight glimmer of light by which she could read the dial of her watch which was supposed to glow in the dark, but didn't. There was nothing to measure time by except her own feeling and that wasn't accurate because her body became a stranger to her mind: transformed by the single, anticipated, yet somehow unexpected ring of a telephone. She was filled with internal rushes so sudden and so distinct the only thing that surprised her was that the sounds within her didn't echo and bounce all over the room.

There was a soft, slow, hesitant, opening sound, heard despite the rushes of internal noises, distinct and separate in the darkness.

It was followed by Marty's voice, hollow and low. "Time?" he whispered carefully and she could hear Stoney moving.

"Ten forty-five."

They all calculated it: the single ring of the phone came at exactly 10:10 P.M. Thirty-five minutes ago. Thirty-five minutes of waiting.

Where was he? Where in God's name was Rogoff?

For Murray Rogoff, the world was a pit of corruption hemmed by lightless cabarets which opened unashamed onto the heated sidewalks, spilling over with wordless, degraded voices emanating from the throats of faceless sub-human inhabitants. In long and hurried strides, direction-less, he strode among them, the anger building into a form-less fury, winding its way from his intestines upward into his chest and lungs, downward into his thighs and knees, until his entire being was one pulsating mass of thoughtless emotion. He flung the touching, inquisitive bodies from him in a horror of contamination, knowing he must find release from the filth in which he found himself.

Wandering the streets of Greenwich Village, his mind could not grasp the steady, clear and certain salvation that somehow he knew was hidden within him, elusive and stolen from him by the narrowed, glinting eyes, the simper-ing voices, the brushing bodies that approached him hope-fully, curiously, lustfully. His eyes burned beneath the encasement of his glasses and he pulled them from his face. His fingers dug at the sockets which itched dryly and ached in response to his rough touch. The sounds became a part of him: part of his being, the blatant noises echoing behind him, around him, before him as he rushed around a corner only to be confronted by the discordant moanings of some singer whose voice came at him as through a long tunnel, reaching out from the cavern of some cafe. His eyes moved constantly behind his glasses again, watching the tourists: gaping, not daring to enter the tempting, sawdust-floored

183

interiors, but their eyes shining in a particular way, fascinated by the strangeness around them, trying to proclaim their own innocence by their reluctance to participate, yet their longings clearly visible, gleaming from their eyes and on their dry lips, licked by furtive tongues.

And all the time, down all the streets, the hunger built within him: the hunger for cleanness and purity and love, which could not be found here on these streets.

Finally, Murray Rogoff stopped, halting in the middle of the street, his mind freed at last from his surroundings. Stretching his arms over his head, his voice raised in a great sob of relief, unmindful of the curious or wishful stares of the other searchers, Murray Rogoff's brain relayed the message that had been there all the time, beneath the turmoil, waiting for him to recognize it.

He could walk through them now, untouched, unused, and uncorrupted. He knew where his freedom and his joy and his happiness was: he knew where love was and the image of Christie Opara destroyed all the vileness around him. With a great feeling of reality, Rogoff carefully looked around him and carefully and purposefully headed in a definite direction.

John Devereaux was a patient man and he had learned through bitter experience that a police officer cannot afford the luxury of impatience. He was accustomed to waiting and he waited with a certainty based on years of experience, but even the certainty could not completely control the spurts of anxiety which pumped irregularly through him.

He sifted the facts once again, for in facts there was something to hold onto: One—subject had located room and entry thereto; two—subject, for reasons known only to himself, had decided not to make entry; three—he had lost all contact with subject; four—he, John Devereaux, could not leave this alleyway if hell froze over, unless instructed to do so by Reardon (and omiGod what must he be thinking?) or until daylight, since subject might change his mind and enter the alley after all. So that *in* fact, the fact was that it was Rogoff who was making all the decisions.

John Devereaux was a man who could think like a machine. He was also a man who could experience very human emotions and during the approximately one and a half hours he had clung to the shadows of this particular alleyway, he felt an exhaustion close to despair and a helplessness bordering on anger and a deep regret that he could not light up a cigarette and inhale just one lungful of nicotine and a sorrow that he could not ease off his shoes and spread his swelling toes.

To keep his brain alert, Devereaux devised small mental games, testing his awareness: scanning an entire line of tenement windows, turning his face, then mentally recalling what each window had contained, in proper order. He wondered what technique O'Neill was using: probably keeping tabs on that nutty babe up there. She was inexhaustible, whatever the hell she was doing. He wondered what they were doing in the room: each one cut off like he was, each working out some kind of mental gymnastics, fighting off sleep, which incredibly could easily weigh them all down. Including him. *Christ, where was the bastard?*

Jimmy O'Neill had known within the first two minutes that the figure in the alley was John Devereaux because if the shapeless form had been the suspect, there would have been a *second* figure in the alley and *that* would have been Devereaux. But there was just one man down there and Jimmy calculated, accurately and sympathetically, what had happened. The bastard had given John the slip and John stationed himself in the target area, and Jimmy O'Neill, through the period of time he spent kneeling and waiting and watching, offered up some fervent prayers on behalf of Devereaux and himself and all the others concerned that the bastard would show.

If there had been any slightest doubt in Jimmy's mind of the identity of the man hidden in the alley—and there really wasn't—that doubt would have been dissipated now.

A second figure had entered the alley and O'Neill's eyes, professionally sharpened by his vigil, picked out the shape as identical with that of the giant he had spotted on the roof over an hour and a half before. Coldly and clearly, O'Neill's mind registered the circumstance: Rogoff is now in the courtyard.

John Devereaux stopped breathing as automatically as a diver who plunges into cold deep water without apparatus of any kind. Knowing that he was invisible within the particular shadow he inhabited, he pressed still closer against the wall, watching the large, agile form moving cautiously but steadily across the courtyard, stopping for a moment, listening, looking without seeing, then moving again. Devereaux's eyes left the suspect for just one quick glance at the window on the second floor behind him, then fastened themselves on Rogoff, assured that Jimmy O'Neill would move out onto the fire escape and begin his climb down the instant Rogoff's body was inside the bathroom window.

The silence within the room was a special kind of silence, not total and complete, but composed of two distinct layers. The first layer was made up of sounds: the sounds of radios and TV sets and whirrings of fans and voices talking behind opened windows and children whimpering their useless protests against the heat. These sounds could be ignored for they were all accounted for and after a while did not have to be listened to: they tended to press together into a kind of steady hum that did not interfere with the concentration required of the inhabitants of the room.

The second layer was distinctive within the room: it was the purposeful silence of the occupants, breached occasionally by a shifting of body weight, a stifled cough. A deliberate, wordless silence enforced by Stoner Martin, his voice softly furious a long time back (when? hours?) when Marty Ginsburg had absent-mindedly begun to hum in the blackness of his closet floor and Stoney had tossed it at all of them: We are waiting this out; get with it. I'll bash the next goddamn head that makes a sound; if it takes all night, we wait!

Her body had relaxed dangerously and Christie was unable to revive the string-tight awareness, the readiness; she was filled with a dull, unreal, sleepy lack of emotion, all feelings had been nakedly bared too long ago, had receded now, and she felt numb and empty.

The sound was soft and sliding: a hesitant, tentative sound which ceased momentarily so that Christie, lying there, the saliva in her mouth not swallowed, waited. She waited for a quick, soft voice of apology: Ferranti, regretting the movement of his numbed leg, or Marty, mentioning a cramped foot, followed by Stoney's angry grunt. But the silence now was completely intensified so that when the sliding sound began again, there was no question of its origin and Christie felt her body, suddenly alive again, begin to fill with terrible pounding, stabbing sensations.

She could visualize the sound: the raising of a body over the window sill, the slow and careful easing of a body into the bathtub, the feet hesitating, the hands extended, taking measure of the room, seeking the doorway. Christie moved carefully on the bed, her teeth clamped down at the sound of the bedsprings, and then she realized that she was not the one who had to maintain an absolute silence. *She* was the one who had to be present, by the movement of bedsprings, by the agonizingly controlled, steady, deep breathing of a sleeper, and she regulated her breath, hearing it fill the room with a peaceful quiet rhythm, though her lungs felt as if they would explode if she didn't suddenly fill them with a huge gasp of air.

The feet were nearly silent, yet Christie could feel the weight of each step as though the feet were encased in lead boots, each step moving nearer, then stopping in the doorway from the bathroom. The absolute silence encompassed her, drew her into the center of a large, inescapable circle of loneliness, and no one existed in the room except Christie Opara and Murray Rogoff. The absolute silence had destroyed Bill Ferranti and Stoner Martin and Marty Ginsburg. Lying rigidly on her side, she was able to pick out the form of the man: huge, hesitant, seeking her, and it was only right that they were alone for she had known all along that she would have to face him out: alone.

Christie saw Rogoff more surely, more certainly, more clearly in that one split-instant of recognition than she had ever seen anyone before in her lifetime, yet her breath continued in and out, softly and without variation, untouched by the stark, pure stab of terror that raced through every part of her body.

"Christie, Christie Opara," the telephone voice called. She heard, as she had not heard in all the nights past when that voice had chanted into her ear, a sound so desolate and empty that all sense of time and place left her and the cold, technical words of a medical report were translated within her brain to the suddenly deformed and frightened boy of sixteen who stood beside her, asking for her help. She felt her hand reach up, felt her fingers make contact with cold and smooth flesh but her gesture had no more reality than a dream.

The abrupt flooding of the room with yellow light and sound and cries and screams and bursts of explosion took her by surprise as though it had all been unanticipated.

She heard the voice, simultaneous with the yellow light, "Duck, Christie!" yet she could not have said whose voice it was that had propelled her off the bed. Her body hit the floor, worked its way immediately under the bed. Whose voice had shouted, "Police!" "Christ! He's got a knife!" "Drop it!"? There was a tangle of voices and sounds, all unfamiliar, crying out at once or in sequence, she couldn't say, all tangled around the other sounds, louder than she had ever heard, yet no louder than the words or the shriek of agony, some nightmare animal voicing unbearable pain, followed by a heavy thud of something coming to rest beside her own body, to share her refuge.

Christie was not aware that her face was pressed into the palms of her hands until she felt something—someone— leaning against her elbow; and then, lifting her face, her eyes were engaged directly by the strange staring eyes which held her with an incredible emptiness, hypnotizing her with their unblinking demands, and her body could not respond to the voices which called her name. She tried to kick away some hands that were reaching for her, pulling at her ankles, trying to drag her from the safety of her hiding place. Instinctively, she bent her knees so that the hands could not reach her and then, no longer able to bear those eyes which were filmed over and lifeless, Christie, in a surge of mindless terror, realized that she was trapped: the right side of her body wedged against the metal leg of the bed frame, the left side of her touching *his* face. Scraping her body against the hard and tearing metal on one side, but more aware of the contact her body made along the entire left side, Christie worked herself free, hands reached for her arms, her shoulders, pulled her to her knees, then roughly to her feet. Her eyes could see sharply now, no longer squinting against the yellow light.

She stood, looking down, fascinated as the thick blood oozed back along Rogoff's skull from a wound low in his forehead, working its way languidly like some gelid insect along the naked, yellow obscenity of his hooded head. Surrounding him in fantastically thick, bright puddles were the emanations of his other wounds, and Christie's left hand, reaching across her mouth, was wet and heavy with slime and she regarded it curiously, not knowing where the blood had come from, for no part of her body felt torn and yet her mouth tasted the thick saltiness of blood and she could see that her shoulder, arm, torso, thigh, calf and sneaker were painted red as though by a wide and careless brush. She stood, waiting to feel the pain of rendered flesh but she felt nothing. Just a terrible, empty calmness.

The room was filled by unexpected faces: Devereaux and O'Neill, and Stoney and Marty and Ferranti, all out of hiding, all plainly visible in the yellowish light and their voices ordering other faces away from the opened door of the room: a myriad of faces, looking, wide-eyed, open-mouthed, asking, staring, their eyes curiously bright; the Homicide men, standing over Rogoff, their faces professionally hard and interested. Then Casey Reardon, with Tom Dell cutting a path for him through the crowded hallway of unknown faces; stolid men who came, regarded the scene wordlessly, not touching the sprawled dead man, but noting the switchblade knife, opened and bloody in Rogoff's right hand, the odd smashed glasses against one wall and the plaid cap, crushed beneath his large black leather shoe.

Christie raised her left arm when Reardon told her to, offering it for his inspection, let him rip the sleeve of her shirt to her shoulder, let him push her along into the bathroom. She watched, fascinated, as the thick red blood thinned to the consistency of watercolor paint while Reardon kept sloshing cold water down the length of her arm. "It isn't from you, thank God," she heard him say, but his voice was unfamiliar and his face was unfamiliar and even his eyes, which tried to hold hers but for some reason could not, were unknown.

A voice, not her own, told him, "I'm all right. I'm all right, just leave me alone!"

Reardon, his hand on her shoulder, did not react or comment as she pulled free of his touch, but just asked her, "You want anything, Christie? Do you need anything—a drink maybe?"

Christie stood rigidly straight, her lips pulling back into a tight and meaningless smile, her eyes narrowed on his. Slowly, deliberately, she raised her right arm, extending the untrembling fingers. "I am as steady as a rock, Mr. Reardon," but curiously, she felt no satisfaction. He left her alone in the bathroom then, and she could not understand her anger or why it was directed at him.

In what sequence they all arrived, Christie could not determine, but the room was taken over by all of those people who have a part in these things, each moving independently of all the others, intent only upon his particular segment of the event. Christie moved closer into the tight little circle that formed in one corner of the room: the circle consisting of Bill Ferranti, Stoner Martin and Marty Ginsburg. Christie, looking at first one face and then the other, was struck by the similarity: each of them seemed washed in a kind of grayness around the lips, which had gone dry as her own lips had, down the nostrils, along the cheeks. Reardon brought some large, expressionless man over to them and he shook hands with each of them, a hard grasp and a quick release, his tiny granite eyes digging at each of them in turn, his bloodless lips telling them they had done a good job. He was brass, but Christie didn't know who, just that he was brass: that much anyone could tell.

The doctor came into the room followed by a hospital attendant. He examined Christie's arm, glanced at her accusingly when he discovered the blood that covered her did not come from her own veins. She wrenched away from him, not wanting to be touched.

Marty Ginsburg extended his right arm, letting Stoney remove his shirt. The paleness spread along Marty's forehead when the doctor swabbed his arm with a large wad of cotton: the blood running down Marty Ginsburg's clothes was from a long, deep cut which started from a point just inside his right elbow and terminated an inch or so short of his wrist.

"But I don't feel nothing," Marty said in wonder, touching his opened flesh, "I just don't *feel* it."

"You will," the doctor said pleasantly, "when the shock wears off, brother, you *will*."

Ferranti knew the blood just under his jaw was from a small deep wound and he held a wet handkerchief against the cut until the doctor finished his temporary bandaging of Marty.

"At least twenty stitches for that one," the doctor said, then smiling, "he doesn't feel it: boy, he will tomorrow. And now, you, what have you got here?" Leaning his head back, the short doctor squinted at Ferranti. "Ah, yes, lucky cut this one. A little to one side and it would have been the jugular vein and then we'd have two for the bag boys."

Stoney, uncut, unwounded, stood beside her, watching. His hand clung to her arm and she could feel the hard kneading pressure of his fingers, keeping her in the room, though her eyes would not follow his, would not look, as everyone else was looking, at the large, lifeless hulk of Murray Rogoff.

The door opened again and Christie turned, seeing the men being admitted, press cards pinned on summer shirts, stuck in hatbands or nonchalantly flashed then put back into a pocket. Reardon backed them into the kitchen alcove, warning them not to touch anything, and their eyes remained on Christie, all their questions directed at her presence in the room, and they grinned, excited by the dark blood down her side. Reardon held them back with a gesture, came to her side.

"*Daily News* and *Post*. They want your picture." His hand straightened her hair lightly. "Look, you don't have to."

She bit her lip, then pushed it out. "Whatever you say, Mr. Reardon."

There was just a smile, not the hard familiar smile, just a smile and his hand pressed hers, leading her to the kitchenette. "Just a couple, fellows, then let her alone; my people have had a rough night."

The reporters directed her, told her how to stand, where to look, pointed at Stoney and Marty and Bill, but mostly the photographers wanted to get a good shot of her: of the side with the blood, and their hard professional voices kept positioning her. Christie looked right through them coldly. The lingering circles of bright haze dulled out all the details of the room as the lights popped at her face. They moved away, finished with her now, aiming at Rogoff, whose eyes would not be bothered by the torturous lights.

A scrawny, wiry boy with a blade sharp nose and almost no lips grasped her arm. "Look, Christie, baby, hop up on the refrigerator, will you, and turn kind of sideways so I can get a good shot of your leg. Let's cheese it up a little!" She thrust his hand from her, meeting his surprised stare; she pulled her lips back and her voice—her own now, low and harsh—threw the words at him, "Keep your hands off me!"

The photographer's face, knowing and shrewd and older than his years, watched her. "Come on, sweetie, don't give me any of that crap! Your boss said we can take pictures, so just make like a good kid and pose."

Christie's eyes hardened and she whispered fiercely, "Get lost, junior, right now!" He turned his back on her in disgust and began edging closer to the dead body only to be turned away by Devereaux and O'Neill who, as Homicide men, had priority and were protecting the corpse until their superior officers were finished with their observations.

She walked down the long hallway, past the people, who pointed and nodded and commented, not seeing them, not hearing them. She felt a strange unreality now: as though the only reality had been back there, in that room, where Rogoff lay dead.

They all rode in the ambulance and when they arrived at the Emergency Ward, Ferranti couldn't put any weight on his right ankle and he leaned heavily on Stoney's arm until the attendant brought a wheelchair: he had twisted his ankle when he had lunged at Rogoff and now the swelling was so extensive that the intern had to cut the sock from his foot.

Christie waited in the Emergency Reception Room while Marty was being stitched up and Ferranti was being sewed and X-rayed. Stoney made the telephone calls to the wives of both men. She was relieved that they hadn't asked her to do it: her voice would have sounded so flat and emotionless they would have been sure the injuries were fatal. Christie called Nora, stated the facts tersely, her voice even and calm and Nora hadn't pressed her, didn't ask anything except, "Are you all right, Christie?" and she had replied, "Yes."

Stoney appeared with two containers of black coffee and she drank the bitter hot liquid, feeling it burn through her without stimulation of any kind. She accepted the cigarette he held out to her. He cupped the match over his own cigarette, regarding it curiously. "Damnedest thing," he said, "I had a butt dangling in my mouth the whole time, drawing on it like it was lit, and you know, Christie, when it hit the fan, when everything popped, all that time, that cigarette just kept clinging to my mouth like it was part of me." He smiled without humor. "Casey took it from my mouth when he came into the room. I didn't even know it was there." They sat in silence, each caught up in the sequence of events.

It was past one A.M. when Reardon arrived at the hospital. Assured that none of his people had been sedated yet, he instructed the reluctant supervising nurse to wheel Ferranti into Ginsburg's room which she agreed to do after a long, hard and revealing study of Reardon's face.

Reardon herded Mrs. Ferranti and Mrs. Ginsburg into the hallway, reassured them that their husbands would survive in good shape and reassured the men that their wives would be delivered safe and well to their homes by Tom Dell. He waved an almost child-sized man with a plump, disinterested face into the room along with Stoney and Christie, and wordlessly, the small man found a chair, which he pulled up close to Ginsburg's bed. Carefully, he opened his

193

little black leather case, pulled a tripod stand from some-where inside the case, twirled a dial on a long roll of white paper, then, his fingers poised over the keys of his stenotype machine, for the first time he looked up, his eyes inquiringly on Reardon.

"While it's fresh in everyone's mind," Casey said, "let's have a run down, beginning with Rogoff's entrance into the apartment. I want to present this to the Grand Jury as quickly as possible."

And then, for the first time, each of them heard how it was; each told his own story and the bits of sound and light and shouting and cries fell into place, the voices now identified, the sudden sounds and words all having been emitted by individual human beings.

Stoney had called out, "Police officers!"; Marty had spotted the knife, calling out, "Watch it!" as Stoney yelled, "He's got a knife!" while Ferranti yelled, "Drop it." It was at Marty that Rogoff lunged and Marty, still not feeling pain, fingered the clean white bandage down the length of his arm. "You'd think with a cut that long—twenty-two stitches —I would have felt something."

Ferranti had seized the powerful arm, trying to wrench the knife free from the unrelenting hand and Ferranti had felt his own wound with more surprise than pain.

"I think I fired first," Stoney said thoughtfully, turning his eyes to Bill.

"I think I caught him in the forehead," Bill said softly, remembering now the startled expression and then the spasmodic twisting of the body.

"I got two off," Marty said. "But I'm not sure if I hit him."

"I hit him," Stoney said. "In the chest."

Reardon signaled the stenotypist, and expressionless, he rolled up his paper, slid the legs back into their hiding place, shut his case, snapped the lock, nodded at no one in particular and left the room.

"Hey, there, Christie," Stoney said, smiling now, "why the heck did you nearly kick my head off? Don't go blank on me: I was just trying to get you out from under that bed."

Yes; she remembered now. Hands reaching for her, pull-

194

ing at her. She shrugged and her shoulders felt very heavy. "I don't know, Stoney; just . . . I just had to get out of there face first, I guess."

His hand ran across his forehead, searching for a bruise. "Any lumps there, Mr. Reardon? That girl has a wicked karate kick."

Reardon was watching her; she knew that. Leaning over Stoney, making his light remarks, he was watching her, as he had been all during the telling of it, but she would not look at him and she didn't know why: maybe because she didn't want him to see whatever it was he was looking for.

Finally, firmly, the supervising nurse came in, stood her ground flatly, crackling with starch and rightful authority. "These men *must* rest now." She held up two little paper cups, jiggling them so Casey could hear the pills inside. "I have orders to give each of them a sleeping pill and *this one*"—her eyes accusingly on Ferranti—"must go back to his assigned room."

Casey stood up, grinned, bowed his head slightly at the surprised woman who was fully prepared to do battle. "Yes ma'am," he said pleasantly, "you're in charge." He winked at the bedded men, his eyes wandering over the square heavy shape of the nurse. "Sleep good, boys, and don't give the nurse any trouble. They act up in any way, ma'am, you let me know."

The nurse ignored him, busily poured water into a tumbler and watched sharply so that Marty couldn't hide the pill in his cheek. Following Casey, Christie and Stoney both turned for a moment, both looked at their partners in a special way, nodding, wordlessly accepting the responding nods.

"You guys have anything to eat lately?" Reardon asked them in the hallway.

"This fella here," Stoney said, pointing at Christie, "had some black coffee which I don't think was agreeable in view of the fact that this fella here is a notorious tea drinker."

"You want a cup of tea or a sandwich or anything, Christie?"

She shook her head. Her fingers touched the dark brown stain on her clothing; Rogoff's blood was still slightly damp and was beginning to stiffen darkly. "I'd like to go home and shower and get out of these things."

"Right. Sam Farrell is standing by with his car to take you home." He looked at his watch, grimacing. "Two A.M. Hate to do this to you, guys, but it's necessary: get home, sleep a couple of hours and be in the office first thing. Nine A.M. okay?"

"You want me in at nine A.M., I'll be in at nine A.M."

He studied her face for a moment, a small, familiar grin pulling at the corners of his mouth, but he bit back whatever words he was about to say. He waved his hand at Sam Farrell who had just gotten off the elevator and had walked directly into a water cooler. Rubbing his thigh, Farrell approached them, his eyes wide and glassy from lack of sleep. "Hey, Sam, you got something on for tomorrow A.M.?"

Farrell dug in his pockets, then came up with a scribbled notation. "You told me to get that tape to the Police Lab, Mr. Reardon, first thing."

Reardon considered for a moment: Farrell lived in the Bronx. "Sorry, Opara, I can't give you transportation in the morning, you'll have to subway-it in."

"No problem," she said shortly, entering the elevator, nodding good night to Stoney, then, her eyes on Reardon's, meeting them fully for the first time in the brief moment before the elevator doors slid shut, she warned him: Whatever it is you're looking for, you won't see it in my face.

JOHN DEVEREAUX's face was marked by deep burrows of fatigue. All the natural lines of some forty-seven years of his life were cruelly evident. His pale gray eyes were oddly flat, surrounded by the redness of long sleepless hours and the consumption of nearly a fifth of Scotch, steadily swallowed, a shot at a time, in a manner that served not to increase his efficiency and alertness but merely as a necessity which enabled him to remain relatively awake and relatively able to continue his tasks.

When Christie Opara arrived at the Squad office and offered to complete his typewritten report, he merely nodded heavily, sliding his chair to one side, watching her push another chair into place before the machine. His eyes seemed fixed in an unblinking stare and every pore of his body exuded the heaviness of alcohol and fatigue. He shook his head over his words, but his voice displayed not a trace of emotion.

"This guy Rogoff," he said heavily, "God. *He kept a shoe box under his bed.*" There was something terrible about the flatness of his voice. He ran a large hand across the disheveled sparseness of his hair. "Shoe box of souvenirs: notebooks and hair clippings. A notebook on you, by the way—it was in his pants pocket last night."

Christie's mind did not hold onto this as a fact: just some words that Devereaux was saying to her. A cold shower and careful makeup hid the fatigue outwardly but her brain was numbed and functioning mechanically.

Devereaux held his hand up, his thumb and index finger measuring. "About an inch of hair in each little box." Then, his words heavy as stone, "There were *seven* notebooks and *six* little boxes of hair clippings."

Christie's mouth went dry as the light gray eyes staring at her revealed no shock and no surprise: John Devereaux had lived with this knowledge for several hours now. *"Seven?"*

197

"Yeah," he said. "We're going to be digging up cases from years back; all over the city. Cases that technically have remained open but haven't been actively investigated for a long time." He was talking more to himself now, "God. There was this kid in Brooklyn three years ago: I worked on it for a while before I got transferred to the Bronx."

"Seven," Christie repeated, and then, it just occurring to her, her own involvement just occurring to her, "seven notebooks and six boxes of hair." Her fingers touched the short hair on the back of her neck.

Devereaux's eyes blinked and he rubbed them. "Hey, Christie, you were real good last night. It was tough, huh?"

"Yes. You had some bad moments yourself, didn't you?"

His eyes were fixed again. "It was worse later; afterward. Jimmy O'Neill and I and some of the other guys from my Squad went to Rogoff's place; spent hours tearing it apart." He rubbed the back of his neck, screwed his face into deep creases, tested his jaw. "That was what you call tough. The brother was there: from Long Island. Poor bastard. He'd been notified and he had to tell the parents. By the time we got there, you could hear the old woman shrieking. A real little woman and his father is a little guy: funny. Rogoff was so big, you know. Jimmy told the brother to get a doc to give the old people a shot to quiet them down but the old woman kept screaming for nearly an hour after she got a shot. The brother came back into the apartment after a while, when the old folks calmed down in a neighbor's apartment and he just kind of stood there, watching us, trying not to get in our way, you know?"

The pale face of David Rogoff had registered in Christie's mind after all: she could see him now.

"You know Paddy Leary? Big guy, heavy set? Well Paddy got a rough mouth, you know, and when we found that shoe box he held it up to Rogoff's brother and he said, 'Nice brother you got there, huh, buddy? Been going around killing all these little girls,' and the brother just stood there and his knees just gave way on him, and Jimmy told him to go into the kitchen and make us a pot of coffee." John shook his head. "Coffee. Christ, and all of us were belting down White Label the whole time."

"Let's get this report typed up, John, okay?"

Jimmy O'Neill, a tall, bony man with a crew cut and boyish face, bore no resemblance whatever to his partner. His cheeks were concave and his eyes were like two bright black marbles. Yet, weariness had made them identical and when he arrived, distributing containers of hot coffee, relieving Devereaux, dictating to Christie, it was the same heavy flat voice, wearily spelling out details, and Christie typed rapidly, looking up in surprise at Reardon's voice.

His sleeplessness, though evident in the heavy squinting of his eyes and bright reddish-gold glints along his cheeks and chin, was more revealed by the hard, artificial brightness of his voice. "Hey, Opara. I didn't think that fast typing was being done by the talented fingers of our Homicide colleagues. Listen, when you get finished I have some rough drafts that need doing, okay?" His hand pulled his loosened tie downward and there were bright red hairs showing at his neck. Reardon looked at his watch, wound it, went back into his own office.

Stoner Martin arrived, waved a quick greeting, hunched himself over a steady series of telephone calls, then informed Christie that Marty was in a lot of pain but Ferranti was feeling pretty good.

Tom Dell entered the office, a package under his arm, rubbing his newly shaved chin. He looked fresh and clean and rested and he carefully placed his hat on the aluminum rack.

"Boy, I feel crummy," he said. "We really should have a shower on the floor."

O'Neill winked at his partner. "Dapper Dell himself, looking like a Saturday night date and crying because he missed his shower."

"Were you out all night?" Christie asked, surprised, because he didn't look it.

"Don't I look weary?" Dell asked, sounding offended. He held up his package. "This is the rottenest neighborhood to try and get a decent shirt."

Devereaux pulled his own sweaty shirt from his neck. "Sonny, you D.A. people kill me. Never go around-the-clock and then some in the same shirt?"

199

Dell shook his head, regarding the two Homicide men distastefully. "We have a little class around here, gentlemen." He shook the package at them. "Mr. Reardon and me, we're not like some other slobs I'm too polite to mention. We meet all emergencies as they come along, but with class and style, at all times."

The men exchanged insults good-naturedly, the weariness receding, the coffee taking hold, their minds resharpened. Dell brought one of the new shirts into Reardon, returned with an electric razor.

"Stoney, Mr. Reardon says can you fix this thing: it buzzes but it don't cut. Me, personally, I wouldn't feel cleanshaven unless I had that nice hot lather all over these tender cheeks, but the boss goes for the electric."

Dell's face was relaxed and unmarked by the long hours of waiting he had spent, the hours searching Rogoff's apartment, the hours driving Reardon from one location to another. He sat down, carefully preserving the crease in his trousers, his feet stretching to the top of a desk.

Stoney brought the repaired razor in to Reardon, then told Dell, "You better get that new shirt on, if you're intending to, son, because the Man says he'll be ready to roll as soon as that red beard is electrified off."

Dell moved quickly, setting his hat on the back of his head, pulling the shirt from the package. "Tell the boss I'll be out front," he called, unbuttoning his shirt as he moved toward the men's room.

Reardon adjusted his collar and tie, scowled at himself in the small rectangular mirror in the Squad room, then turned to Devereaux and O'Neill. "I just spoke to your Squad Commander, fellas. You finish your reports?"

They nodded. "He wants you both; better grab a bite. Jesus, it's lunchtime, isn't it? He's got some brass coming over and he wants you there."

"Yes, sir."

"Martin and Opara, stick around. I'll be back in about an hour." The amber eyes, sharp and clear again, caught her expression of annoyance. "Chin up, Opara," he said lightly, tossing a copy of the *Daily News* at her. "How often do you get mugged on the front page?"

Christie watched him leave, her eyes angrily on the dark red cowlick. Her mouth fell open when his hand pressed the lock of hair down and he turned at the door, grinning directly at her. Damn him.

Devereaux and O'Neill made short, muttered phone calls, explaining to long-experienced wives that they weren't to be expected until they arrived home. Resigned to their continuing tour, they left for their own office. Christie and Stoney, paced by each other, typed rapidly, piecing together the seemingly endless reports which Reardon needed for the case file. Christie had called her brother's home, spoken briefly to her sister-in-law, assuring them she was fine. She had tried to engage Mickey in conversation, but he was too excited and too obviously annoyed by the interruption: Aunt Alice was taking him and all his cousins and two neighborhood kids to the movies and yeah, he saw her picture, yeah, it was swell and gee, he couldn't talk now, Mom, because *Mary Poppins* was going to start in ten minutes and yeah, he would see her later and yeah, goodbye.

It was four o'clock before Reardon returned, and Christie wondered if he and Dell had gone somewhere and slept for a few hours. They both looked rested and starched and fresh. Christie felt exhaustion in every part of her body and a strong and growing resentment at being in the office. She wanted to be home; under the shower, in bed. Reardon scooped up the stack of papers, took his time reading them. Dell handed her a copy of the afternoon *Post:* her picture was on the first page. Not reading the copy, just staring at the photograph, she hated the girl, standing there, legs apart, thumbs hooked into the pockets of her dungarees: she looked like some delinquent arrogantly admitting she had stolen an old woman's pocketbook.

Stoney's voice was sad. "Christie, Christie. You got to learn not to glare at those men with the cameras, because baby, they got the final word."

Reardon walked rapidly from his office, not breaking pace as he crossed the Squad room. "C'mon, c'mon, let's get going, fellas. Dell, you get the wheels out front? Come on, Opara, let's move it."

Following Reardon, she exchanged glances with Stoney,

who shrugged. "Just do what the Man says and follow where the Man leads."

Sitting slumped in the back seat of the Pontiac, not taking part in the conversation, Christie slid her wristwatch around, checking the time, but the sharp voice from the front seat informed her, "It's five-fifteen, Opara. What's your problem?"

"No problem, Mr. Reardon, none at all."

He directed Dell into a parking slot that was clearly marked "Doctors Only," then hurried them through the hospital lobby, ignoring a nurse who tried to tell them something about "visiting hours"; he stabbed the button of the elevator and waved at the nurse as the doors closed. "Come on now, Opara, let's see your best visitor's smile." Christie stretched her lips, showing two rows of white teeth. "Great," Reardon said. "That'll send Ginsburg into a relapse for sure."

Striding past the floor nurse, Reardon called, "It's okay, it's okay, don't worry about it," and he hurried them along, despite the fact that the nurse was rushing around the small desk behind which she had been toiling over official records.

Reardon flung the door open and his voice startled the other two patients sharing the room with Marty Ginsburg.

"Well, exactly how long do you intend to hang around this place, Ginsburg? How long do you think I'm going to carry you?"

The two other patients leaned warily into their pillows and stared at the group of intruders.

Incredibly, it seemed that Marty had lost a considerable amount of weight; his large cheeks were drawn and empty like airless balloons and his lips were white and pulled back in a half smile. He offered his left hand to Reardon. "I'd give you my shaking hand, boss," he said in an odd imitation of Marty Ginsburg's voice, "but as you can see, it's a little out of order right now."

Reardon stood beside the bed quietly for a moment, his eyes a different color than Christie had ever seen them: softer and with an expression of concern. He leaned close to Marty and said something the others couldn't hear and Marty nodded once, heavily, as though in reassurance. It was so quick an exchange that Christie wasn't even certain it had taken place for Reardon turned easily to meet the outraged nurse and his face was animated again and his voice was loud and playful. "It's okay, honey, relax. You just take very good care of this guy here and watch out for his stitches." He leaned into the startled face. "This guy has skin like leather: when it starts to mend, those stitches might go flying all around this place like bullets."

Marty joined in some light banter and his voice, oddly enough, sounded familiar again. They followed Reardon out of the room and Christie could hear the nurse warning Marty to settle down, but the woman's voice wasn't really angry.

Bill Ferranti was sitting up in bed, reading a magazine, his cheeks a healthy pink. He was having some difficulty keeping his head in a comfortable position because the bandage covering his neck wound was bulky, and he touched it when Christie asked how he felt.

"This is a little annoying. I don't see why they made the bandage so large. The cut actually is only about an inch."

"An inch?" Reardon asked. "Boy, it's a good thing they have that cast on your ankle or I'd have you up and out." His voice softened and his fingers touched the cast lightly. "I understand you have a fracture?"

Ferranti made a clicking sound. "That really surprised me. It didn't hurt that much. In fact, it doesn't hurt now, just feels a little uncomfortable."

Reardon's fingers moved along the cast for a moment and Christie noted a kind of gentleness in the gesture, but Reardon's voice was tough and mocking again. "What a hell of a Squad: two of my guys flat on their backs and you"—he turned to her—"plastered all over the front pages." There was no special expression when he faced her, just that amused, hard grin. "Comes the cold weather and I can just hear you all groaning with aches and pains. Anything hurt you, Opara?"

"Nothing hurts me, Mr. Reardon."

No one seemed to notice the coldness of her voice. If Reardon caught it, nothing in his face indicated that she had even spoken. "Boy, you guys sure knocked the D.A. for a loop," he said. "He was so impressed he almost smiled. Not quite, but almost." He snapped his fingers. "Damn, I almost forgot. I put you all in for promotion and commendation. Not you, Stoney—you got nowhere to go, but they might give you an extra medal. The D.A. endorsed the recommendation but that doesn't mean anything. We'll have to see what the availabilities are."

Then, brusque again, "Well, let's move. Ferranti, you stay put, I'll have to think up something good for you—we must have a case where a guy on crutches will come in handy."

Ferranti signaled Christie to his bedside and Reardon impatiently called out, "Make it fast, will you, Opara, we're ready to move!"

Christie, puzzled by the deepening color rising along Bill's cheeks, leaned toward him.

"Christie," he said hesitantly, "I want to apologize."

"Apologize? For what?"

Ferranti licked his lips, adjusted his horn-rimmed glasses. "Last night: when the lights went on and all the action and everything, well, in all the confusion and all"—Ferranti took a deep breath—"well, some of the *language* that was tossed around—well, some of it was mine and frankly, I wasn't even aware of it. But lying here all day, thinking about it, well, I realized all of a sudden some of the words I used and I want to apologize to you."

Christie felt a giddy sensation, a lightheadedness. She reached for his hand, pressing it firmly to keep herself steady. "Bill, in all the noise and confusion, I think I probably added my own touch of 'blue' to the atmosphere, only under the bed, I doubt anyone heard me. At least, I *hope* no one heard me. Anyway, apology unnecessary, but accepted. You take care now."

"You too, Christie. You were great. Really. Just fine."

Reardon was involved in some animated conversation with the nurse who followed his every word and gesture with a delighted, if somewhat wary, smile and her only comment, repeated several times, was "Oh, you cops!"

Reardon was humming in the elevator and Christie wondered where this surge of energy had come from: he must have slept a few hours. The cool breeze felt good against the clamminess of her dress and Christie let it envelop her, consciously enjoying the cleanness of the air, not listening to the men, not even aware of their voices, until she felt Stoney pressing her hand. "You take care, little one," he said, waving to them.

Dell handed Reardon the car keys. "I checked with Communications and Homicide and the office and nobody's looking for us, boss. You got a full tank."

Christie felt a sense of relief now: Reardon was going home. She was finished for the day; she could go home, get Mickey. Reardon had a tight hold on her arm and was propelling her toward the Pontiac. Tom Dell called to her, "See you, Christie, take it easy."

Reardon opened the car door for her. "Come on, Opara, get in. Hey, do you know that your mouth is open?" Edging her into the front seat, he leaned toward her. "Dell has to subway it home tonight. The boss is driving. Any questions?" He held up his hand. "Don't ask any questions, just do like the boss tells you—fasten your seat belt."

She clicked the seat belt, feeling the metal buckle press against her stomach. She didn't look at him, sitting beside her now, but she felt a renewed wave of anger growing: at him. Everyone else was going home; everyone else in the Squad was finished for the day. But *she* had to drag around, probably type up a hundred more reports. She folded her arms and dropped her pocketbook beside her feet.

Reardon drove the way he did everything else: quickly, expertly, impatiently. Christie sat biting the inside of her cheek, refusing to ask him any questions in response to his lack of any explanation. She didn't even notice what street they were on when he suddenly slammed on the brakes and backed into a parking space.

"What luck: they must have known we were coming. C'mon, Opara."

She debated sitting there, waiting for him to walk around and open the door for her, but he was headed down the block, waving his hand for her to follow. He didn't slow his pace, so she walked rapidly until she was alongside of him. He grasped her arm and steered her into a doorway.

"Here we are," he said easily, as though they had both

been looking for a particular location. It was a restaurant and the coolness sent a momentary chill along her shoulder blades and some man approached them, smiling expansively, shaking Casey's hand, taking hers, nodding approval, walking them past all the other tables to a booth isolated in the semidarkness. Christie slid into the dark red leather seat indicated by the man, identified as George, and Casey sat opposite her, leaning his elbows on the table, regarding her with an amused expression.

"Hey," Reardon asked, "when did you eat last?"

Christie shrugged.

"Well, you are going to eat now. And I mean eat. George doesn't give me a menu: he just brings food. And you better smile, because George is a very sensitive guy and he watches like a hawk: the first bite of everything he brings. He waits and watches. You better keep that face of yours under control because I'll murder you if you hurt George's feelings, because if you do, I'm dead here."

She started to answer, to say something to him, but George appeared carrying two drinks on a tray, smiling and beaming at Casey and then at Christie. "Scotch on the rocks for Mr. Reardon and for the young lady, something very *special*." He carefully placed a white frothy drink in a cocktail glass before her and stood, waiting, the smile hovering. His hand gestured. "Taste it, young lady, and you let me know."

Christie sipped at the liquid; it was cool and creamy and sweet in her mouth, then warm in her throat. "It's very nice," she said, then seeing the smile was not completed, she sipped again. "Really, it's delicious."

George's face expanded and he made a circle with his thumb and index finger and headed for the kitchen. "See," Casey said, "George's feelings are very delicate."

Christie tasted the drink again. George's feelings. Why should she be concerned about the feelings of some stranger named George, who stood there waiting, demanding her reaction? She turned her wrist; the damn band was too loose and she could never see what time it was. Reardon's hand shot out and grasped her wrist.

"Relax, Christie, you're with the boss."

She pulled her hand away, recognizing the voice, the familiar taunting voice. Whose voice had it been last night, asking her if she were all right, over and over again, asking if *she* were all right, as if only *she* of all of them would be the only one not to make it?

"Mr. Reardon, I'm tired. I'm not hungry. I'm just tired. I don't want to upset your friend George, but I think I probably will because I don't think I'll be able to eat anything so why don't you just explain it to him because I really want to go home now."

"Too late," Reardon said, smiling over the tangy, steaming delicacy that the waiter placed before them and, automatically playing a role, Christie nibbled at a corner of something, not tasting it, smiling up at the man, who wouldn't move away until she had swallowed. Her fork played over the plate, her fingers locked tightly around it. Reardon was talking about the food, then something about wine, about which wine went with what food and about fragrance and aroma and bouquet and vintage. He uncorked a bottle, pouring a small amount into a sparkling glass, sipped it, signaled acceptance to George somewhere behind her, then poured some for her and urged her to drink it and she did.

In one swallow, Christie let it rush down her throat, ignoring Reardon and his voice, telling her that isn't the way you drink wine, as though the technique of drinking wine mattered, as though their sitting here mattered.

"Christie, look up at me." The voice was sharp but she could see only a blur facing her. "Christie, let it out," Reardon said, and she heard her own voice, hard and unfamiliar, "Leave me alone, Mr. Reardon. I'm fine. You didn't think I would be, did you? Well, wet-nurse one of the others—*not me!*"

His chin was raised but she couldn't really see him. His face was lost in the shadows, in a kind of darkness that was enveloping him, but she could still meet him head on. If he had to dig at her, that was his problem not hers.

The voice was familiar, mocking and sarcastic, and his

207

words were rapid and mean. "Jesus, I hope you're not getting the idea that I'm wet-nursing you. Hell, you're one of my guys, right?"

"Right," she said, unaware she had spoken.

"You're one of the best, right?" He was leaning forward now, his hands flat on the table alongside his drink, and his voice was low. "It didn't touch you, did it? None of it reached you, did it? It said in the *News*—it said Christie Opara was cool and calm as if she'd just taken a walk around the block. It said you were the calmest officer present on the scene. Like ice. Is that what you're like, Christie? Because—hey—that's a damn good thing to be: *like ice!*"

His words pierced her like a steady barrage of sharp bright needles but she didn't recognize him: he was a dark shape, darker than the darkness surrounding him, the clearest shape she had ever seen in her life, moving toward her, and she opened her mouth to protest, to tell him, to strike back at him, but a low sound came from within her and her breath caught and she could not form the sound and she could not breathe in or out. And then, it was as though light had suddenly shattered the intense darkness of the room and the room changed, unfamiliar and unknown. Christie reached out for something to hold on to and there was something—someone—beside her now, holding her tightly, and she tried to wrench away because it was Rogoff and his hands, dead, could not hold, but hands held her now, biting into her shoulders, pressing her face against the clean fresh smell of a new shirt and the hands were easing their hard grasp now, the pressure relaxing, and it was Reardon's voice and Reardon's hands, moving through her hair, pressing her face against his chest.

"Okay, Christie," he intoned, chanting it over and over, until the words began to have meaning, "okay, Christie, let it out, Christie, let it all out, it's okay now, Christie, it's all over."

She eased back now and he released her and she touched her face, looking at the colorless wetness which was not blood: not this time. He dug around in his back pocket, wiped her face, told her to "blow," then he blotted her eyes again.

She leaned back, taking the handkerchief from him, blew again, avoiding his eyes. "I'm sorry," she said. "I guess I'm the first member of your Squad who ever cried all over your shirt. And a new shirt too."

He turned her chin roughly to him, forcing her face up. "Don't apologize, Christie. You've a right to cry it out. Hell, I think men would be a lot better off if they sobbed it out occasionally. There'd be a hell of a lot less boozing and a hell of a lot less ulcers and a hell of a lot less everything else." He grinned now. "But I'll tell you, I thought I was going to have to belt you one, and George never would have understood that."

She leaned back feeling more tired than she had ever felt in her life: but it was a good, empty tiredness. She opened her eyes, saw George with his tray. He registered no reaction to the fact that Casey was seated alongside Christie. Casey looked at her, then at George.

"George, I hate to do this to you," Casey said, rising, extending his hand to her, "but this young lady has become ill." He quickly added, "Not from the drink or anything, gee, no. You see, she's been exposed to the German measles and just look at her. She's all blotchy and I haven't had the German measles and I'm going to just stick her in a cab and send her home right now. I certainly wouldn't want her spreading her germs all over this place."

George moved his head discreetly. "What a shame," he said. He balanced the tray against his body and lifted a heavy aluminum cover just enough to permit a steamy fragrant aroma to escape. "Another time?"

Casey placed a five-dollar bill on the tray. "Right. And next time, George, when the lady is over the German measles, I'll starve her for three days and then you can stuff her for a whole evening. She needs a little fattening up, don't you think so?"

George smiled. "Thank you, Mr. Reardon. Yes, I will plan something very special. Any time, Mr. Reardon, you come any time. You too, miss."

The evening had darkened with long jagged red remnants streaking across the edges of the sky. Christie sniffled into the handkerchief, then jammed it into her pocketbook. Reardon held the car door open for her, ordered, "Fasten your seat belt."

Christie leaned her head back, closed her eyes and did not listen to his terse telephone conversation or his grunt of satisfaction when he placed the receiver back into position and switched the mobile telephone to the "off" position. "We're off the air and we are going to stay off the air." He turned his body toward her, his arm on the steering wheel. "Christie, where do you want to go?"

Her eyes traced the white vinyl of the car ceiling and the weariness seemed to be dissolving and she thought for a moment.

"Not home?" he asked. "Not yet, right?"

Her tongue touched the corner of her lips and she started to say something, then stopped, and he told her impatiently, "Look, Opara, you name it—you got it."

"The beach," she said.

"The beach," he said flatly. He started the car, pulled into traffic, disregarding an irate motorist who had to come to an unexpected, brake-shrieking halt. "Not P.J.'s? Not Top of the Sixes? Not the Four Seasons?" He glanced at her, then muttered to himself, "It figures. Okay, Opara. The beach."

Reardon fought every car in sight, cataloguing the inadequacies and low intelligence of all the drivers on all the streets and parkways between Manhattan and Queens. Christie dozed, half listening to the one-sided arguments which finally subsided into an occasional snatch of song: he had a nice voice, musically strong and certain. She opened her eyes as he cut the motor.

"Where are we?"

"Riis Park," Reardon said, *"The beach."* Then, as she looked around, "This is a closed-off road, used for military vehicles at the Army installation over there. Some people don't believe in signs"—he pointed to the official no admittance poster—"but, hell, this is an authorized vehicle, right?"

"Right." She got out of the car and he slid across the seat and stood beside her.

"Well," Reardon said, "we're at the beach. What do we do now—strip and go swimming?"

She shook her head slowly and walked onto the sand, wordless. Reardon followed her halfway to the water's edge, then squatted on the cool sand. She had thought, back at the restaurant, that she had purged herself of it, but he knew she hadn't. He watched her move tentatively along the shore, her body caught by the strong pale moonlight, a small shadow on the deserted beach. It was the loneliest sight Reardon had ever seen.

He knew she could not accomplish it alone and he walked toward her. He saw her shudder as his shadow crossed hers; the air rushing from the ocean was cold and wet. Her face, as she turned to him, was contorted by pain and her eyes were empty and she tried to say something but the words stopped at her lips. She was too drained to cry and too exhausted to attempt to explain what she felt.

"Come on up on the beach. It's too cold here." He took her arm and led her to a mound of dry sand and she sat when he did. Reardon began speaking, his voice a little uncertain, his eyes on the ocean. "About sixteen years ago," he said, "I was in Korea. Right off the beach there was a jungle. It was cold on the beach, but it was hot in that jungle: like steam heat. You had to keep your eyes sharp and the damn sweat seemed to bubble up in your sockets. You had to look around in that goddamn tangle of hot weeds and trees and you had to spot those bastards: they were hidden all around us. We were part of a large encampment of Marines getting ready to push on. There hadn't been any sniping for several hours, but they were there. You could *feel* them there."

Reardon dropped his head for a moment and was silent. She had never heard his voice sound like this before: it was hollow and frightening and she wondered if he was going to continue.

"You could feel them there," he repeated, "watching you. But it was hot and you got careless. *I* got careless. Standing orders were to wear combat helmets at all times." Reardon turned and his eyes did not leave hers. "I was a lieutenant: twenty-four years old and invulnerable. I took the damn

211

helmet off and put on my overseas cap to keep the sweat out of my eyes. I set it on my forehead and dropped my hands." He outlined the gesture. "And then I heard the shot. It never even knocked my hat off: went right through, clean, and I heard a small noise in back of me." He ran his hand roughly over his face; his voice was harsh and bitter. "My sergeant was dead before he hit the sand. The bullet penetrated his helmet. I turned him over and there was a small red mark in the center of his forehead. He was a boy: a kid."

Reardon shifted so that he was on his knees, facing her. "Do you understand what I'm saying, Christie?" She stared at him dumbly and he grasped her shoulders. "Listen carefully: *that bullet was mine. It was meant for me.*" His voice was cold and positive. "*There was no bullet in that room last night meant for you.*" He saw the quick intake of breath; his words began to penetrate and she seemed immobilized. "All the bullets were meant for Rogoff. They were directed at Rogoff and they hit Rogoff and they *killed Rogoff. Not you.* His death had nothing to do with you."

He relaxed his hold, then stood and walked down the beach, his mind relinquishing the scene he had just described to her, filling with the clean cold sight and sound of the ocean. It was a long time before he returned to her and he was surprised that she had fallen into a deep sleep. She was curled on her side, her cheek resting on her folded arm. He knelt beside her. Her face was more than pretty now: relaxed, at peace. He touched her cheek and a frown pulled at her forehead. He traced it away gently without disturbing her sleep.

Reardon locked his hands around his knees and watched her. She aroused so many conflicting emotions in him. She looked, in sleep, so completely vulnerable: that was one part of it, his feeling of wanting to protect her. But she was a tease in some ways; no, not really a tease, but provocative, then suddenly innocent. And fresh. Tough: not really tough, strong was a better word. She *tried* to be strong and she had great pride. Reardon watched her move slowly, then her body relaxed again.

It all went deeper than just physical desire, though that,

of course, was present. Not that she was particularly desirable: thin, flat, wiry, but the way she moved, sure of herself, confident, a little defiant and guarded.

He pressed his forehead against his knees, not looking at her now. Because if he continued to look at her, he would reach out for her. Christ, he hadn't wanted this. Never this. There had never been anything like this before. He had been to bed with many women and it had always been a casual thing, understood on both sides, taken for the mutual pleasure that was involved. His relationship with women other than his wife had never even gone into a relationship which could be called an affair. There had been many others: attractive women easily available and attractive women not easily available, but always it had involved nothing more than a mutual desire.

He and his wife had an understanding, going back some fifteen years: back to when his twin daughters were born. It was bitter and involved and he owed no explanations to anyone: not to his wife or to himself or to anyone.

Reardon licked his lips. His tongue lingered between his teeth and he looked at Christie again. This was different and this wasn't what he wanted. He thought of Nora Opara: *Christie is someone very special: she cares.*

She moved her arm, then slowly straightened her legs in a long stretch. Her face was puzzled for a moment, then she smiled. "I really slept," she said.

Reardon stood up and brushed his jacket. He sounded annoyed. "I'll be carrying sand around with me for a week. Damn, my shoes are gritty. You better get up, Opara, it's getting cold. That's all I'd need—to have you on the sick list too." He looked around quickly. "Hey, where's your pocketbook?"

"I left it in the car."

"In the car? With your gun and shield? Great. You could get a complaint for that, you know that, don't you?"

She wasn't certain if the anger was genuine but when he told her to get up, without offering assistance, she brushed herself off and followed him to the car.

She pulled the gun and shield from her pocketbook, at his insistence. "There. Nobody broke in and took them." She

213

tossed them back into the pocketbook and snapped on her seatbelt, then pressed the doorlock after he slammed the door shut. She glanced at him, but he was starting the motor, his head ducked down.

"Damn it, look at the time. Do you know how long we've been here?" he demanded.

"Apparently, too long."

Reardon didn't answer. The silence which encompassed them was heavy and tense and confusing. He changed so rapidly, so completely, from one moment to the next. His face was set in that familiar, hard expression and he gave no indication that he was aware of her presence beside him in the car. He squinted, then leaned forward and slowed the car down. He had pulled into the driveway of a diner.

"You hungry?" he asked, finally turning to look at her.

Christie leaned back, her cheek against the vinyl backrest. He let her study him and his face seemed to relax. Calmly, she looked for all the things she had learned about him: the different facets of Casey Reardon appeared and disappeared. It was a comfortable, honest silence now and she saw the small, familiar grin at the corners of his hard mouth. She thought of what he had told her on the beach without wondering why he had told her. Whatever his reason, it seemed to have clarified something within her. She knew that he had revealed something very personal and she felt, now, that he had regretted it. That was what had made him angry. He had been angry at himself.

He looked amused and that triggered her own reaction: the set of rules between them was well defined. She turned slowly and looked through the windshield. "I'm hungry," she said, "but I wouldn't eat in that greasy spoon. There's a very nice drive-in about a mile further down. On the left side of the parkway."

Reardon's eyes glinted. "Opara, you are pushing," he said, but he started the car and backed out of the driveway. He whistled through his teeth in that annoyed way, yet, at the same time, he seemed to be happy.

Christie wondered if she would ever get to understand him. Casey Reardon was, indeed, a very complicated man.

>>> If you've enjoyed this book and would like to discover more great vintage crime and thriller titles, as well as the most exciting crime and thriller authors writing today, visit: >>>

The Murder Room
Where Criminal Minds Meet

themurderroom.com